Mask
of an
Angel

Ed Harvey

Dedicated to Tom Currie
A man of integrity
A gentle sense of humour
And love of family

Acknowledgements

My thanks to…

My darling Sue…for her love, support, and advice.

The experts…
Dave Tadd, my forensics guru; Rob Layton, sub-aqua; Doug Day, police procedural; Toby Hutton-Gee and Gaz Godfrey, helicopters.

Those who have helped edit the manuscript…
Akiyah Clements, Jean Macpherson, Maggie Foulkes, and Marcia Redmonds, and Jane Thomas who proofed the proof.

1

Lydia Jones hated funerals and spent ages wondering what to wear and what say to Stewart after so long. She opted for smart casual - her hair tied back in a ponytail, a white blouse, black jeans and jacket. She decided not to worry about what to say. She'd rarely been tongue-tied - part of being a cop, she'd always assumed.

Rosemullion Hall was like an old friend, but as she crossed the lawn to the family's private chapel Jones felt unsettled by the hundreds gathered to pay their respects and troubled by the sudden death of Richard Lander, a man she'd grown to love and admire.

She joined mourners and took the short flight of steps to the chapel. Ahead, she saw Stewart Lander accepting sympathy and exchanging a few words. It was obvious his father's death had hit him hard. He looked older than the last time she'd seen him - more than the ten years that had passed - but crying out from those deep green eyes was a loneliness the sudden loss had inflicted.

'Lydia?' His handshake was firm, but his face had registered his surprise. 'It's been a long time. You're the last person I expected to see.'

'Really?' She took his hand. 'I loved your father like he was my own. I wanted to be here, no matter how difficult for both of us.' She paused and then asked, 'and where's your fiancée?'

'Kate was with him when it happened. She was so distraught that we agreed it would be better if she stayed up in London.'

It was clear he was struggling. His lower lip began to quiver and Jones was convinced he was about to start crying, but he took a deep breath and said, 'At least the old man was able to give us his blessing.'

After the service she left the chapel and, not relishing the prospect of a wake, felt a rush of relief when she saw DS Brenda McLeish and DC George Tregunna talking to a doorman at the front of the Hall. Their presence meant one thing...a major incident that required her immediate and undivided attention.

She sighed, hoping Brenda would behave.

Tall, heavy set and bosomy, Brenda McLeish was born in London's East End, left school before A-levels, joined the Met police, met Angus, moved to Glasgow, and then transferred to Falmouth when he took over *The Crows Nest*. She'd brought with her a man-management style honed during years in Vice. She would, so legend had it, frighten off punters cruising the streets by pinning them against a wall and saying, 'Listen, sweetheart. I'll give you two options. Stay the fuck away from here or I'll cut your dick off and post it to your wife.'

Superintendent Hinkson stood next to Jones and they watched the two officers make their way over.

Celia Hinkson was one of the few women to hold a senior rank in Devon and Cornwall's Police Service and when Jones transferred from the Met, it was the Super who'd looked out for her.

Hinkson lit a cigarette. 'Loose saddle?'

'A new stable girl. Inexperienced. Bridle and saddle weren't tightened correctly. Saddle slipped.'

'But he was wearing a riding hat?'

'Yes, but fell awkwardly, broke his neck, and never regained consciousness.'

'PM?'

'Accidental death. Case closed.'

Hinkson returned the cigarettes and lighter to her handbag. 'You've known the family a long time?'

'Yes, Ma'am. Richard Lander sorted things when my parents were killed. I lived here until I left school.'

'At Rosemullion?'

6

'Lady muck, me.' Jones tried to smile. 'He was a wonderful man.'

Hinkson nodded. 'And how's Lizzie?'

'Fine.' Jones felt blotches on her neck, a giveaway she'd been cursed with since her childhood. 'She's just finished a tour with The Royal Philharmonic, staying at her flat in London.'

'Give her my regards.'

'Yes. Thank you. I will.'

Jones heard a polite cough and turned to find George Tregunna with his craggy face and unfashionably long hair, standing alongside DS McLeish.

'Sorry to disturb you, Guv,' Tregunna said.

'I'll be a minute.'

'Body's been washed up on a beach near Pendennis,' Brenda McLeish said. 'We've got a car waiting for you.'

'I said, I'll be a minute.'

'Time and tide...'

'Brenda?'

'Yes. Guv.'

They watched McLeish and Tregunna retreat to the squad car. 'How's George?' Hinkson asked.

'Taking it hard. Hanging on in there.'

Her list of clichés fell short of *fucked up*.

'No chance of a reconciliation then?'

'It's not looking good. His wife's made her mind up. Separation, divorce: same old.'

'Best keep an eye on him.'

'Yes, Ma'am.'

Jones closed her eyes and lifted her face to the sun. The truth was George was underperforming and it was down to her to sort him out.

'I'll leave you to it, Inspector.' Hinkson stubbed out her cigarette and joined others making their way towards a large marquee.

7

Jones hurried to the Hall's entrance and climbed into the passenger seat of the unmarked car.

'Sorry about this, Guv.'

'I'm not, George.' She turned to McLeish. 'Body on a beach, Brenda?'

'Found near Pendennis Point.'

'And we've been called in because?'

'Alarm raised about two hours ago. Local Uniform assumed you'd want to take a look. Not a pretty sight. Crabs and gulls in attendance.'

'Do we have ID?'

'Not yet, Guv.' McLeish flipped to the next page of her notebook. 'Male, early forties. Diver. SOCO on stand-by. A race against time, next high-tide just after eleven.'

They drove along a road teeming with holidaymakers heading for beaches at Meanporth or Swanpool. At Little Dennis they parked between two Incident Vans, changed into forensic suits and made their way to a seaweed-covered cove that had been cordoned off by uniformed police. News of the discovery had spread and sightseers were testing the officers' patience as they craned to watch Sebastian Coleman examine a body floating in a large tidal pool.

Jones stopped halfway down the path. 'So, we have an unidentified corpse that no-one's reported missing?'

'Probably an emmet with a skin-full.'

'If he was hammered, George, he'd be sleeping it off somewhere, not trussed up in neoprene. As soon as his nearest and dearest realise he's missing they'll come calling.'

They made their way to the edge of the pool and the crowd, perched on the rim of the car park, murmured in anticipation.

'Fucking vultures.' McLeish shook her head.

Sebastian Coleman, Home Office Pathologist, stood up as they approached. He was a small man, short, thin and dapper, with a receding hairline and half-moon glasses that made him look like an elderly professor who'd grown tired of his students' questions. He glanced at the incoming tide. 'You don't have much time, I'm afraid. I'll know more once I've got him on the slab, but much of the forensics may already have been washed away or buried in the sand. Crabs and gulls have been busy. You'll want to be present during the PM, I presume?'

'Let me know when.' Jones knew better than to ask for details this early in an examination, but couldn't resist a stab at the time of death.

'Too early to tell. The dry suit will have affected core temperature and slowed rigor mortis. Lividity's fixed.' Coleman took a stainless steel probe, circled a purple-blue tinge around the victim's mouth, and then added, 'there are traces of sputum: a mixture of saliva and mucus from the respiratory tract.'

'Caused by?'

'I'd say his ascent was uncontrolled. His lungs will tell us more.' He struggled to his feet and removed his latex gloves. 'OK. I'm done here. Shall we say two-thirty this afternoon?'

'We have a date.'

Jones waited until Coleman had been led through the expectant onlookers, then turned her attention to the corpse in the water.

Usually, dead bodies float face down. This one was buoyed by the neoprene dry-suit and propped up by an aqualung and was floating on its back. The diver's head was partially submerged and hidden from the vultures in the viewing gallery by an inflated lifejacket.

Jones looked across at McLeish and Tregunna.

'Your shout,' she said.

9

She watched them wade into the pool and heave the corpse upright. As they did, its head flapped about like a near-decapitated doll.

'Jesus Christ.' McLeish said. They struggled with the weight of the body. 'What a fucking mess.'

'OK...' Jones tried to normalise her breathing. 'We have dry suit, life-jacket, aqualung, octopus rig...' She hesitated. 'Mask? Where's his mask?'

She spent several minutes studying the damage to the diver's face, soaking in the detail, her breath shortening.

'Come on; let's get him out.'

She called for assistance and two uniformed officers helped drag the corpse onto the sand. As the body lurched to one side, it came to rest facing the crowd and a murmur of horror and disgust scattered amongst them and cameras flashed.

Jones walked over to an officer at the barrier. 'Keep them back. Forensics will need to comb the area before we let souvenir hunters loose. What the..?' She pointed at a man she vaguely recognised, who'd slipped the cordon and was close to the corpse. The flash of his digital camera was incessant. 'For Christ's sake get him away from there. Get them all away.'

She paused, catching second wind and, as she walked toward Tregunna and McLeish - both seemingly unable to look away from the hideously disfigured face - she heard McLeish say, 'Where's the dignity in that, eh George? Where's the fucking dignity?'

Alan Gooding, the Conservative Chief Whip, waved Geoffrey D'Ancey towards an armchair in his office at the House of Commons.

'David's tied up. Asked me to brief you.'

'But, I had a message. His secretary was insistent. He wanted me at Number Ten, immediately.'

'Matters of State, beyond his control. He sends his apologies.' Gooding shrugged. 'How was your journey?'

'I came up early this morning. The train was on time for a change. It gave me a chance to prepare for the 1922 Committee meeting.'

'How's Emily and that charming daughter of yours? It seems ages since we've seen them.'

'They're fine. They're at a funeral.'

'Richard Lander's?'

'Yes.'

'Tragic loss. A riding accident?'

'So it seems. I wanted to be here, of course, but sent my apologies.' D'Ancey sat down.

'Tea or coffee?'

'Coffee.'

'David wanted you to know…we've appreciated your work from the backbenches.' Gooding passed him a coffee and took a sip of Earl Grey. He opened a file and glanced at the list of Standing Committees and Royal Commissions D'Ancey had been part of. 'Impressive.'

'Thank you.'

'We've also enjoyed watching you in The House. It's good to see the Opposition squirm.' Gooding smiled, thinly. 'And your Constituents are impressed.'

'An increased majority at the last election, pushing Labour into fourth behind the Lib Dems and the Greens.'

'Quite so.' Gooding seemed distracted. 'Yes, well, quite so.' He sipped his tea, replaced the cup and dabbed his mouth with a fresh, white napkin. 'But we cannot afford to bask in past glories. We must prepare for the next election and make sure the electorate give us the mandate to rule without the shackles of a coalition. The tide is turning and we must be prepared. We'd like you to be part of that preparation. You'll be a Minister of

11

State for the Home Office. You'll oversee Government policy on immigration, police and national security.'

'Front Bench?'

'Yes, when speaking on behalf of the Coalition. And you'll attend cabinet meetings when required. Of course, you'll have to stand down from the 1922 Committee.'

'A pity, but I understand.'

'You'll appreciate that this is an important step in your Parliamentary career?'

'Of course.'

'There's one other matter.' Gooding faltered. 'For the Americans, shooting themselves in the foot is a national pass time. Every time the President announces a new appointment skeletons come rattling out of the cupboard. Draft dodging. Pot smoking. Tax evasion...'

Gooding leaned forward. 'If you have any skeletons, Geoffrey, you walk out of here and we'll say no more. We cannot afford a scandal. David's judgment, the integrity of our Party and the opportunity to offer the electorate a real alternative will be jeopardised if, after the Cabinet reshuffle, the tabloids splash you over the front pages. You understand what I'm saying?'

'No skeletons. You have my word.'

But Gooding wasn't finished.

'Most of us have a vice or two. We might drink too much on occasions, loneliness might drive us into the arms of another woman...'

D'Ancey laughed. 'I enjoy wine with a meal and a cognac afterwards, but that's about it.'

Gooding stood up and turned his back.

'There are those who'd mention Geoffrey D'Ancey and gambling in the same breath.' As D'Ancey rose to protest, Gooding spun round and held up his hand. 'No, wait, sit down and hear me out. There are those who say you like more than a flutter on high-days and holidays. There are those who'd like to see you fall flat on your face and would jump at the chance to fuel the insatiable appetite of the gutter press.'

'Alan...' D'Ancey clasped hands together. 'You're right, before the good folk of Falmouth put their faith in me, I did gamble occasionally. Nothing big. Everything kept within reasonable limits. I'd spend a few hours after a long day unwinding, playing poker or roulette. But I never allowed it to get out of hand.'

'And recently? Last weekend, for instance?'

D'Ancey sighed. 'I met up with a friend. We rolled a few dice, no more. How did you..?'

'A columnist in one of the Sunday broadsheets put it most succinctly. You are, he wrote, one of our *most talented* backbenchers. Everything about you will be public property. We need to be sure.'

'Even you have enemies.'

'But I don't give them stones to throw, Geoffrey. If you want to be involved in the Party's future...'

'Alan. I've told you. No skeletons.'

Gooding glanced at his watch.

'I'm late for a meeting,' He said, and took D'Ancey's hand. 'And for goodness sake,' he said, 'let's see more of Emily.'

'OK, people. Listen up.'

Kate Madison walked onto the set of *Ask the Minister* at ITV's South Bank complex and stood in front of the backdrop - two armchairs and a coffee table - where the fortnightly interviews were staged.

The production crew were scattered across an empty audience amphitheatre. They were taking a break and hadn't looked up from their rolls and coffee.

'So, what d'you want first?' She asked, her mid-Atlantic drawl clattering amongst the fishpoles and the lighting bars. 'The good news or the frigging bad news?' She waited, shook her head, and then looked down at her clipboard. 'OK. The good news...Downing Street's just released details of a Cabinet reshuffle. There's a new kid on the block. Geoffrey D'Ancey. Anyone know anything about him?'

Some of the production crew looked at each other. They shrugged and shook their heads.

'No. Me neither. Anyways...he's been invited to Friday's show as a warm up for the main event. Lyn and Derek, see what you can dig up on the man they call Judge Geoffreys. Go back to his days on the Bench and see if there's any substance in his reputation. He lives in a manor house outside Falmouth. Married into the aristocracy, would you believe? He'll be here this afternoon. Get me something I can work with.' She flashed a smile. 'OK that's about it.'

'Miss Madison.' It was one of the crew. 'What's the *frigging* bad news?'

'Chris has gone AWOL.' She waved a script above her head as she walked off the set. 'Don't ask me, I'm only a gofer. But if he's not here by Friday, someone will have to step up to the plate.'

'I don't suppose you have anyone in mind?'

She turned. 'Not off the top of my head, no.'

'Really? Thought you'd jump at the chance.'

'Hadn't crossed my mind.'

'It's academic, anyway,' said another of the crew. 'Chris has never let us down. He'll be here.'

*

14

The corpse had been placed on the pathologist's table in the morgue at Truro's Royal Cornwall Hospital.

Diving gear - including aqualung and lifejacket - had been removed and Jones was examining them, careful not to compromise any forensic evidence.

She spent several minutes examining an octopus rig attached to the top of the aqualung. Dials at the end of three of its tentacles showed the amount of air left in the aqualung, the dive's duration, and the depth dived. The silicon mouthpiece - the demand valve - was connected to a fourth tentacle, whilst a spare demand valve was connected to a fifth. This spare would have to be used - Sebastian Coleman explained - if a dive buddy got into difficulty and needed to share air, or the main demand valve developed a fault.

'And do they often develop a fault?'

'Modern equipment is very reliable. Serviced regularly, it's rare for anything to go wrong. Bit like the human body really.' He smiled. 'Trouble is, of course, it's all too easy not to bother.'

Jones examined the mouthpiece. 'Things have come a long way since I did my PADI course ten years ago.'

'You've noticed that both lugs are missing?' Coleman picked up a stainless steel probe and pointed at the jagged silicon the diver's teeth would have gripped. 'Bitten off in a moment of terror, quite probably.'

His mortuary technician, a young woman in her mid-twenties, moved about the light, airy, cold room with great efficiency. Jones watched as she sorted instruments on a trolley, stripped away the diving hood and the rest of the neoprene suit and then removed the dead man's socks, jeans, underpants, a shirt and t-shirt. She placed them carefully on a large stainless steel bench.

'No shoes?' Jones asked.

15

'He would have had to take them off to get the suit on. They'll be kicking around somewhere.' She raised her right eyebrow and smiled.

'Shall we begin?' Coleman said.

Once the corpse was naked, it wasn't long before surgery began to reveal the true nature of death and provide Jones with her first substantive clues.

It was seven forty-five by the time she got away and the day had settled into a balmy summer's evening. She was tired and hungry and the humidity dragged on her like a heavy woollen coat. She decided to take time out before returning to the Incident Room. She parked at the Maritime Museum and strolled along the quayside. The air was muggy and contrasted sharply with the clinical, antiseptic chill of the morgue and the smell of seaweed helped banish the nausea she'd experienced during the autopsy.

In the town, the gaiety of holidaymakers, the smell of fish and chips, and the bustle of traffic made her feel light-headed and she realised she hadn't eaten since a round of sandwiches with Brenda McLeish and George Tregunna at lunchtime. What she really wanted to do was to go home and feed her cats, but there were too many unanswered questions and, given this was her first big case – her first as Senior Investigating Officer - she knew she'd have to return to the station. Equally, she reasoned, she couldn't work on an empty stomach, and decided to grab a steak pie and wash it down with a diet coke. Half an hour later, she caught news of the body's discovery on the pub's TV and reluctantly decided she couldn't put work off any longer.

Back in the Incident Room, she cleaned two large, magnetic whiteboards, sat at her desk and stared at the empty melamine. She glanced down at a report George Tregunna had processed, critical of its brevity, and scanned another relating to the couple who'd found the body.

'Above and beyond, DI Jones?'

She'd always considered Superintendent Hinkson as attractive, without being beautiful, but this evening she seemed oddly sensual in a blue, low-cut gown, a diamond necklace and a collection of bracelets.

'Good evening, Ma'am. Just tying up loose ends.'

'How's that aunt of yours?'

'Oh,' said Jones, rattled by the sudden intrusion into her private life. 'Pulling through. I'll try to get to see her next weekend. The stroke's left her partially paralyzed. Speech has been affected.' She laughed, hollowly. 'For someone who loved to gossip, using an alphabet-board's driving her crazy.'

'Well, if you need time.'

'Thanks. Appreciate it.' She hesitated. 'You must be going somewhere, Ma'am?'

'Very astute, Lydia.' Hinkson smiled. 'The costume's for the University's Summer Ball.'

'Very nice.'

'Makes a nice change.' Hinkson pulled cigarettes from a handbag. 'Electronic. Synthetic nicotine. What will they think of next?' She walked over to the empty whiteboards. 'Making progress, I see?'

Jones smiled at Hinkson's gentle sarcasm and dogged determination to feed her addiction. 'I'll know more in the morning, Ma'am. Sebastian's promised to get his report to me ASAP.'

'Your first impressions?'

'I'm not convinced it was an accident.' Jones started to illustrate on a whiteboard. 'We have a body.' She wrote the word *Diver* in the middle. 'We found ID in his jeans.' She wrote *Chris Baldwin*. 'If he's our man, the media will be all over us.'

Jones waited for Hinkson to make the connection and when she did the Superintendent said, 'TV's serious side?'

'He fronted last year's award-winning series, *Britain and the Middle East*. Took over *Ask the Minister* about two months ago.'

'That's all I need a dead celeb on my patch.' Hinkson paused. 'Cause of death?'

'I'll know more tomorrow, after Sebastian's finished the autopsy.'

'Clothing, personal effects? Nothing missing?'

'His clothes are being examined.'

'Tomorrow, I presume?'

'Tomorrow, Ma'am.'

'Update me at noon.' Hinkson drew on her synthetic cigarette, the menthol vapour stinging her eyes as she exhaled. 'Baldwin's not local?'

'Lives in South London.'

'We'll need to find family or someone close and arrange for a formal ID. I'll contact Commander Hobson at Scotland Yard.'

'Charlie Hobson?' Jones asked.

'You know him?'

'When I was with the Met.' Jones was distracted, momentarily, by images of the affair she had had with Charlie Hobson - Sergeant Charlie Hobson, as he was then. 'He's made Commander?' she asked.

'Yes, about a year ago. All this promotion. Must be something in the water,' Hinkson said. 'Apart from dead celebrities.'

Jones was convinced she saw a smile flickering at the corner of her mouth.

'Anyway,' the Superintendent said, 'I'll ask Charlie to make some enquiries on our behalf.' She returned her cigarette to its box. 'Now, go home, have a stiff nightcap - wash away the smell of formaldehyde.'

'Wish I could, but Brenda's issued a three-line whip. Team talk.'

'Pub Quiz?'

'Finals on Friday. We don't stand a chance. Daniel Green's in the PAWS team. They've won every year since he joined them. Brenda's thinking of nobbling him. Make things less one-sided. Works at the local library, knows the location of every book.'

'Pity he's not a cop. He'd probably clear our backlog in days.'

'Whatever,' Jones said. 'He gives me the creeps. He was there this morning, at the crime scene. He'd slipped past Uniform and was taking photos of our dead celeb.'

2

The bed in his room - the spare room - was small and uncomfortable and George Tregunna had been awake for most of the night. They'd spent the evening trying to maintain the pretence of normality but, as usual, he and Maureen were unable to bridge the gulf between them.

If he'd had an affair, or beat her, anything he could rationalise...

They'd known one another for a long time, had a history. They'd been camping in North Wales long before parents realised they were more than just good friends. They'd walked along the cliffs and had sex in secluded coves. They'd talked of a family. Maureen had always wanted kids. He wasn't fussed. Maybe if he had been. But nature had had the last laugh. Sick joke, really, impotence: *his* impotence, *his* sterility, *his* male infertility.

She'd always said it wasn't important as long as they were together. That was then. Now, his home was a twelve-by-six box room.

Of course, he'd assured her time and again that he'd let her have the house and make sure she was provided for. There was no need for lawyers. They'd work things out amicably. But, she'd gone away for the weekend with a girlfriend and a letter from her solicitor arrived soon afterwards, taking him to the cleaners.

She didn't want to talk about it. She was sorry, but had to think of her future. Oh, and yes, she did love him, would always love him, but she was no longer *in* love with him. Whatever that meant.

He looked at the alarm clock he kept on the floor by the bed. He'd counted down the small hours and tried to concentrate on cases he was working on, but had found it difficult.

At four-thirty, he got up and was standing barefoot in the kitchen, making a cup of tea, when he glanced at the wooden knife rack next to the draining board. He took the cleaver, felt its weight in his hand, looked up at the ceiling and imagined her lying in their king size. He shuddered with horror at what had skipped through his mind. He fought for breath, bowed his head and was unable to stop the tears. It was the first time he'd cried since he was a kid and it was, he realised later, a merciful release.

Cold was seeping from the flagstones and his feet felt like blocks of ice. He replaced the knife, used a piece of kitchen roll to blow his nose, took his tea into the lounge and, after brushing yesterday's paper to the floor, sat on the sofa and glanced around. They'd spent ten years hard graft converting the barn they'd bought for a snip. It was in a village just outside Falmouth and, even in today's market, it was worth a small fortune. But Maureen had hankered after London's bright lights and a penthouse overlooking the Thames. It would be, she once told him, within spitting distance of West End theatres, cinemas, and classy restaurants and George...George would have been promoted to Inspector. DI George Tregunna.

That was never going to happen. It was time for him to move out and start over.

Rita and Henry Harrison were not only creatures of routine but also of ritual. Each chapter of their lives seemed to be choreographed as if to replicate previous episodes...there were, for instance, eggs for breakfast, boiled for three minutes (finely judged by the sand-timer bought as a souvenir on the Isle of Wight), accompanied by slices of Mother's Pride cut into soldiers and dunked in the yoke's rich fluid; and the weekly visits to the Post Office to collect pensions, followed by a stroll across the Common and lunch at the pub; and visits to the doctor to pick up prescriptions and to check on Henry's ticker and Rita's diabetes.

It was such routine and dependability that made Rita and Henry ideal foster parents, a role they'd performed for over twenty years until their retirement four years ago. They'd fostered a succession of 'poor little mites' who'd stayed with them until the Courts decided their fate. As well as being playmates for their only child, these 'mites' had added something special to their lives. Many kept in touch by letter, or by dropping by to show-off their own fledgling families and update them on careers, past-times, hopes and dreams.

All, but one, had been a delight, sharing their home, their gentle regimentation and their love. But they would never forget the shame their son, Jonathan, had endured. Shame that had driven him from their home and the community he'd grown up in; shame that haunted him through his days at college; shame that had destroyed the anonymity he'd sought in the armed forces.

They'd never doubted his innocence. He'd only ever wanted a kiss. Adolescent. Naïve. No more than a kiss. But Jennifer had made such a compelling victim and accused him of attempted rape. It was an accusation he'd taken with him to his grave.

His sacrifice, in the deserts of Afghanistan, had robbed them of their son soon after he'd completed training with 7 Squadron Special Forces. They would never be able to forget the day an officer from his regiment stood in their lounge and told them that he was missing.

Not *missing in action, presumed dead*. Just missing.

For a few days it made the news. His helicopter had gone down, all other personnel accounted for - five dead, several injured – and, when he wasn't listed among the casualties, the most plausible scenario was that he'd been kidnapped. This, they'd been told, was not unheard of, but Rita and Henry knew that the Taliban usually ended up executing their captives. His regiment had been desperate to find him and several reported sightings had raised hopes, but his body was never recovered.

Breakfast over, the dishes left to dry, Henry collected mail from the *Welcome* mat and Rita sorted the laundry. She'd just closed the washing machine door and set the programme when she turned to find Henry standing at the door to the utility room.

He had an envelope in his hand. 'Guess what I have here?' he said.

'Judging by that stupid grin, I'd say it wasn't a bill.'

'Correct.' He smiled, teasing her. 'Now, what is it we've been waiting for all this time?'

Rita's face suddenly lit up. 'It can't be. I don't believe it. Is it?'

Henry nodded.

'Really?' She held out her hand. 'Come on. Don't be mean. Show me.'

Henry turned and, as fast as his dodgy ticker would allow, he led Rita a pied-piper-paper-chase around the kitchen table, waving the letter aloft.

After three circuits, they stopped, Henry breathless and Rita no nearer catching him.

'These…' Henry fluttered the letter before her. '…are tickets for Friday's *Ask the Minister* at Kent House, on the South Bank.'

'*Ask the Minister*? Oh, dear.'

'What?'

23

'That's politics, isn't it? I was hoping for one of those cooking programmes where they invite someone from the audience to help the chef.'

'Well, I suppose we don't have to go.'

'What? Of course we'll go. I wouldn't miss it for the world.'

'But you just said...'

'Never mind what I said. Let me see. Let me see.'

She grabbed the letter, finished reading the instructions, and then looked at Henry.

'Friday? This week? But, I haven't got anything to wear. Everything's so old and shabby.'

Henry smiled. 'Well, we've got some pension left. Let's pop into town...see what we can find in the sales.'

The cottage was in Mawnan Smith, a village just outside Falmouth where her parents had planned to retire. Jones had been up since dawn. She was a morning person, and loved the calm a new day brought. She was sitting in the conservatory sipping tea when she heard something clatter through the letterbox. She went through to the hallway and picked up a flier advertising facilities at Port Navas Yacht Club. She went back to the conservatory and sat in the window overlooking the garden, glanced at the flier and wondered if promotion would mean she'd have more time. More responsibility meant more civilised hours, didn't it? Maybe she should take up the flier's offer. Port Navas was far enough from Falmouth to get away from work, yet close enough to be able to respond to serious incidents.

'Fat chance,' she mumbled, and threw the flier onto the bin.

She went into the bathroom and looked at herself in the mirror. The light shining from a fluorescent strip was unforgiving and exaggerated the shadows beneath her eyes and made her skin look sallow.

Not for the first time, niggling insecurity sidled up and muscled its way into the forefront of her mind, and she began to wonder how much longer Lizzie would put up with her unsocial hours or if, in the end, neither of them would want a relationship in which they spent more time apart than together. It was the first time, since Emma, she'd felt this way about anyone, but there was always *something* - another obstacle, another hurdle - to negotiate.

She resolved to talk to Lizzie about how she was feeling, but didn't want to precipitate anything. She also changed her mind, retrieved the flier from the bin and resolved to use its invitation as an excuse to visit Port Navas. Maybe she'd meet someone: someone to help take her mind off things. Someone wealthy would do, unattached, with a yacht moored in the estuary. Someone looking for a skinny redhead, liked cats, and wanted to settle down, have a couple of kids.

She thought of Lizzie, felt disloyal and wanted to cry, but didn't. Instead, she looked at her watch and got ready for the day ahead, the niggling insecurity settling in her gut.

'Are you familiar with Boyle's Law, Inspector?'

It was ten-thirty and, despite a change of clothes, Sebastian Coleman looked tired. He'd worked through the night, he'd told her, to complete the autopsy.

'Science and me parted company a long time ago,' Jones said, 'but I think they mentioned Boyle's during a

PADI course in Magaluf a few years ago. Something to do with gases?'

'Without an understanding of how compressed air behaves at depth, there'd be many more fatalities around our coast. It's why training is so important. It might seem obvious, but the deeper a diver goes the greater the pressure on them and on the air in the aqualung. On the surface, the pressure is one atmosphere...'

'One bar?'

'Yes, more or less. At ten metres, the pressure is two bar. At twenty metres it's three bar. Etcetera. Simple rule of thumb...the deeper you go, the less air you'll have and the sooner you'll have to come up. We know Baldwin dived to 40 metres...'

'Five bar?'

'You catch on quickly, Inspector. Yes, five times normal atmospheric pressure. At that depth it's easy to become so disorientated that it's difficult to tell which way is up or which way is down.'

'The Martini effect?'

'More accurately known as nitrogen narcosis.'

'The raptures of the deep.'

'At best, divers experience a false sense of wellbeing, as though mildly intoxicated. At worse nitrogen narcosis can impair decision making, induce anxiety and, at depths below 50 metres, result in hallucinations, hysteria and terror. Divers have even been known to remove their mouthpiece and go into a trance.'

'Do you think that's what happened?'

'I don't know. I'll let you have my full report in due course, but I do have some suggestions to make.' He sat at his desk and motioned Jones into a chair opposite him. 'Baldwin died between eight on Sunday evening and the small hours of Monday. He'd dived to 40 metres, where his lungs would have been full of air at a pressure five times greater than normal. During the dive, nitrogen had saturated every joint in his body. Then, for reasons we may never understand, he accelerated at a lethal speed towards the surface.'

'He didn't decompress?'

'If his ascent was uncontrolled he wouldn't have been able to stop on the way up. The nitrogen would have expanded, shattering joints in the elbows, knees, wrists, ankles, and hips, as well as the vertebrae in his neck and spinal column.'

'So, if he'd survived...'

'He wouldn't have survived. Even if we'd got him to a decompression chamber, the damage to his lungs, heart and brain would have been irreversible.' Coleman paused. 'What I do know is that Chris Baldwin was alive when he entered the water. Something happened at depth. He must have panicked and held his breath during ascent. When he reached the surface, he probably bobbed about like some ghastly buoy supported by his lifejacket and must have spent several minutes in the most excruciating agony. He did not drown, as you might assume, although he did ingest some seawater, either during his ascent or on the surface.' Coleman took a handkerchief from his pocket.

'You'll forgive me,' he said, wiping his eyes. 'These all-nighters are a bugger.'

'There's nothing else that might explain his death? No alcohol or drugs?'

'No. His stomach contents included the remains of a meal - salad, pasta and chicken - eaten about two hours before he dived. Our diver didn't smoke, had perfectly healthy tissues in the heart, liver, kidneys and spleen. The only foreign bodies I found were slithers of silicone - the lugs of his mouthpiece.' Coleman wiped his eyes again.

'You must be exhausted,' she said.

'I learned a long time ago that the dead are reluctant to share their secrets if you make them wait.' He smiled and sat forward. 'Just before you go, there are a couple of other things that might be of interest.'

'Please.'

'His nostrils have been torn and there's bruising on the upper lip. Someone forced his mask off after smashing it into his face.'

'Which means he wasn't diving alone?'

Coleman looked at her like her teachers used to when she'd said something stupid.

'I mean,' she said, blushing, 'it wasn't an accident. Not just another poor sod who'd pushed it too far?'

'Have you ever panicked, Lydia? How do any of us know what it's like when something goes wrong at 40 metres, in almost zero visibility? Did he dive alone? I don't know. Did he dive with someone or was someone waiting for him on the seabed?'

'Waiting for him? What, in the middle of the English Channel?'

'Not as far fetched as you might think, not with the technology that's available these days. They could, for example, have used sonar and satellite to navigate to a wreck a mile or so offshore, where they weighed anchor. Our diver used the anchor line to guide him to the bottom...'

'Where someone is waiting? Which would suggest the skipper had been briefed.'

'Who knows? It's a possibility. There again, maybe I'm out of my depth?'

'No.' Jones was already sifting the information. 'Grateful for anything.' She looked up and saw Coleman grinning. 'Yes, OK, I get it...out of your depth.'

'Oh, there is one more thing.' He pulled a photograph from an A4 envelope and pushed it across the desk. 'The tattoo is fairly recent. The colours are still vibrant and the scab's yet to heal. It's just below what you women call the bikini line. His pubic hair has been shaved. The re-growth is a few days old at most. The design is small, delicate.'

'What do you make of it?'

'It's a dove.'

'Meaning what?'

Coleman shrugged. 'Your guess is as good as mine, but Aphrodite kept a dove as a pet. It became the symbol of love...'

'Oh, my God.'

Kate Madison felt faint and breathless, unwilling to believe her eyes.

She'd been reading a profile of Geoffrey D'Ancey when one of the floor assistants had shown him into the control room. He'd looked across at her but, as far as she could tell, he hadn't recognised her.

But she'd known. Instantly.

He'd arrived late at Kent House - ITV's South Bank studios - without apology, and made it clear he had more important matters to attend to. 'Will this rehearsal take long? I'm needed at the House. There's an important division. The Whip has expressly requested...' Thus, he introduced himself, dispensing with any of the usual social niceties.

'Please. Sit down, Sir,' Madison said. 'Thank you for coming at such short notice.' She shuffled her papers, but the room became airless suddenly, too close and too warm, and nausea rose from deep within her stomach, catching in her throat and forcing her to gasp.

'Will you excuse me?' she said, and stood, spilling her papers onto the floor. She hurried past him and out through the control room door.

One of the producers looked away from a bank of screens, shrugged, smiled, and said, 'Nerves. She'll be back in a minute. Would you like a coffee?'

She made it to the women's cloakroom just in time to throw up into one of the sinks. The vomiting continued, each convulsion more empty and painful than the last.

As the trauma subsided, she gulped cold water from the tap, splashed some over her face and stared into the mirror.

'Sweet Jesus.' She fought to compose herself and eventually her breathing returned to normal. She glanced at her reflection, checked her make-up, spiked her cropped blond hair, took a final rinse of water, spat it out, and reapplied her lipstick.

'Back to work Kate Madison,' she told herself. 'You don't get an opportunity like this every day.'

It was soon after the City Hall clock struck twelve and Jones was standing in the Superintendent's office, police headquarters, in Courtleigh House, Lemon Street, Truro.

'I like my officers to be punctual,' Hinkson said.

'Yes, Ma'am.'

Jones guessed that the Ball the previous evening had taken its toll. Certainly this was a more business-like and far less approachable Celia Hinkson and, dressed in a crisp white shirt, regulation tie and uniform denoting her rank, the Superintendent sat behind a large Rosewood desk.

'So, what have you got to tell me?'

Jones summarised the autopsy's findings and then laid several items of diving equipment on the desk - the lifejacket and a small bottle to inflate the lifejacket, and gauges showing the amount of air left in the aqualung and the depth dived.

'The gauges show Baldwin dived for about twenty minutes and had enough air to make a safe ascent.'

'So, his equipment failed?'

'Everything checks out, but if he did have a problem, and was an experienced diver, he'd be unlikely to panic.'

'And was he experienced?

'Not sure. Need to find out where he trained.'

'A good place to start, don't you think?'

'Yes, Ma'am.'

'So, where does that leave us?'

'This is an older style of lifejacket, called an ABLJ: an adjustable buoyancy lifejacket. The deeper the diver goes, the heavier he becomes and this...' she picked up the small bottle. '...can be cracked open by turning the valve, forcing air into the jacket and adjusting buoyancy. If the crack is short, a small amount of air is injected.'

'And if the valve is left open?'

'The jacket will continue to inflate.'

'Until it bursts, presumably?'

'There's a safety valve that purges any excess air.'

'So?'

Jones went over to a whiteboard and sketched a boat on choppy waves.

'Divers at a depth of forty metres.' She wrote '40m' at the bottom of the board. 'Twenty minutes into the dive, Baldwin's dive-buddy smashes his mask and rips it off.' She drew the hull of a wreck embedded into sand and, using an irreverent style of cartoon, drew a diver's face, mask shattered, eyes wide in panic. 'Diving masks are manufactured using tempered glass.'

'Then it must have been difficult to smash.'

31

'Whoever attacked him probably used a pneumatic hammer. Splinters of glass were found embedded in Baldwin's face, and there were cuts and bruises around eyes and nose.' Jones sipped water from a bottle. 'After ripping his mask off, the assailant inflated Baldwin's lifejacket and removed his weight belt, using the quick release.'

'Weight belt?'

'He didn't have a weight belt. At least we haven't found one. When they're wearing a dry suit, most divers need several kilogrammes of extra weight to get below the surface. To ditch a weight belt is lunacy.'

'And the result...' Hinkson got up, walked over to the whiteboard, took the felt-tip pen from Jones, and drew an arrow from the seabed to the surface. '...we have a diver, without a mask, with a lifejacket propelling him to the surface like a sea-to-air missile.'

When she first started to use the apartment in St James's Square, Kate Madison hadn't appreciated how convenient it would be. It wasn't just its proximity to her work as well as the shops, cafés, theatres and cinemas of the West End, but with London's Heliport less than fifteen minutes away she could leave Rosemullion Hall and be there in less than two hours.

After rehearsals at Kent House, she took a taxi to the apartment and as she waited in the lobby she exchanged a few words with the security guards, and then took the lift to the penthouse. She let herself in, took a can of coke out of the fridge, emptied it into a crystal tumbler, and added a slug of brandy from the decanter on the sideboard.

She walked into the bedroom, stripped, ran herself a bath and laced it with oils she'd bought from Harrods. As the bath filled, she swirled the water, testing the temperature and allowing bubbles to slip sensuously through her fingers.

Whilst she waited, she sat on the edge of the bath and made a call.

'Hi. It's me.'

'Sis, where are you?'

'At the apartment.'

'How are things?'

'Busy. You?'

'Quiet.'

'Good. Just keep your head down.' She ran her fingers through the water again. 'You've got my new passport?'

'Yeah. I'll drop it off at the front desk in a brown paper bag.'

'Very melodramatic.'

'Eh?'

'Never mind.' She sensed he was hesitating. 'What?' she asked.

'Nothing. Well…I've had to call in a few favours. Cost me more.'

'Money's not a problem.'

'It'll need to be cash. I'm more or less full time at the Club and the renovation is costing a bomb. So, if you could see your way to subbing me?'

'I said it wasn't a problem.'

'And that information you wanted?'

She sipped her brandy and coke. 'Well?'

'He's a compulsive gambler.'

'And?'

'He's lost heavily. Doesn't have the readies. Creditors are really pissed off.'

'Perfect.'

'Another brown paper bag?'

'Yeah, as much info as you've got. Drop it off with the passport.'

'I'm thinking...' he said.

'Oh, God.'

'No, seriously, why not let the loan sharks do your dirty work?'

'You know me better than that.'

'Yeah.'

The conversation dried, until he said, 'Information doesn't come cheap and it's not easy from this distance. I might as well buy a season ticket on the train.'

'Would I leave you high and dry?'

'No, it's just...'

'Yeah, I know, you're getting impatient and tired of waiting.' She turned off the taps. 'Get everything to me by twelve tomorrow. I've got to go out. I have some shopping to do. I need a little number to die for.'

'And the money?'

'I'll leave it in the usual place.'

She cut the call, gave the bubbles a final swirl, stepped into the bath and eased herself down. She lay there for several minutes. The warm water, awash with perfume, not only relaxed her, but also brought a broad smile to her face. She looked around at the extravagance of this, one of her favourite rooms, and giggled, measuring the journey she had made.

She lay there for three-quarters-of-an-hour, running more hot water when necessary and gazing into the mirror on the ceiling, comfortable with her body - unlike so many women obsessed by their bottom, or their legs, or their breasts.

She stared at her body. Her breasts were firm and full and, in the mirror above the bath, she watched her hands stroke, caress and cup them, and when she pinched her nipples a wave of lust, desire and anticipation coursed through her groin. She lifted her hips and slid her hands below the water. She opened herself up, felt her moist lips and, gently, began to massage her clit. She moaned, climaxing, and sank back into the warmth of the bath and into a light sleep.

When she woke, the water was cold.

She shuddered, climbed out, and enveloped herself in a towel.

The House of Commons would adjourn soon and she didn't want to be late. She wanted to look her best - smart, sophisticated - and chose a beige linen suit and white blouse. She laid them out on the bed before applying her war paint. At the dressing table, she looked at herself in the mirror. 'Drop dead gorgeous,' she said, and lifted her glass, toasted her reflection, and downed the remainder of the brandy.

Geoffrey D'Ancey may have come back into her life, but this time she held all the aces.

It was agreed. As Senior Investigating Officer, Jones would not only lead the investigation, but would also be responsible for keeping Hinkson informed so that the Superintendent could keep her superiors off her back and the media at bay.

The latest generation H.O.L.M.E.S had been installed and this not only reduced the need to footslog - checking facts, statements, comparing incidents across the country – but also minimised the risk of human error. Since its introduction in 1986, H.O.L.M.E.S had been a potent weapon in the fight against crime and ranked alongside fingerprints and DNA. The power of the H.O.L.M.E.S software meant that every scrap of information could be collated, retrieved, interrogated and cross-referenced, no matter how trivial, irrelevant, or unrelated. And it was this cross-referencing facility that had made the biggest difference.

Jones stood in front of a magnetic whiteboard in the Incident Room and pointed at a sketch of Baldwin's face that was held in place by a fridge-magnet of a uniformed police officer.

'The likeness is pretty good,' she said.

Someone sniggered.

'What?' she asked, thrown momentarily, wanting to make a good impression, blood coursing up her neck. 'Did I say something amusing?'

'Sorry, Guv. The magnet. Good likeness. PC Plod.'

'I meant the sketch of Baldwin. It's the best we've got 'til we can lay our hands on a photograph. Now, if you've done taking the piss?'

She hesitated.

'There's swelling here and here.' She pointed at the top lip and under the eyes, and then passed photocopies around. As each member of the team studied it, she invited George Tregunna to take the floor.

Tregunna didn't get to his feet, but turned in his seat.

'Baldwin was wearing clothing under a dry suit. We recovered his wallet, BSAC membership card linked to a leisure centre in Richmond-upon-Thames, and a security pass for ITV's headquarters.' He consulted his notebook. 'We've run background checks. He inherited a house near Richmond Park a few years ago. It's worth a few bob.'

'Married?'

'As far as we know, he lives alone, Guv.'

'Anything else?'

'He's well-known to the local boys as a celeb, but no previous, no misdemeanours, no traffic violations.'

'OK. Thanks.' Jones turned to Brenda McLeish.

'There are only five dive shops left in Falmouth. The recession's put paid to the rest,' McLeish began. 'They all sell new and second-hand gear, but none of them hire out anything except bottles. Two shops have boats that run from the harbour - day trips to wrecks with groups of divers, fishing expeditions, sight seeing. Business is slow. They'd remember if anyone bought a complete set of gear, but...' She picked up the lifejacket. 'No-one's used one of these for a very long time.'

'Past its sell-buy-date?'

'Technology's moved on. Most use a buoyancy control device connected directly to the aqualung. Much easier to operate and safer.' McLeish looked around, as if checking that she still had everyone's attention. 'Apart from shops, there are several dive clubs, including a BSAC Branch in Falmouth. They meet once a week for lectures and a few pints. I popped in last night on my way home. Showed them the lifejacket Baldwin used.'

'And, what did they make of it?' Hinkson said.

Jones was unsure how long she'd been standing at the back of the room and she watched as the Superintendent took out a cigarette, looked like she was having second thoughts and put it back, unlit.

'The dive club's D O,' McLeish said, 'wanted to put the lifejacket in their museum, but he didn't seem particularly interested in Baldwin's accident.'

'Does the Dive Officer have a name?'

'Tony Simpkiss.' McLeish consulted the notes she'd taken. 'Aged about thirty. Big fella. Bit of a temper on him, especially when his authority is questioned.'

'Authority?' Jones raised an eyebrow.

'Anything to do with diving, the D O's word is law.'

'Odd, don't you think,' Hinkson said, 'that he wasn't interested in the death of another diver?'

'Quote…'McLeish read…'*Accidents happen all the time. It's a dangerous game. People die.* He gave me a lecture about how *merciless* and *indiscriminate* the sea can be and told me about one famous wrecker who'd lost a son diving for treasure in fifteen metres of water.'

'Treasure?'

McLeish checked. 'According to Simpkiss, there are at least two-hundred-and-fifty-thousand wrecks around the British Isles. Most too deep to dive.'

'Thanks, Brenda,' Jones said. 'Visit any boatyards still in business.' She turned and looked at the faces of her team. 'Anyone got anything else?' She waited as they responded with pursed lips, shrugs, raised eyebrows and shake of heads. 'OK. Just one more thing. We need to keep a lid on details as they emerge, so keep eyes and ears open and mouths shut. No idle chitchat over a pint. I want to make sure the press and public only get to hear what we want them to know. Understand?'

She gave everyone tasks for the day before turning to Superintendent Hinkson.

'Did you get a chance to contact Charlie Hobson to ask if he could run background checks for us? Apart from the obvious profile, we need to know what brought Baldwin down to Cornwall. I don't believe that he came to dive. If he had, he would have brought his own gear.'

'Yes, I've spoken to Commander Hobson. He claims he doesn't have anyone to spare. Don't know why, but I got the impression he'd prefer to see you up there, in person.' Hinkson raised an eyebrow and smiled. 'You're booked on this afternoon's Flybe flight from Newquay. You've got a couple of hours to go home and pack.'

*

38

Kate Madison had been watching proceedings from the public gallery. She'd been surprised how close she was to MPs, how small, how intimate, in fact, the House of Commons felt. It had been a long session, lasting all afternoon, but Geoffrey D'Ancey had missed the first hour, delayed by a problem in a shop in Regent Street. From her vantage point in a café across the road, Madison hadn't been able to see what all the fuss was about, but she'd enjoyed stalking him, knowing the real fun was yet to come.

When, at last, the division bell sounded, she knew it wouldn't be long before the MPs would peel out of the chamber to vote, and she watched as D'Ancey followed the rest of his party into the lobby. He was chatting to one of his fellow MPs and seemed relaxed and cheerful.

After ten minutes, they returned to the chamber and, as they waited for the Speaker to announce the result, she saw D'Ancey check his watch several times. His eyes were bright and piercing, crow's feet defining rather than detracting. His hair was dark, greying at the temples and longer than most in the Chamber. This she had to admit made him look younger and more dashing. His body was slim and upright, tall, and commanding. She guessed he must be about fifty and, whilst age was immaterial, she made a mental note to check. Part of being thorough, she reminded herself.

Her patience was rewarded and she followed him from the House of Commons towards Great George Street. He moved swiftly, walking against the flow of traffic. It was six forty-five. The pavement was teaming with commuters heading for the Underground or clambering onto buses as they made their way home. D'Ancey flagged a taxi and, as he gave directions to the driver, she hailed another.

'Follow that cab.' She couldn't believe what she'd just said and giggled out loud.

'You OK, darling?' The cab driver looked at her in his rear-view mirror.

'Yes, yes, I'm fine. Thank you for your concern.'

'No probs, love.'

They inched along in the rush hour traffic until lights at the junction of Horse Guard's Road and Birdcage Walk changed in their favour. D'Ancey's taxi sped past Buckingham Palace and Grosvenor Place before turning left along Chapel Street, through to Belgravia Square. It stopped outside an impressive Georgian townhouse and D'Ancey got out, paid his fare and took the few steps to the front door.

She checked her appearance in the glass panel that separated her from the cab driver.

'Very nice, darling.'

'Thank you.'

She paid him and left a handsome tip.

'Thanks love. Nice one.'

Yes, she'd gambled. He'd remember such a generous fare. But the detail? Unlikely.

'*She was tall, like. Long dark hair. Good tippa.*'

She stepped out of the taxi, took the flight of steps to the front door and waited as D'Ancey fumbled in his jacket pocket for his keys.

'Good evening,' she said, her face partially hidden in shadow.

He turned around and looked startled. 'Oh, oh, it's you. I wasn't expecting…didn't recognise…'

'We need to talk.'

He checked his watch. 'I'm attending a reception at Westminster Hall in an hour.'

She sensed his eyes wandering freely over her body, then back to eyes accentuated by long lashes and sharply defined high cheekbones. Her nose was small and fine. Her mouth large and full lipped, cherry-red, and smiling.

It was a package she hoped he'd be unable to resist.

She guessed he would have been alarmed when he realised she was standing there. He'd been in public life long enough to appreciate the risks: terrorists targeting individuals or the public en masse; organised crime; muggers, pickpockets and bag snatchers. She wondered if he'd considered a bodyguard and if promotion would mean that he'd be entitled to one? He would, she knew, be used to attention and, at any other time, he might have brushed aside unsolicited advances. But she'd watched the early evening news, and it had been a good day for Geoffrey D'Ancey that included his promotion and the safe passage of the Immigration White Paper's second reading.

Watching him relax, she assumed that any alarm bells had been silenced not only by the effort she'd made, but also by the fact that she wasn't exactly a stranger.

She moved closer, knowing that her perfume would fill him, as it had others, with a desire to know more.

'What are you doing here?' he asked.

'I need to talk to you privately and in confidence. I could come to the House of Commons, but when you hear what I have to propose, I'm sure you'll understand why discretion is essential.' She'd emphasised the words 'propose' and 'discretion', and hoped the inflection in her voice would swamp any misgivings he might have about her presence outside his London home.

'And the nature of this *proposal*?' he asked.

'I'm offering you an opportunity to become rich beyond your wildest dreams.'

He laughed. 'As I think you know, my dear, I already am.'

'You've been relying on your wife's fortune. This is her apartment, not yours.'

She moved closer, fighting the nausea that robbed her of her composure earlier that day.

'Your affairs are in a mess.' She smiled. 'I want to help. Meet me for a drink at The Ritz, tomorrow. One hour is all I ask.' She lent forward, her body close, her perfume filling his senses, and whispered. 'Who knows where this might lead?'

'And my wife?'

'Lady Emily will know what you choose to tell her.'

She walked down the steps, turned and smiled her biggest smile. 'I look forward to seeing you tomorrow at the Ritz. Shall we say, one o'clock?'

She hailed a taxi and returned to her flat.

Her evening had just begun.

Jones was met by uniformed officers at Gatwick Airport and driven through the rush hour to Richmond-Upon-Thames.

She popped into Lizzie's flat, dropped her bag in the bedroom, left a note suggesting a table for two at a local Italian restaurant, and then walked to Richmond's leisure centre. She was directed to the bar where she found the sub-aqua club's chairman.

He was an elderly, rotund man, and was staring into an empty glass. She flashed her warrant card and was about to ask about Graham Baldwin when he said, 'Too many people take the plunge without proper training. It's too bloody late when something goes wrong. You can't beat a good club and good training. Theory and practice, take it from me.'

It was clear he'd been drinking for some time.

'Let me tell you, Inspector,' he continued, 'the three cardinal rules of diving. One: never dive alone. Two: plan your dive. Three...' He stared into the distance.

'And the third?' She didn't have time to humour him.

'What?'

'Rule number three?'

'Oh, yes. Make sure you're gear's in good condition.'

'And how would you rate Mr Baldwin as a diver?'

'One of the best. God rest his soul. Can't believe he's gone. Accident, papers say.' He looked up. 'That right?'

'Did he have a particular dive partner?'

'Simon, the D O, he's the one to ask. He'll be on the poolside. Well, must be off. Nature calls.' He fumbled for his wallet. 'My business card, should you require any further assistance.' He slipped from the stool he'd been sitting on and disappeared into the changing room.

Jones shook her head, went through to the women's changing room and walked through to the poolside.

The Dive Officer, a short, powerfully built man in his early thirties, was busy setting up tanks and connecting demand valves for novice divers.

'The old boy suffered an embolism a couple of years ago, complicated by a minor stroke,' he said after Jones had mentioned her encounter. 'Can't dive. Can hardly walk. Finds solace in the sauce.'

'So, it needn't be fatal?'

'We train everyone to return to the surface slowly, but if they mistime stops they can end up in a decompression chamber.'

Voices, laughter, and the clatter of changing-room doors echoed around the pool as club members drifted in, sat on benches and waited for the D O. He finished checking the equipment before passing control to one of his instructors and taking Jones back to the bar.

Simon Dansk ordered a mineral water.

'Must have been good for the club to have a celebrity on its books?'

'Yes. An attractive guy. Changed girlfriends as often as men change their underwear.' He smiled. 'But he was dead serious about his diving.' He faltered. 'Sorry, that sounded tasteless.'

'No particular girlfriend?'

'Not until about a year ago and then, one evening… We meet in the back room of the *Saracen's Head*, you know the pub down by the river?'

'One of my old haunts.'

'He turned up with a real stunner.'

'She was learning to dive?'

'Took a few lessons. She had instructors falling over each other, but didn't stick at it. Chris seemed keen on her. Brought her to a party at the end of April. After that, I don't think I saw her again.'

'You remember her name?'

'No. No I can't.' He seemed to be confused. 'I'll ask around.'

'And treasure? We found a gold doubloon in his jeans. Could that have come from a wreck?'

'Treasure?' Dansk laughed. 'Inspector, do you think that I'd be sitting here if it was that easy? The chances of finding a wreck are slim enough, but a wreck with treasure? A porthole, maybe, or brass hacked off with a pneumatic lump hammer. These are the treasures of the club diver. But real treasure? You could sit on a brass cannon or the hull of a Spanish galleon, and never know it. The sea swallows, distorts, covers and camouflages. Sorry, that's a line from one of my lectures…Anyway, it doesn't give up its secrets to the likes of you and me, or Chris. No, Inspector, an enormous amount of money, patience and luck is needed to locate a wreck worth plundering. And, even if you found one, you'd be subject to the laws of salvage. It's more likely that his gold coin was purchased at a museum gift shop or at auction. Salvagers often raise funds for projects by selling off artefacts.'

'Thank you, you've been very helpful.' She got up to go. 'Oh, just one thing: where were you on Saturday the 4th and Sunday the 5th June?'

'You can't think..?'

'Elimination. Name of my game.'

Dansk took his time, Jones growing impatient.

'The weekend?' she said.

'The Club dived at Swanage, Saturday morning.'

'Not Falmouth?'

'Not for the weekend. We leave Cornwall for the Whit week or the summer.'

'And were you in Swanage?'

'Yes. I took the inflatable down Friday evening. Stayed at the *Smuggler's Inn*, had a few beers, and was in bed about midnight. We dived Saturday and Sunday, then drove back to London in the evening.'

'And Mr Baldwin didn't join you?'

'No.'

'Did he say why?'

'I haven't seen him for a couple of weeks. He's been busy with his new series, *Ask the Minister*. Next one's due this Friday, I think.'

'So, he packed his diving gear and drove all the way down to Falmouth?'

The D O shook his head. 'No, he must have hired gear down there.'

'I don't follow.'

'I've got his equipment. We're using it for training. It's in the back of my van. I even took it to Swanage, expecting to see Chris. It's here today, on the pool slide.'

'And the treasure?'

'Look, Inspector.' He rubbed his eyes and seemed to be irritated. 'There are always rumours, and Cornwall's a hotbed - smugglers, sunken treasure, pirates, wreckers lighting beacons to lure ships onto rocks and plunder the spoils. It could be an individual - someone who's found

45

a wreck and is stripping it, gradually. He might need an extra pair of hands, or finance. God knows. I'll tell you what...' He leant forward and tapped the bar. 'You can't tell me Chris died accidentally. He was too good and too careful.'

Jones nodded. 'I'd appreciate a list of club members and, in particular, the names of those who *weren't* in Swanage at the weekend. Uniformed officers will be in touch.'

'Inspector.' He underscored his words by pointing at her. 'Chris would never have dived alone. I don't believe his equipment failed, and even if it did, he would have coped.We train for emergencies. Something catastrophic must have happened down there. I've no doubt he dived *with* someone. And that *someone* killed him. Someone who must have been a bloody good diver.'

Westminster Hall is one of the oldest parts of The Palace of Westminster and dates back to 1097. It was constructed during the reign of William Rufus, the son of William the Conqueror. For many years, the Royal Courts of Justice met in within its walls and the trials of Thomas Moore, Guy Fawkes, and Charles 1 took place there. Brass plaques commemorate monarchs who've lain in state including Edward VII, George V, George VI and Queen Mary, and it was from there that the coffins of Winston Churchill and the Queen Mother began their final journey.

That evening some of the wealthiest and influential of London's business community had been invited to join the Mayor of London at a lavish banquet. Security was the organisers' highest priority and biggest headache.

TLS, a company owned by Terrance Leadbetter, had installed a surveillance system and Leadbetter had spent that afternoon supervising final checks. Long before the first guests arrived, five TLS operatives were stationed in a control room. They'd been vetted by Scotland Yard and were monitoring live pictures from every part of the Hall on a bank of TV screens.

As guests gathered, armed police officers dressed as waiters and carrying trays of hors d'oeuvres, looked distinctly ill at ease. But the champagne flowed and it wasn't long before the Hall rang to the banter of the elite at play.

Terrance Leadbetter sipped a juice and waited for Geoffrey D'Ancey to arrive.

He arrived late, unaccompanied, and it was obvious to Leadbetter that he had no intention of staying long. It was important, Leadbetter knew, that D'Ancey showed his face, pressed the flesh, and allocated time to his constituency Chair who had, according to Leadbetter's contacts at Gatwick, flown from Newquay that afternoon and was staying overnight at Claridges.

Leadbetter waited until D'Ancey was between flutes of champagne, took two charged glasses from a passing waiter and walked over to join him.

'I hear congratulations are in order?'

'Good news travels fast, Terrance.'

'I see the path ahead,' Leadbetter said, waving his arm in an arc, as a mystic might. 'Promotion to the Front Bench and, after the next election, Conservative Minister for..?'

'That will be for David to decide, but I've made no secret of my preference for the Home Office.'

'Including national security, I presume?'

D'Ancey laughed and placed a hand on Leadbetter's shoulder. 'Never miss an opportunity, do you?'

'In my business, shrinking violets whither and die.'

47

Leadbetter raised his glass.

'Your good health...Minister.'

They stood along the West Wall and looked towards the Gothic-style partition at the southern end.

The hubbub seemed to swell into the arched roof and everything seemed to be going according to plan when a glass smashed on the floor a few metres away from the Mayor. Leadbetter could feel the tension in the air. He imagined a dozen security officers reaching for their handguns and wondered how operatives in the control room had reacted. Then the culprit held his hands in the air and apologised - 'Sorry. Sorry everyone' - and a waiter was sent to find a mop.

Leadbetter fished a wallet from his tuxedo.

'Missing anything?' he asked D'Ancey.

'Good God. I thought I'd seen the last of this.'

D'Ancey opened the wallet. 'Cards and money gone. I suppose that was inevitable. How did you..?'

'Our surveillance cameras picked you up walking along Regent Street. We've had our eye on a scam involving several retailers, including the shop where that attractive young blond caught your eye.'

'She...?'

'Picked your pocket. She works for a professional outfit.' Leadbetter handed him an envelope containing a DVD. 'A snippet. It shows you strolling along Regent's Street. I didn't download the incident inside the shop. Didn't want it to fall into the wrong hands.'

'As long as it doesn't end up on YouTube.'

'Do you want the police involved?'

'Of course.'

'But, no actual harm's been done.' Leadbetter put a hand in his pocket and produced D'Ancey's credit card.

'How..?'

'We made a citizen's arrest, all part of the service we provide. But, you should check your bank account, see if any withdrawals have been made.'

'What are you saying, Terrance?'

'A man in your position, so easily distracted by a short skirt and a pair of shapely legs? There are those who'd make hay and question your judgment.'

Leadbetter looked across the Hall and noticed a large lady in a billowing lilac gown. She was steaming in their direction and Leadbetter detected a shift in D'Ancey's demeanour.

'You're right. This incident should be handled with the utmost discretion,' D'Ancey said. 'I'll leave you to ensure that this doesn't see the light of day.'

'And, when the Conservative Home Secretary needs advice on security?'

D'Ancey moved forward to greet the Chair of his Constituency. He took her chubby hand and kissed her chubby cheek.

'Allow me to introduce Terrance Leadbetter,' he said. 'A man I would trust with my life.'

3

George Tregunna looked a mess.

He was standing at the back of the Incident Room and, as far as Brenda McLeish could tell, he was finding it difficult to concentrate on the briefing. She noticed that one or two shirt buttons and their button-holes were mismatched. His grey suit was rumpled and shabby, and his hair was limp, greying around the temples, aging him beyond his forty-three years.

At the end of the briefing, she followed him into the corridor. He opened a pack of cigarettes, found it empty, crushed it, and threw it into a metal waste bin. 'Sums up my life: empty packet of fags.'

'Very poetic, George. Didn't know you smoked.'

'Man of mystery, me.'

'Wife kicked you out?'

'Renting a flat. One room, with shared facilities. Beginning of the end.'

'Sorry. Seriously, it's sad when things fall apart. Still, might be the best thing that's happened to you in years.'

'How'd you work that one out?'

'I don't want that hangdog expression around me for much longer.'

'That bad?'

'You're not a happy bunny, George. Haven't been for a long time. You should see a doctor. Depression's not something to be swept under the carpet.'

'I'm not depressed.'

'Go see your doctor.'

'Just need to get my life sorted.'

'George...' McLeish sighed and lent against the wall. 'Depression is nothing to be ashamed of. It's a disease and needs treating. Go and see your doctor.' She smiled. 'That's an order.'

'Even if I wanted to, my digs are in a different area. I've got no idea where the nearest surgery is.'

'Here...' McLeish fished out a pen and her note pad, flipped open her mobile, checked through the pre-sets and wrote down a number. 'This is our doctor. He's used to working with basket cases.' She smiled and watched him pocket the number. 'Fancy some nosh later?'

'Angus cooking?'

'No. I wouldn't subject you to that. We've got a new chef.' She walked along the corridor, stopping outside the lady's washroom.

'I'll pick you up at six,' she said.

'I'll get there under my own steam.'

She wagged a finger. 'Don't let me down, George.'

'I'm not suicidal.'

'That's better, more like the George we all know and love.' She walked over and slapped him on the shoulder. 'Beginning of a new chapter, you'll see.' She ran her hand under the lapel of his jacket. 'We'll make a start this evening. Six o'clock.'

'A start?'

'New image, George. A new image.'

She walked back dowm the corridor, pushed her way into the washroom and looked at herself in the mirror.

'Ugly bitch,' she mumbled.

Kate Madison arrived at The Ritz and chose a small alcove at the back. She placed a document case on the seat beside her, removed her sunglasses and ordered a pot of Darjeeling. Unlike many patrons, this was not a treat to be savoured, unlikely to be repeated, way beyond normal budgets.

51

Whenever she was up in town, she 'took tea' and the management treated her accordingly, reserving the best table whenever she phoned and ensuring staff were vigilant. She tipped well, knowing that such generosity supplemented meagre wages and reinforced the image she'd been cultivating.

She toasted her reflection in a large mirror beside her table, checked her appearance and recalled the fun she'd had the evening before, yesterday evening, when she'd followed Geoffrey D'Ancey from Westminster Hall into China Town...

She'd sat in a pub opposite the restaurant where he was having a drink with a young Asian woman. She'd waited until they'd finished and followed them to his Club in Park Place. Once there, she'd paid off her taxi and stood in the shadowed entrance of a jeweller's shop. She'd watched him enter the Club, unaccompanied. His companion used the fire escape after it was opened from the inside. An hour later, the young woman left. She closed the fire escape behind her and hurried towards Piccadilly, seemingly unaware of the eyes that tracked her as she turned the corner and disappeared.

And now, as one of her favourite waiters at The Ritz placed a tray in front of her, all Kate Madison had to do was sip her tea and wait...

'I'm so glad you could make it.' She rose as D'Ancey was shown to her table. 'Would you like some tea?'

He glanced at his watch.

'Something stronger, I think.'

He ordered a double gin-and-tonic. The waiter looked across at her. 'I'm fine, thank you. Perhaps later.' She let the words linger and then said. 'How did the vote go?'

'As expected. A Government majority, but a little too close for comfort.'

'The Opposition's been very successful lately.'

'The curse of coalition. It's not easy working with a bunch of tree huggers.' His drink arrived and he raised the glass in salute. 'Good to see you again.' He drained half and lowered his glass, but whilst his eyes smiled, his mouth set hard. 'Tell me. What are we doing here?'

'Well, I suppose you might say that I've *selected* you,' she began, slowly. 'Let me explain.' She took the document case, but didn't open it - in fact it was empty, but he wasn't to know.

She glance around and lent forward to ensure their conversation wasn't overheard. 'Your financial affairs are in a mess.' She sipped her tea and looked at him over the rim of the cup. 'I shall go into detail later, but you've been frequenting a small gaming club in Soho for the past three years and lost a fortune. Recently, you lost a substantial amount in a poker game. Creditors won't wait forever.' She laid a hand on the document case. 'You needn't be concerned. I am totally discreet. If anyone is aware of your problems, they didn't hear it from me.'

'My wife?'

'Lady Emily's been bailing you out.' She lifted her right eyebrow, as if challenging him to deny her next assertion. 'But I'm not sure how she'd feel about the young Asian women you entertain at your Club in Park Place.'

'So, this *is* blackmail?'

She took another sip of tea and replaced the cup. 'Given what I know, it would be easier to bleed a stone,' she said, and saw the colour rise in his cheeks.

He downed the rest of his drink and managed to find his voice.

'You seem remarkably well informed.'

'You're a man of high expectations. I mean to match or exceed those expectations and convince you I'm dead serious.' She tapped the document case. 'I want to help.

53

I have information. A merger. Huge profits for those in on the ground.'

He lent forward and glanced around, just as she had. 'This smacks of insider dealing,' he said. 'It would be inappropriate for me to be involved.'

'Yes, I agree. Insider dealing's illegal and since the banking crisis it has been easier to catch a cold than make serious money. I'm talking about a perfectly legal enterprise for those who have the balls for it. This is something that could make millions, for both of us. I just need to know if you're in or out?'

Before he could respond, she continued.

'Look, we can't talk here. Is there somewhere we can go that is...' she smiled '...less public?'

He dipped his head - in resignation, she hoped - and looked at her, his eyes weary, his face drawn.

'Why are you doing this?'

'You want the truth?'

'Yes.'

'Can you handle it?'

'What?'

'The truth.'

'Yes, yes, of course.'

'My assessment of your finances is accurate. We both know that. I can help you fix things. But, to be honest, that's not the only reason I invited you to tea.'

She took a final sip. 'Can't you tell?' She held his gaze, feigning embarrassment.

'Tell?'

'Geoffrey...' She used his name for the first time with crippling effect. 'I'd do anything for you.' She put her cup down and lowered her voice to a whisper. 'I'd like to see you. Tonight, if possible.'

'We could go to my Club?'

'Sounds perfect.'

'I have an apartment reserved for when I'm attending the House. But, the Club has rules...'

'The fire escape will do nicely.'

'How did you..?'

'I'll reveal *everything* this evening. Shall we say eight o'clock?'

'Eight would be perfect,' he said.

'I must go,' she said, suddenly, and signalled to a waiter. 'Put this on my account, would you?'

She stood up. 'Until later.'

George Tregunna walked passed *The Crow's Nest* several times. Months of eating out of cans and cartons - months of processed food, washed down by chemically enhanced beer - had robbed him of the spark and passion he'd brought to both his job and the early years of his marriage. Now, everything was an effort.

The divorce settlement would leave him without a home. He'd probably have to part with a third of his salary to keep up the mortgage payments on *her* house for the next fifteen years. And, adding insult to injury, he'd been slapped in the face by the take-it-or-leave-it attitude of the property agent who'd found him a one-room rental for another third of his salary.

But, as he stood outside the pub door, he realised that there could be serious consequences if he dared to defy Brenda McLeish and it was that realisation that drove him into the lounge bar...that, and free food, decent grub, home cooked, lashings of gravy, mash to die for, washed down by a jug of real ale.

'Right.' McLeish breezed into the bar. 'Let's get shot of everything you're standing up in.'

She didn't give him a chance to reply.

'You didn't honestly think I was going to let you eat in our pub looking like a tramp, did you?'

She took his hand, pulled him through a door leading to the pub's private quarters, up a flight of stairs and into a bedroom with ensuite shower room.

'Lounge and kitchen through that door. In a couple of weeks, you'll be able to call this home and tart it up as much as you like. The pub's cleaners will run a vacuum over it once a week, your laundry can go in the van on Mondays, and you'll be entitled to one free meal a day as payment for the security you'll provide for the brewery.'

'So, I'm a night watchman now, am I?'

'Once word gets out that we've got round-the-clock police presence, only a nutter would chance his luck.'

'And you, and that long-suffering husband of yours?'

'We're getting our own place, putting down roots at last, starting a family.' She looked at him. 'Well, don't stand there gawping like a stranded monkfish. Strip, shower. There's change of clothes on the bed. Be ready to shop 'til you drop.' She moved closer to him, her face inches from his. 'And don't even think about climbing out of the bathroom window, George Tregunna. I don't like being messed about.' She walked over to the door turned and grinned. 'I'll explain as we go.'

He was standing in the middle of the room.

'Go where?'

'First, your digs. I want all your old tat bagged up and sent to a charity shop. When was the last time you sent stuff to a dry-cleaners? No, don't tell me, it'll make me sick. I've got a friend. She's having a sale. Last year's stock. We're gonna give your credit card a bashing.' She walked out, then popped her head around the door. 'You've got ten minutes and counting.'

*

56

'Hallo stranger.' Jones had used her key to Lizzie's apartment and was carrying a large bunch of flowers.

'What's this, a peace offering?'

'Come here, give us a hug.'

As they held on to one another, Jones soaked up the warmth of her body and tried not to crush the flowers.

'I've opened a bottle of bubbly,' Lizzie said. 'Help yourself.' She put the bunch on the kitchen worktop and searched through several cupboards before she found a vase.

They'd met two years ago at a party following the orchestra's final night at the Festival Hall. Jones was attending a training course in London and was reluctant to accept Charlie Hobson's invitation to accompany him to the concert, not only because she wasn't keen on classical music, but also because she wasn't sure how she felt about seeing him so long after their affair. But he'd persisted, and she'd given in, and thrown something together, and was determined to make the most of the evening.

After the concert, they were invited backstage and Jones had jumped at the chance - seeing it as a way of delaying any after-date awkwardness - and had dragged Charlie through the maze of curtains until they found members of the orchestra and crew celebrating.

Lizzie James had joined the party, shyly, to great applause. As the soloist for the evening's recital of a Rachmaninoff piano concerto, she'd earned a standing ovation and praise from professional colleagues who'd gathered to celebrate another successful season.

Charlie Hobson had introduced Jones to Lizzie and probably wished he hadn't when he was left high and dry and the girls spent the evening chatting, laughing, and dancing.

Despite several unsatisfactory affairs with unsuitable men Jones certainly hadn't imagined she'd fall in love with another woman but, as she stood in the kitchen and watched Lizzie cutting stems and arranging the flowers, she remembered the instant attraction she'd felt for her - those huge brown eyes, full, ever-smiling lips, and small broad nose.

'Good day?' Lizzie placed the vase under a tap.

'Gathering background info on Chris Baldwin. You?'

'Exhibition at the Tate Modern. Rehearsals...'

'For the tour of Asia?'

'KL, Singapore, Hong Kong.'

'You said, over the Chianti, last night.'

'I can't turn down invitations. They'll dry up if I do. There's so much competition.'

'Sometimes, I just wish...'

'I know. So do I, but...' Lizzie shrugged. She placed the vase on the table. 'When are we going down to Cornwall?'

'Thursday or Friday. Depends.'

'I'm assuming...' Lizzie tilted her head and Jones knew she was in trouble. 'That we've got this evening together?'

'I'm going out. Charlie Hobson.' Jones smiled, and shrugged. 'A drink. Come if you want to.'

'Hence the flowers?'

Jones hesitated. 'Charlie says he has a proposition to put to me.'

'Of course he does. Unfinished business. That night we met? He was smitten. I could tell.'

'Smitten?' Jones laughed and took Lizzie in her arms. 'Didn't stand a chance once I'd met you.'

'Be careful he doesn't slip under the radar.'

Jones looked puzzled.

'You know what I mean. Once bitten.'

'Smitten? Bitten?' Jones laughed. 'I'm not interested in him. End of story.'

58

'Glad to hear it.' Lizzie fussed the flowers. 'They're beautiful. Thank you.'

'What are you doing about food?'

'Takeaway. Indian, probably.'

'I'll order an extra biryani.'

'Flier's in the top drawer, next to the sink.'

'Can I use your phone? Mine needs recharging.'

'Help yourself, it's in my handbag…'

Jones picked it up, but didn't open it immediately. 'This new?'

'Impulse. Couldn't resist it. Shop in New York.'

Jones noticed that she'd blushed. 'Lizzie?'

'You promise me you won't shout at me?'

Jones was going to ask, 'Why would I shout at you?' but knew the answer the instant she looked inside.

'Oh, for God's sake, Lizzie.' She eased the canister out of the handbag. 'How the hell did you get it through customs?'

'Wing and a prayer.'

'Jesus.' Jones hesitated. 'You do realise that this is illegal?'

'I won't tell if you don't.'

'Jesus Christ.'

'I bought it for protection, but if it makes you feel any better, I'll get rid of it.'

Jones dropped the pepper spray into the handbag.

'Look, I can understand why, but just don't…'

'Don't worry.'

'It's not you I'm worried about.'

'I know, your job…'

'No. Well, yes. My job. God, I don't know, just make sure you read the instructions and know how to use it. OK?'

Lizzie wrapped her arms around her waist.

'Are you listening to me?' Jones said.

'Don't worry. I'll read the instructions. I promise.'

59

Lizzie grinned.

'Now, what time you meeting Charlie?'

'Eight.'

'So, we have time?'

'Before or after I ring the Indian?'

'Place an order, but tell them to deliver in a couple of hours.'

Geoffrey D'Ancey asked the taxi driver to include his tip in the receipt, got out and took the short flight of steps into the Explorers and Travellers Club where he was greeted by musty air mingling with the smell of restaurant food.

There was also a familiar face smiling at him from behind the front desk.

'Good evening, Tommy.'

'Good evening, Sir. Early tonight.'

'I have some business to attend to.'

It was a coded message.

'Of course, Sir.' Tommy lent forward, as if wanting to ensure they weren't overheard. 'Everything to your satisfaction yesterday, Sir?'

'Yes, timing was perfect.'

'I'm not being funny, Sir…' There was something else on Tommy's mind - something that concerned him far more than money. He looked about again, nodded at a couple on their way to the restaurant and waited until they were out of earshot. 'Last night one of your…one of your guests walked through reception, bold as brass, and…'

'I know who that was. It won't happen again.'

'Risky, that's all. We agreed, the fire escape?'

'Understood, Tommy.'

It was D'Ancey's turn to check the lobby.

'I'll put something in my expenses to compensate for your anxiety.

'Very generous, Sir. I wasn't trying…'

'Tommy. Please. Stop worrying. Now, this evening.'

'Will you be dining, Sir?'

'What time is it?'

'Five-to-eight.'

'Perhaps you'd arrange for a menu to be brought up?'

It was another coded message.

Tommy nodded. 'Immediately, sir?'

'About five minutes, Tommy.'

Kate Madison waited in the same shadowed entrance to a jeweller's shop she'd used twenty-four hours earlier, until someone unlocked the fire escape door and pushed it open. She slipped through and took the lift to the sixth floor.

He was standing at the door to his apartment.

She walked from the lift and stood before him. She'd unbuttoned her cashmere three-quarter-length coat and her dark hair cascaded across her shoulders. Her linen jacket was also unbuttoned and she wore a pristine white blouse, tight across her breasts.

'May I come in?' she asked.

'Yes. Yes, of course. I'm sorry. You quite took my breath away. Come on in. Here, let me take your coat.'

She slipped the coat off, walked across the room and stepped through open doors onto a balcony.

She lent against the handrail and glanced briefly at the view across Green Park and towards Buckingham Palace. She looked down at a flowerbed beneath the balcony and pressed the handrail into her hips.

She turned, stepped back inside and closed the doors.

'Are you cold, my dear?'

'No. I was just admiring the view.'

She tapped her document case. 'Work?'

'A drink,' he said. 'I've got a rather good brandy.' He opened the cocktail cabinet.

She glanced at the photographs of the Royal Family above the fireplace, the two cream sofas, and the coffee table. She placed the document case on the floor against the coffee table.

'Your good health.' He handed her a glass containing a generous measure of brandy.

'Here's to a long and fruitful relationship.' She raised her glass.

'I'm confused,' he said, leaning forward and running his fingers through her hair. 'Why the wig?'

'I have my reputation to think of. I wouldn't want the tabloids to capture me skulking around in the shadows, using the fire escape or spending time in a gentleman's room.'

'You have nothing to fear. I have a reputation to protect as well, you know.' He smirked. 'It suits you. Most unusual, blue eyes, long dark hair.'

She smiled. 'As long as it's not too distracting.'

'Perhaps we should postpone business until later?' He walked over to one of the sofas. 'Come and sit down. We have so much to discuss.'

She sat next to him.

'Earlier today,' he began, 'you said that you had 'selected' me. I didn't quite understand what you meant by that.'

'I also said that I was a long-time admirer. In truth, Geoffrey, I find you extremely attractive. Few men have such a...' She looked down at her glass. 'Oh, gosh, how can I put this? Very few men possess such a devastating combination of intelligence and power. And...' She looked directly into his eyes. 'You have such a physical presence.'

'I had no idea you felt this way.'

'Why would you?' She sipped her brandy and averted her eyes again. 'Your financial misfortune is temporary. I can help you, if you'll allow me to.'

'But why me?'

She held up her empty glass.

'Could I have another one of these?'

'Yes, yes, of course, but please, go on, don't be shy.'

'It's…well…it's a bit embarrassing really, but being this close to you…' She giggled, took the glass he'd recharged and sipped her brandy, feeling its warmth in her stomach, settling her. 'Mustn't have too much. I don't want to do anything I might regret.'

'Oh, I'm sure you're in complete control.'

He used the back of his hand to caress her cheek.

She tilted her head to one side, away from his caress.

'I must confess I've made every effort to learn as much about you as I can.' She laughed. 'Your Who's Who makes interesting reading. There's even talk of you being Prime Minister, one day.'

She waited, allowing her sycophancy to soften him up and then she struck the deal that most men need to hear when playing away from home.

'You're able to distinguish between the different relationships in your life. I know I can never be part of your personal life, but I needed to tell you how I felt. You're discreet, which is why no one knows I'm here tonight.'

'My wife?'

'Lady Emily need never know. This is just between you and me.'

She lent over and kissed him on the cheek and then stood up, placed her glass on the table, removed her jacket and led him towards the balcony.

63

There, she stood to one side and waited for him to open the doors. 'Thank you, kind sir.'

'My lady.'

She stifled a giggle and pressed a finger to his lips.

'Don't want to disturb the neighbours, do we?'

The evening had closed in and the balcony dark. She rested against the handrail, her back towards him. He followed, put his arms around her, and nuzzled into her neck. She felt the cold steel of the handrail pressing into her hips, sighed and turned to face him. 'At last we are alone.'

She allowed him to kiss her and felt his passion rise as he became more urgent. His hands snaked up to her breasts and, as he pressed against her, his breathing became laboured.

She found his zip and pulled the fastener down.

'Here, let's change places,' she whispered, her voice low and seductive, warm against his ear. 'Lean back, against the handrail. It'll be easier and more comfortable for you.'

They swapped places and he perched on the handrail, still fondling her breasts. He spread his legs.

'Good,' she said. 'Now, relax. Close your eyes.'

She fumbled with his zip once more and, as he threw his head back in anticipation, his centre of gravity shifted and she struck, driving upwards with both hands.

He fell backwards and down - arms flapping, mouth gasping for air, his cry cut short on impact. And then there was silence - his body was impaled on spiked railings surrounding the flowerbed beneath the balcony.

She walked back into the room, calmly, picked up the document case, opened it, removed several photographs and scattered them on the sofa. She downed the last of her brandy and collected her jacket and coat. Before she left, she stepped out onto the balcony and looked at his body convulsing in its last seconds of life.

*

Jones hurried across Richmond Green...past the theatre's Victorian façade, past people dying for a fag on the pavement outside *The Cricketers*, and past the grand houses that muffled the grumble of traffic inching along George Street.

She was on her way to see Charlie Hobson and felt a rush of guilt. She could still smell Lizzie's perfume and passion. She should have stayed with her. It was there, in Richmond, where they'd spent the early days of their relationship. And, it had been fun despite the separation, the travel, the intensity of their jobs, and the raised eyebrows. Good days that seemed so long ago.

Hobson had reserved a table at *The Saracen's Head*. The terrace overlooked the Thames as it flowed beneath Richmond Bridge. She glanced at the muddy water and noticed swans paddling past, riding waves with dignity, their necks, long and elegant.

'Sorry I'm late,' she said.

After an awkward moment when neither seemed sure what to do next, they kissed one another on the cheek.

'It's good to see you again.'

'And you, Charlie.'

'A pint OK?'

'A half.'

'Of London's finest?'

'A half.'

A waiter took their order.

'Glad you could get away,' he said.

'Not without consequences.'

Their drinks arrived and she took a sip, a taster, like wine, allowing it to linger in her mouth and awaken her taste buds. In truth, she felt very uncomfortable.

'There's an opening for you here,' he said. 'If you're interested.'

65

'Thanks, but Cornwall's home.'

'A long way from the action.'

'I've got all the excitement I can handle.'

'Lizzie still part of your life?'

'I'm forgiven?'

He looked confused.

'The evening that Lizzie and I...at the concert? I wasn't intending...' She faltered. 'Just didn't see it coming.'

'Neither did I.' Charlie looked like a small child. 'But if ever, you know, it doesn't work out.'

'She's very perceptive, Lizzie,' Jones said. 'She said you'd want to jump my bones.'

'She didn't.' He laughed and supped his beer. 'She wouldn't say that. She's too sophisticated. You might, but not Lizzie.'

'What? So I'm not sophisticated?'

'It's not the first word that comes to mind.'

'Bloody cheek.' She sipped her beer. 'I told her I'm not interested in you.'

'Don't pull your punches, do you?'

'Never did Charlie. You know me better than that.'

He snorted, shook his head, and sighed. 'Could have had something special, you and me.'

'Charlie.'

'Remember Magaluf?'

'Charlie.'

'You learned to dive. I learned to swim.' He snorted. 'You were very patient with me.'

'It's a gift.'

'I'd hoped, you know, you, me, we...'

'It's not going to happen, Charlie.'

'She's a lucky lady.'

'Yeah.'

They sat in silence and Jones found refuge in the sea-of-faces enlivened by the location and the drink.

'How'd you murder someone, Charlie?' she asked, almost absent-mindedly.

'Murder? This work?'

'Yeah, given the number of different ways and given that we've encountered most, what would you choose?'

'Slow, painful and undetectable.' He stressed each word. 'If I wanted to kill someone, I'd want them to know what was happening, I'd want them to suffer, and I'd want to walk away. No comebacks.'

She glanced at him. 'Wouldn't take risks would you?' She shifted in her seat. 'They took Chris Baldwin down to 40 meters. Dark, cold, visibility shit. Why didn't they just chop him up into little pieces?'

'And feed him to a stray dog?'

'I'm serious. It just doesn't make sense.'

'Amateurs. Trying to make it look like an accident?'

'Unless, of course, it *was*.'

'And he became disorientated, kept going down.'

'Raptures of the deep?'

'Talking of raptures...'

'Charlie.'

They returned to their beer. Clouds gathered and, as spots of rain became more persistent, punters began to drift inside or call it a day.

'I was serious,' he said, 'about us.'

'There's no us, Charlie. Never will be. Sorry.'

He shrugged, his face set in resignation, and ordered another drink.

They sat, protected by an awning and Jones enjoyed the freshness bought by the rain. She sensed him squirming on his seat and hoped to God he wasn't going to plead undying love when his mobile clamoured for his attention.

He listened, ended the call. 'Sorry, got to go. A member of Her Majesty's Government's just been found dead at his Club.'

*

An hour later, just before ten - Lizzie already in bed - Jones was lying on the sofa in the living room, picking at cold biryani and reading the letter her aunt had written before the stroke.

Although she was unsure what the word actually meant she thought *ironic* sounded about right. Ironic that she'd offered to buy her aunt a laptop with a web-cam and sign her up for cheap Internet calls. But her aunt was terrified of anything technical and Jones was always too busy to write. At least, that's how she'd rationalised her irregular response to her aunt's newsletters. Even before the stroke, phone calls had often been hurried, truncated by something that cropped up at work. 'Got to go aunty,' she'd say. 'It's my mobile. Someone from the station. Duty calls.'

She spent a couple of days with her immediately after she'd been taken into hospital but, since then, work, and the cost of the six-hundred-mile-round-trip, had made it increasingly difficult.

Her promotion, she guessed, would make it nigh on impossible.

She'd considered asking for a transfer to London.

She'd be closer to Lizzie.

Lizzie.

Someone she hadn't told her aunt about.

The old girl would never understand.

At ten-thirty, she was in the shower when the phone rang. She grabbed a towel and hurried into the lounge.

It was Charlie Hobson. He told her about Geoffrey D'Ancey.

'Jesus. All hell will break loose back home. First Baldwin on the beach, and now...'

She looked down at the puddle of water soaking into the carpet. 'Hang on a sec, Charlie.' She carried the phone to the bathroom, lodged it between ear and shoulder, and tried to dry herself.

'Someone will have to go and see D'Ancey's wife.' Hobson said. 'She'll need to come up to London for the formal identification.'

'I'll contact my Super.' She pulled a clean bra over one arm, but couldn't do it up and let it dangle.

'You've met her?' he asked.

'Lady Emily? Yes. I crewed for her a couple of years ago.' She grabbed a pair of knickers from her case.

'I'd heard she can be difficult.'

'Doesn't suffer fools.'

She managed to get the knickers on and, flushed with success - but with the bra still dangling - she dislodged a pair of jeans from a pile of clothing.

'Shit,' she muttered, as the whole lot fell on the floor.

'You OK?' he asked.

'Can't multi-task.'

'Congratulations, by the way. Your promotion.'

'Snap.' She was still trying to get dressed. 'Look, Charlie, I'm going to put the phone down and call you back in five minutes, OK?'

She did and they swapped information about both cases, brought each other up-to-date and discussed other avenues of enquiry.

'I need a favour,' Hobson said.

'I'm listening.'

'You've made a start on Baldwin, and I'd like you to be involved in D'Ancey's death.'

'Makes sense. Our local MP.'

'You'll probably need an extra pair of hands. Don't have anyone spare, do you?'

'Like I've got officers sitting around, drinking coffee, and waiting for something to do?'

69

'Two days…three, tops. Get you back to Falmouth by Friday or Saturday.'

She sighed and bit her lip. She knew Lizzie would be pissed off by the delay. She fought the urge to block the request, but knew he could pull rank or cut her out and go straight to Superintendent Hinkson. Besides, she'd decided that George Tregunna could do with a change of scenery. 'I think I've got someone who fits the bill.' She checked her watch. 'I presume you'd like us to start in the morning?'

'I'll book the overnight train. It'll get your foot soldier into Paddington at five-thirty in the morning. You'll be there to meet him?'

'You're brutal.'

'You'll square it with Lizzie?'

'No problem.'

'Sure?'

'She's good as gold.'

'Well, if you ever…'

'Don't hold your breath, Charlie.'

Fortunately for Tregunna, it was McLeish who found him and not one of the patrol cars detailed to track him down.

She'd tried his digs and *The Crow's Nest* and had drawn a blank. She'd tried a pool hall he'd begun to frequent and was told he'd left at least half-an-hour before. She'd driven down Falmouth High Street, parked at Custom House and found him propping up a pint in a corner of the *Quayside Inn*.

She looked at him.

He'd aged, and the bags under his eyes seemed to be stuffed with dirty laundry - dark, red rimmed, bloodshot whites. His hair was longer, probably unwashed, and the suit he'd bought in her friend's boutique was already crumpled and stained.

She decided that she'd have a word with Angus. If anyone could sort Tregunna out, her husband's school-of-charm was probably the best medicine.

'You sober, George?'

He looked up at her, his grin lop-sided. He tipped his glass towards his mouth and slurped down the last of his drink.

'What's this crap?' She took the glass, sniffed and glowered at him. 'Now I know you've hit rock bottom. Lager top? For Christ's sake.' She took the glass over to the bar and muscled her way between two middle-aged men who were discussing the weekend's cricket.

'Get him a large, black coffee love,' she said to the barmaid. 'Bring it over, would you? Thanks, you're a doll.'

She sat down opposite him.

'Balloon's gone up, George. It's all hands on deck. You're off to London.'

'What?'

'Special assignment. Overnight train. Sleeper. Give you a chance to sober up.'

The coffee arrived and she took his hand, forcing his fingers around the cup. 'You can drink yourself stupid when you get back from London. I might even give you a hand, but tonight...' She looked into his eyes. '...I'm fucked if I'm going to let you off the hook that easily.'

4

By the time Jones had arranged for George Tregunna to be driven to Truro station to catch the sleeper it had gone twelve.

She called Superintendent Hinkson not only because she felt she'd want to know about Geoffrey D'Ancey immediately, but also because she didn't relish the idea of McLeish driving up to the Elizabethan home of a titled lady and breaking the news that her husband had been found dead.

She could have kissed the Superintendent when she said, 'Tell McLeish to pick me up in half an hour.'

They were shown into the drawing room and asked if they'd like tea. They declined and stood like bookends either side of a huge fireplace that was - McLeish had seen enough Hollywood movies to know - typically Elizabethan.

Even this relatively small room was imposing enough to render them speechless and they stood, gazing at tapestries, the stained glass windows, old oil paintings depicting hunting scenes, and the furniture that looked both exquisite and impractical. McLeish found it difficult to imagine lying on the chaise longue underneath the far window, reading a copy of *Hello!* and munching her way through a packet of cheese and onion crisps.

Lady Emily entered, elegant in a silk kimono, her long, luxurious auburn hair framing her pale, delicate face.

'Superintendent Hinkson, what brings you here in the middle of the night?'

'I'm afraid I have bad news, Milady. Would you like to sit down?'

'I'll stand, if it's all the same to you?'

'Of course, as you wish.'

Hinkson assumed she would be impatient to hear what had happened, but was surprised by the strength in her voice.

'Well, Superintendent?'

'I'm very sorry to tell you, Milady, that this evening your husband was found unconscious at his Club in London. He was certified dead by a police physician on the way to hospital.'

Both McLeish and Hinkson had been the bearer of bad news on numerous occasions and were hardened to the natural responses of shock, disbelief, and anger, but Lady Emily remained calm, dropping her head briefly before asking, 'How did he die?'

'We can't be sure until after the post-mortem.'

'Did he fall over and hit his head? Was he drunk? Was he shot? Stabbed?'

'I'm afraid I'm not in a position to confirm anything at the moment, other than we understand he fell from a sixth floor balcony.'

'And a police physician was called?'

'They felt it was important to maintain an element of discretion until you'd been informed and until the cause of death had been established.'

'When can I see him?'

'We'll need you to make a formal identification. I can arrange for a car to drive you to London.'

'My chauffeur will take me.' She walked over to a telephone and dialled a single number. 'Is Alexandra back yet? Ask her to join me in the drawing room.' She covered the mouthpiece. 'Would you like some tea?' She spoke into the phone again. 'And bring some tea and a few of your homemade biscuits. Thank you.'

'After you've returned from London,' McLeish said, 'we'll want to interview you.'

'And you are?'

Hinkson intervened. 'Sergeant McLeish is part of the investigative team working with Inspector Jones. The Inspector's already in London.'

'So, you're treating me as a suspect, are you Sergeant?'

'It would help,' McLeish said, 'if you could confirm your whereabouts this evening between, say, six and ten.'

'And how do you imagine I could be in London, kill my husband, and be back here in time to be insulted by you?'

'Fly?' McLeish folded her arms across her ample chest.

Hinkson stepped in.

'You would want us to be as thorough as possible, Milady. The Sergeant's questions are no more than routine. Your cooperation is appreciated.'

But, McLeish wasn't interested in appeasing either of them. 'We'll need a comprehensive breakdown of your husband's business interests, his itinerary over the past few weeks, and access to his personal and business computers. We'll also need to question each of your staff.'

'I will not have my life turned upside down.' Lady Emily looked like she was building a head of steam when the door opened and a young woman wearing a white dressing gown hurried into the room. She looked at Lady Emily who motioned her to her side. 'Alexandra is my daughter.' She looked intently into her eyes and squeezed her hand. 'These are police officers, my dear. They're here on official business.'

'What's so urgent it couldn't wait until the morning?'

McLeish smiled. Although she was barely out of her teens, Alexandra had the same challenge in her eyes as her mother and was obviously a chip off the same block. Her long, dark hair was tousled as though she'd just got out of bed, which, given the hour, she probably had.

Alexandra looked at her mother.

'Bad news, I'm afraid, my darling. Your father's been found dead at his Club in London.'

'Oh, my God,' Alexandra said, apparently stunned rather than distressed.

Lady Emily held her hand and turned to McLeish.

'Whilst we will assist you in any way we can, I don't want the smooth running of the Hall affected or my staff upset. Is that clear?'

'That may not be possible.'

'Did I make that sound like a request, Sergeant?'

McLeish looked at Hinkson, who nodded.

'There are complications.'

'If you mean his death wasn't straightforward, then say so.'

'Too early to be certain, but it's possible your husband was murdered.'

'Well, I gathered that.'

Tea arrived and Alexandra seemed to have recovered enough to pour. She handed cups round and sipped from her own. 'Murdered?' she said. She put the cup on a side table and then munched absentmindedly on a biscuit. 'Murdered?' She seemed to be in two minds. 'Good God.'

'We'll travel up in the morning and stay in London for a few days,' Lady Emily said. 'If you need to contact us, you'll find us at The Savoy.' She got up, her tea untouched, and took Alexandra's hand 'Now, if you'll excuse us? Goodnight, Superintendent. Sergeant.'

*

The sleeper to London was delayed by half-an-hour and arrived just after six. As it slowed into Paddington and hit the buffers, George Tregunna woke, sluggishly, from a deep sleep.

Jones was there to meet him and, after a leisurely breakfast at an all-night diner, they deposited Tregunna's bag in left-luggage, then made their way underground and caught a District Line tube.

Nine stops later, they fought their way off the train and on to the platform where they were blasted by warm air funnelling down an out-of-service escalator. They stopped at the bottom of the motionless escalator and looked up. Each step seemed that bit bigger than the one before and Jones glanced around, hoping there'd be a lift. There wasn't and, after being jostled by half a dozen commuters who seemed unfazed by the challenge ahead, they began the ascent. By the time they'd climbed to the top, Jones realised how out of shape she was. She resolved to do something about it when she got back and had more time.

They came out opposite The Houses of Parliament as Big Ben struck eight, mist rising from the Thames.

'Haven't been here since my last year at Primary school,' Tregunna muttered. 'We met a real live MP. Showed us round. God, it was boring.'

They chose a coffee bar across the road, sat at a grubby window overlooking the chaos of rush hour and watched as commuters, wrapped up against the early morning chill, stop to buy the day's Financial Times from a street vendor or a take-away coffee and doughnut from the café.

'Bit of a shock at eight o'clock in the morning.'

'Give me the cliffs and surf anytime.' Jones glanced at Tregunna, wondering if he'd need an agony aunt, and decided to play it by ear, keep him occupied, and take the opportunity if and when it arose.

'You OK?' she asked.

'Headache.'

'Night on the tiles?'

'That and the log saw in the bunk above me.' They looked at one another and Tregunna dragged up a smile from somewhere. 'The bloke I shared the journey with. If snoring was an Olympic event...' He shook his head. 'Any progress on D'Ancey?'

Jones sipped her coffee, grimaced and slid the cup to one side.

'Official line's a suspicious death. Her Ladyship's on her way to make a formal identification.'

'But, there's no doubt he was murdered?'

'Always some doubt, I suppose.'

They ordered another coffee.

Rush hour traffic increased. As commuters hurried in and out of the café, the door spent more time open than closed, the fluctuating noise making conversation almost impossible.

They left and crossed to the public entrance to the House of Commons where Jones spoke to police officers carrying Heckler and Koch G36C rifles. They were asked to produce their warrant cards and were searched before being told to wait whilst their appointment with the Conservative Chief Whip's Office was confirmed. Ten minutes later, a uniformed officer came through the portico entrance and led them along a seemingly endless warren of corridors. He paused outside a small anti-room and told them Alan Gooding was not yet in the House.

They were invited to wait in the room.

Jones sat on a high-backed chair and Tregunna stood at the window and stared at traffic on the Thames.

'How's the Super?' Jones asked.

'Not a woman I'd want to cross.'

'A ball breaker, eh?'

'Aren't they all?'

77

She let it go and took out a new notebook from her document case. 'It's registered in your name.'

'Got a pen, Guv? It was all a bit of a rush after you called last night. I've moved into digs. Bit chaotic. Not sure where everything is.'

They spent the next half an hour going back to basics, examining the motive, opportunity, and modus operandi for both victims.

First up: Chris Baldwin.

Tragic accident or murder? Who'd want him dead and why? What leads did they have and which lines of enquiry would be most productive? They'd already prioritised his place of work and his home.

Jones described her visit to Richmond Leisure Centre and Tregunna outlined developments down in Cornwall. Uniformed officers had been visiting guesthouses, hotels and pubs and Brenda McLeish had checked several dive shops and boatyards and was trying to make sense of a gold doubloon found in Baldwin's jeans.

'The man's a TV celebrity for God's sake,' Tregunna said. 'Someone must have seen him.'

'What's your gut tell you?'

She watched him pacing around the room, probably trying to shift some of the effects of the long, overnight journey.

'An accident?' he said.

'Charlie Hobson, Scotland Yard, reckons we could be dealing with amateurs.'

'I just don't get it. Why go to all the trouble of killing someone at 40 metres, when a bullet in the head would have been so much easier?'

'Maybe you're right. Maybe it was an accident.'

They moved on to Geoffrey D'Ancey.

Jones brought Tregunna up-to-date and included the investigation carried out by the Metropolitan Police and the evidence collected by SOCO.

'He'd been entertaining,' she said. 'There were two glasses in his room, with lipstick on one and prints on both. The lab boys are on overtime; DNA results should be with us early next week. You never know, we might strike lucky and get a match.' She waited, a smile flickering at the corners of her mouth, but Tregunna seemed unmoved by her clumsy wordplay.

She continued. 'There was no sign of a struggle. His trouser fly was undone, but everything was...how would you say?'

'Behind bars?'

Jones laughed. 'Very good, George.'

'The media's all over it, like pigs-in-pooh.' Tregunna rummaged in his jacket and handed her a scrunched-up copy of the *Metro*. 'It's an early edition. I picked it up at Paddington.'

Jones scanned the front-page. Given the limited time the editor had to put the paper to bed, the lead article was surprisingly detailed.

'Someone might come forward,' she said. 'I'll get the press boys to issue a statement as soon as we've got something worth shouting about.' She hesitated. 'Lady Emily is staying at the Savoy. I'd like a crack at her.'

'You don't think she..?'

'Always start close to home.'

'A professional hit?' Tregunna offered.

'Unlikely. The MO doesn't fit.'

'Organised Crime?'

'Possibly, but there's something I haven't told you...'

The door opened.

'If you'll come with me?'

A middle-aged woman in a tweed skirt and light blue blouse ushered them along a corridor that echoed, Jones imagined, with the footfalls of the great and the good as well as - given the scandals of recent years - the wicked and the corrupt.

The woman stopped outside a door and knocked.

Alan Gooding was sitting at his desk. He looked tired and gaunt; his hair greyer than Jones remembered from a talk show she'd seen a couple of weeks back.

'A sorry business,' he said.

'Appreciate your time.'

'I've already spoken to officers from Scotland Yard, but that was before the exposé in today's *Mail*.'

'I haven't had a chance…'

'Here, read it.' Gooding pushed the newspaper across the desk, but didn't wait for Jones to finish reading the article. 'This could damage the Party and our chances at the next election. Tea?' Gooding got up, walked over to a side table, and poured.

'I'm sure it must have come as a quite a shock to his family as well,' she said.

'Yes, of course. David has already spoken to Lady Emily.' Gooding handed them a cup and stood at the window. 'I presume we can't rule out Terrorists?'

'We're keeping an open mind.'

'COBRA met last night and the Government's been advised by both MI5 and the JTAC. It was decided to maintain the present terrorist threat level at *Moderate*.'

'Moderate?' Tregunna said, pen poised.

'*Terrorist attack possible but not likely*.' Jones filled in the blanks. 'Family aside,' she said, 'the timing would seem a little unfortunate.'

'I don't follow,' Gooding said. He turned away from the window and returned to his desk.

'You've just announced a Cabinet reshuffle and Mr D'Ancey was due on tomorrow's *Ask the Minister*. The newspapers have been touting him as a rising star.'

'You sound as if you're enjoying this Inspector.'

Jones didn't take the bait. 'This is not about me sir, or you sir. It's not about the Party, or those who've got egg on their face. It's about the body in the morgue, those left behind, and making sure no-one else is bereaved.' She shook her head, fighting her impatience. 'This is a murder enquiry and I'd appreciate your...' She hesitated when Gooding picked up the *Mail* and became engrossed in the article. She glanced at Tregunna and rolled her eyes. 'Of course...' She waited for Gooding to look up. Her next few words were perfectly weighted, not only to put him firmly on the back foot, but also to wipe the smugness from his face...

'The gutter press will be much more interested in Mr D'Ancey's predilection for sex with children.'

'Sex?'

'With children. We found photographs at his Club.'

There was a long silence and Gooding tidied his desk, his breathing laboured. 'Do you know,' he sat upright, suddenly, 'he had the temerity to sit there, right where you are, and assure me there was nothing the press could get their teeth into.' His face was drawn and haggard. He rubbed his eyes, dragged fingers down his face, and sighed heavily as though spent by the significance of the exposé. 'It's difficult to know who to trust these days,' he said, more, it seemed, to himself than the detectives. 'A man's word is no longer his bond. After all we've stood for over the years...' He hauled his body upright and appeared to try to shake off his despair. 'So, Inspector, what evidence is there to link Geoffrey to the photographs?'

'Investigations date back to 2001. An Internet-based paedophile ring known as The Wonderland Club. At the time there were several arrests, but it was rumoured that some of London's elite were involved...lawyers, high-ranking police officers and senior politicians. Arrests continued, but the trail went cold.'

'Has Geoffrey been under suspicion?'

'Not to my knowledge.'

'So these could have been planted by someone with a grudge against him, an ex-con, say, sent down during his days at the Bar?'

'That's possible, yes. Computers in his office, flat, and home have been seized.'

'Mud sticks, doesn't it? Another scandal. Sex with children, for God's sake...'

'There's one photograph more damning than the rest. It's probably the one the *Mail* referred to this morning. It was taken by someone using a digital camera. It shows Geoffrey D'Ancey with a girl in her mid teens. His face is clearly visible, but he's got his hand over her mouth. It covers most of her face, but it's not difficult to see the terror in her eyes. We're treating it as rape.'

'Jesus wept.' It was Gooding's turn to shake his head. 'So, someone must have been there, taking the photograph whilst he...? And it'll be published?'

'Not for me to say.'

'There can be no doubt it's him?'

'None whatsoever. It's my guess that whoever left this particular photograph in his room wanted to make sure we knew what he'd been up to: child abuse; rape.' Jones allowed Gooding time to absorb the seriousness of the allegation.

'Rape?' he said, bristling with defiance. 'That photograph won't stand up in court.

'It will, when we find the girl.'

'OK. Listen up, people.' Kate Madison walked across the stage in Studio 3.

The technical crew were testing lighting and sound for tomorrow's programme, but Madison felt uneasy.

Baldwin's death had hit the nationals, was featured on news channels, and had spread across social networks like a virus. She'd been told that members of the crew had been fuelling the rumour factory.

Here was a celebrity, with a face as familiar as a Sunday roast, with a distinguished career behind him as a special correspondent in hotspots around the world. He was a popular choice during the hunt for someone to host *Ask the Minister* – an appointment that cemented his position as a serious political commentator.

'Take five everyone,' Madison said. 'I want your full and undivided attention.' She waited until they'd assembled in the amphitheatre and then stood before them, clutching her clipboard to her chest.

'You'll have heard about Chris's accident?'

'It was murder,' one of the lighting crew called out, breaking her rhythm. 'The police are treating his death as suspicious, and that's good enough for me. We all knew Chris. He was as serious about his diving as he was about international politics. Someone topped him, for sure.'

'As far as I'm aware, the investigation is on-going and nothing official has been announced.'

She glanced down at her clipboard, before hugging it back into her chest. 'You'll also know that one of the guests lined up for tomorrow's show was found dead at his Club last night. Again, there's been nothing official but, if it is homicide, I want to be one step ahead of the competition.'

'And if it's a double hom-i-cide?' a set designer said, stressing each of the syllables, echoing her mid-Atlantic accent and drawing a mumbled show of disrespect from the rest of the crew.

She heard several snigger and the impasse lingered until one said, 'So, Kate, what about tomorrow? Are we going ahead?'

'As far as I'm concerned, the show must go on. I met with the Directors this morning. We have a schedule of guests and an invited audience.'

'And where are they going to get someone to front the show this late in the day?'

'I've been asked to step into the breach.'

This was greeted with silence.

'I hope I can count on your support? These are difficult times for all of us, but I look forward to working with you. We'll rehearse this afternoon, as scheduled.' She turned to leave, then added, 'The police want to interview everyone later this morning.' She checked her clipboard. 'They'll use the canteen and one of the ancillary offices. In the meantime, people, let's get back to work.'

Before she could leave, one of the researchers, who'd provided much of the background material on the guests for the show and who'd worked closely with Chris Baldwin, called from high in the auditorium.

She turned to face him.

'Chris was not only a brilliant interviewer,' he said, 'but he was also a friend. We're shocked and saddened by what's happened, but I'm sure we'll all do our best to make tomorrow's show as polished and professional as possible.'

This was greeted with nods and scattered applause.

Kate Madison smiled. 'Thanks. Now, let's…'

'You see,' he said, 'I was just wondering how *you* are feeling?'

'I'm as upset as everyone.'

'I just assumed,' he continued, 'that given your close, *personal* relationship with Chris, you'd want to take time out, to help you come to terms with your loss.'

Madison's head dropped. She stood, silently, and then turned to face him.

'Chris and I went our separate ways several months ago, but we remained good friends. Of course, I share your sadness and have special memories of a very kind and gentle man.' She paused. 'For sure, Chris would have wanted tomorrow's show, his show, to go ahead.' She appeared to wipe away a tear from her cheek. 'Now, if you'll excuse me?'

Jones wondered whether it was a sense of awe that had rendered Tregunna speechless as they walked from Westminster to Kent House - passing the London Eye, the South Bank Centre, and the National Theatre - or whether he'd retreated into his own world to lick his wounds and work out how he was going to pick up the pieces. She watched him look across the Thames and then down at the walkway. He scuffed his feet and kicked out at a plastic cup. The strike, that sent the cup spiralling over the riverside wall, was one of resignation, it seemed to her, rather than aggression and Tregunna's face was locked in a grimace, his jaw muscles working overtime. She decided to leave him to it and, as they made their way towards the studios, she tried to recall a programme she'd seen a couple of weeks back.

She'd been flicking through channels and had settled on a programme charting ITV's history. She'd found it hypnotic, she reasoned later, because it reminded her of her childhood, growing up in Putney, on the south side of the Thames. The ITV logo and the theme tune had been part of the life she shared with her parents. They'd loved the comedy and the variety shows and the soaps. And, as she watched the documentary, she'd realised that her ambition to join the Met had been sparked by shows she seen on Saturday evenings. Police dramas that she'd found compelling at the time but now, whenever she watched reruns, she found embarrassingly naïve.

The documentary had included a tour of the nine studios and twenty-one floors of Kent House. The camera had lingered a the canteen where stars, directors, producers and technical staff enjoyed subsidised food and uninterrupted views - west to Waterloo Bridge, east to Blackfriars, and north, across the Thames, towards Victoria Embankment and some of London's grandest buildings.

She glanced across at The Embankment - a stone's throw from Somerset House where births, deaths and marriages used to be registered - and wondered just how much *sadness* Chris Baldwin's friends and colleagues had felt when they'd heard of his death. *Sadness*, she'd decided by the time they found the entrance to Kent House, would be a useful yardstick to use to judge the emotional response of those who'd shared his professional life.

They were greeted by security guards who frisked them and x-rayed Jones's document case before handing them over to a young man who escorted them across the lobby and into a lift. The corridor connecting the top-floor suite of offices and studios was long and narrow. The walls were covered by photographs of household names: stars of ITV's sitcoms, comedies, soaps and dramas, their faces as familiar as family.

They were shown into a room filled with equipment: consoles, television screens, sound and lighting controls, and editing suites linked to banks of computers.

They'd agreed to share tasks.

Whilst Tregunna interviewed the production staff, Jones would home in on Baldwin's boss...

'I hope your questions won't take long, Inspector,' Dr Ian Carter, Head of Programming, began. 'Chris was in

Cornwall. None of us were there. We should all be eliminated from your enquiries.'

'You'd want us to find his killer?'

'Of course, but we have a schedule and rehearsals for tomorrow continue after lunch.'

'Then let's not waste any more time, shall we?'

The interview was punctuated by interruptions from members of Carter's crew anxious for decisions about a tribute to Chris Baldwin that would air later that day.

'Rush job?' Jones asked.

'We keep archive material on anyone considered part of the national psyche. He made his name reporting from places such as Baghdad, Chechnya, and Damascus, and was recognised as something of an authority on the Middle East. He spoke French, Russian and Arabic.' He hesitated. 'You don't suppose this could be linked to his time in the Middle East, do you? Some sort of retaliatory hit by extremists?'

'Seems unlikely. No one has claimed responsibility. Besides, they'd have put a bullet in his head, poisoned him, or slapped a bomb under his car.' Jones wanted to steer Carter away from speculation. 'Is there anything else you want to tell me about him?'

Carter had known Baldwin for a number of years and was aware of his interest in sub-aqua diving, but knew little of his social life. He seemed unperturbed by the death of someone who was, Jones assumed, pivotal to the success of the show.

Carter sighed wearily. 'I've been in this game a long time, Inspector. Of course, one's never inured to the loss of a colleague, especially one so talented. Chris will be sadly missed, but we've already found a replacement and life, and the show, will go on.'

Jones wasn't sure how to calibrate her measurement of *sadness*, but decided Dr Carter's *grief* was unlikely to register on any scale. She shook her head. 'The loss of two people must have been a body blow?'

'Geoffrey D'Ancey? Whilst any death is regrettable, if the revelations are true, it'll be a blessing in disguise.'

'It must have made you feel uncomfortable, so close to inviting a paedophile onto the show?'

'It'll give us more time to interview our main guest and, if you like a flutter Inspector, I'd take the bookies' odds on Labour to win the next election. With this little scandal, who's to say they won't?'

'I'd like to meet Mr Baldwin's replacement.'

'Kate? She's been with us since March last year. She works as an assistant to one of our Producers, but has had experience in front of camera. She's a natural.'

'A natural?'

'The camera seems to love her. Simple really, but rare.' Carter rose. 'I'll see if she's available and send her along. But now, if you'll excuse me, I really must get back to work.'

Jones found her attractive from the moment she walked into the interview room. She was tall, willowy, and had long legs that were accentuated by a short skirt and high heels. Kate Madison smiled and sat in the chair opposite. She wore her hair close-cropped and had such vivid blue eyes that Jones wondered if she wore contact lenses.

'Dr Carter seemed oddly unmoved by Mr Baldwin's death,' Jones began.

'Pompous ass.'

'You're American, Miss Madison?'

'No. I spent a couple of years studying and working there. The accent kinda rubs off.'

'You worked in television?'

'Mainly.'

'Difficult to break into in the States.'

'I worked my way up from making tea and running errands.'

'To?'

'Eventually? Assistant producer with CBS. I fronted the news occasionally if 'The Talent' didn't show up.'

'Impressive.'

'For one so young?' Madison smiled. 'I worked my butt off, trusted no one. You learn quickly.'

'I'm curious...' Jones looked at her, elegantly poised, her legs angled to one side, hands relaxed and interlaced on her lap. 'Why..?'

'Did I leave the States when I had the world at my feet? Simple really. Despite everything LA had to offer, I was homesick. I'd had a blast studying at Berkley. I worked on film sets at Universal Studios before I was invited to become part of a progressive news team. But working in the media is like living in a pressure cooker. The heat's on twenty-four-seven. Know what I mean? If I'd stayed much longer, I'd have burnt out by the time I was thirty.' She shifted uneasily in her chair, a small movement. 'I was in a relationship that was on the skids...' She grimaced. 'Then, one morning, I was caught in traffic on the freeway and saw a bumper sticker...' She used her right hand to trace the words through the air. '*Don't mess with me. The gun I'm carrying is loaded.* Did my head in. Know what I'm saying? Scary or what?'

'You didn't carry a gun?'

'After seeing that? You bet I did. In LA, a gun's as commonplace in a gal's handbag as a compact.'

She smiled, and Jones wasn't sure if she was joking.

'Tell me about Chris Baldwin.'

'You know, I've been wracking my brains, trying to think of something but...' She shrugged. 'I'm sorry.'

89

'Let's see if this helps, shall we? How well did you know him?'

She blushed. 'We dated for a few months when I first arrived at the studios.'

'A serious relationship?'

'He'd wanted it to be, but I'd moved on.'

'And you have no idea what he was doing in the West Country?'

'Diving, I guess.'

'And where were you on the night he was killed?'

'So, it was murder?'

'Looks like it.'

'Gosh, how awful.' She shook her head slowly, her hands fidgeting in her lap. Jones noticed her American accent had softened and blended with something oddly urban, estuarial.

'Am I a suspect?'

'Most murders are committed by those closest to the deceased, and until we're able to eliminate you from our enquiries...'

'I'd read somewhere that he'd been killed on Sunday, or early Monday?'

'As far as we know.'

'That's easy then. I'd left Cornwall, early evening.'

'What time?'

'Say seven-thirty.'

'On Sunday?'

'Yes.'

'From which airport?'

'We have our own helicopter. An EC135. Our head of security doubles as our pilot.'

'Head of Security?'

'John Hartley. He came highly recommended. Well, he'd have to check out, wouldn't he?'

'And he's installing what, exactly?'

'CCTV, new alarm system, and a panic room.'

'Panic room?'

'Somewhere I can hide, lock myself away if someone breaks in. Anyway, you can check the pilot's log for details.'

'Where did you land?'

'London Heliport. I had some research I needed to catch up on. I went to our apartment in St James's Square, had a bath, watched a movie, and turned in at about midnight.'

'Alone?'

'Inspector, please, spare my blushes. Yes I was alone. My fiancé was at home in Cornwall. He comes up to town when his business demands, but prefers the quiet of the country.' She looked down, paused fleetingly, then looked up and said, 'we lost his father recently. It's been a difficult time for all of us.' She sighed and smiled weakly. Her teeth were white and uniform - cosmetic treatment that left Jones wondering what else had been fixed. 'My job keeps me here five days a week. The security guards at the apartment will confirm what I've just said, and you can always check the CCTV.'

'Did you see Mr Baldwin when he came down to Cornwall?' Jones asked.

'No. I had no idea he was there. Why would I? He was probably diving with his club. When we first started dating, he took me along to a pool in Richmond. I tried a couple of times, but with all that gear on, even in two metres of water, I felt claustrophobic, you know?'

She shuddered.

'What sort of man was he?'

'Chris? He was lovely. Gentle. Kind. Romantic.' She sighed heavily. 'Made me laugh. Important in a man, don't you think?'

'So we're led to believe.'

'Stewart and I...we are very, very happy, but...' She seemed hesitant. '...His father's death has cast a terrible shadow over us. He was a wonderful man. We got on so well. He was so supportive.' She drew breath. 'He was killed in a riding accident.'

'Richard Lander?'

'Yes. How did you..?'

'I was at the funeral. I hadn't seen Stewart for a while.'

'What a coincidence? I'll tell him that we've met. I'm flying down on Friday evening, after the show.'

'And you'll be in Falmouth until?'

'I'm not sure. When we prep the next show, I guess.'

'You didn't attend Richard Lander's funeral?'

'No.' She dropped her head and Jones could see tears at the corners of her eyes, and wondered just how easily she was able to turn on the waterworks.

Madison took a tissue from a box on the table and dabbed her eyes.

'I'm sorry. His death was such a terrible shock. I was with him when he fell. We often rode together. I'm afraid I just couldn't face...Well, you know?'

'Surely, his son would have appreciated his fiancée by his side?'

'It was Stewart who suggested I came up to London. I was upset, as you'd imagine, but I also think he wanted to grieve alone. Some men are like that, aren't they?'

Jones rose and collected her document case. 'I'll be down in Cornwall sometime over the weekend. I'll be in touch.'

'Perhaps you'd like to come to dinner?' Madison said, and her face lit up.

She was, Jones reckoned, stunningly beautiful - fine features and a rare symmetry.

'We're hopelessly in love,' Madison said, 'and we've avoided talking about the past. I'm not sure I want to know about Stewart's other girl friends. It's tricky. He used his influence to get me this job and introduced me to Chris Baldwin. For a time I was...' She faltered, and her face flushed with apparent embarrassment. 'Oh, this is going to sound awful, but I was sort of double dating. I didn't tell Stewart about Chris. It wasn't serious. Least ways, I wasn't serious. And when Stewart and I grew closer and had a future together...'

'You dumped Mr Baldwin?'

'Sounds very clinical when you put it like that, but yes, I ended the relationship.' Madison stood up. 'I'm sorry. I have to rehearse. I'd appreciate it if you'd be, well, you know?'

'Discreet?'

'Thank you for being so understanding.' Madison hesitated. 'Have we met somewhere before?'

'I think I would have remembered.'

'I guess.' Madison lent forward and touched her arm. 'I was serious about dinner, by the way.'

Jones found Tregunna in the canteen.

They took a tray, queued up, and chose a main course and pudding. They found a table by a window and, after marvelling at the view, they settled to their lunch. They watched a television's Who's Who queue for their lunch.

Some faces they recognised, but couldn't put a name to, others were vaguely familiar, but they couldn't place the programme. Then the cast of a popular soap came in, chattering and laughing.

'Odd, isn't it, how we feel we know these people, just because they're on TV?' Jones said.

93

'You could go and talk to them like they were mates.'

'The curse of fame.'

'Yeah. But imagine just how pissed off they'd be if no one made a fuss?'

They sat in silence and watched an endless queue, plates held out in expectation, stars making choices and joining others at tables across the canteen. Tregunna pushed his fish pie around the plate and Jones assumed his loss of appetite was another side effect of his marital problems. She decided not to nag him and spent the time checking off stars until she'd finished her lunch.

Over coffee she asked him to bring her up to date.

'I spoke to the crew individually. Most seemed to like Baldwin.' He checked. 'One said he was an interviewer who knew how to *dig beneath the surface without being intimidating or disrespectful. A throwback to the days when interviewing was an art and not a battle of egos.*'

'Days of old, eh? Good. OK. Get someone to cross-reference each statement with H.O.L.M.E.S. Is anyone worth interviewing again?'

'Not really, but most don't have a lot of time for Kate Madison. Something about Union regulations. Equity cards are not easy to come by, but Miss Madison arrived from the States early last year and got the green light to work in record time. Someone pulled strings.'

'I think I know who.'

'Others don't like her manner.'

'Too in your face?'

'Too bloody rude.'

'Gunning for her? Jealous?'

'One of the younger women came over to dish the dirt and didn't pull any punches.' Tregunna checked his note pad. 'A girlfriend dated Baldwin. He dumped her when Madison came on the scene.'

'And you're suggesting what? That the girlfriend was somehow involved in Baldwin's murder?'

94

'A long shot?'

'Interview her again. Maybe Chris Baldwin's got a dark side. Well done, George.' Jones sipped her coffee. 'Now, for the rest of the day, you're on your own. It's time for a spot of gardening. Start with Baldwin's home. Anything that'll help pinpoint why he went to Cornwall, who he went to see, and who would want him out of the way. There's a forensic team on stand-by.'

She waited for Tregunna to finish taking notes.

'Got it,' he said.

'Good. In the meantime, I shall be taking tea with Lady Emily.'

'At the Ritz, no doubt.'

'The Savoy, actually.'

'It's a rough life…'

There was hint of a smile in Tregunna's eyes and Jones began to wonder if the change of scenery might, as she'd suggested, be what the doctor would have ordered.

'Then, I'm back at D'Ancey's Club,' she said. 'Make sure we haven't missed anything. A DVD was found in D'Ancey's jacket. Scotland Yard are studying it, as well as CCTV of a reception at Westminster Hall. They're also making enquiries at hotels, restaurants, theatres, and clubs within a five-kilometre radius of the city centre. I'll liaise with Charlie Hobson and see what they've come up with. After you've given the house the once over, collect your luggage. There'll be a car to ferry you to Lizzie's apartment. I'll meet you there for dinner. I'm cooking.'

'I'll bring some wine.'

'We're flying back to Cornwall tomorrow. Gatwick. Check-in, seven-thirty.'

'Flight? Pushing the boat out a bit.'

'I want you in good shape when we get home.'

*

Over breakfast at Paddington, earlier that day, Jones had taken Tregunna on a trip down memory lane. She'd reminisced about her holidays at the cottage in Cornwall and trips to Taunton with her father to watch Somerset play cricket.

She'd also told him about her home in Putney and walks with her parents in Richmond Park. She couldn't remember why the park was called *Richmond* – except, of course, that it was close to one of London's most exclusive areas, the Royal Borough of Richmond-upon-Thames. She knew that members of the royal family lived somewhere in its grounds and that the park had become a sanctuary for wildlife. It was a haven that was under threat, she'd told him, from commuters who used it as a short cut, tourists who flocked to torment its deer, and day-trippers who left rubbish spilling from its bins.

As his patrol car made its way through the park, it wasn't long before Tregunna understood what Jones had meant...when, through the rear window, he saw a family try to sneak up on a herd of fallow deer, only to startle them into flight.

As they skirted the Pen Ponds and the White Lodge Plantation, his driver told him that to buy a property within striking distance of any one of the Park's nine gates would 'leave a serious hole in most people's pockets.' It was, obviously, a very expensive area and Chris Baldwin's house was only a couple of roads down from Sheen Gate. Tregunna made a note in his pad.

As the patrol car slowed to allow a small herd of deer to cross the road, it struck Tregunna that if Baldwin had grown up near here he would, almost certainly, have played in the Park, and fished for newts, ridden his bike, flown his kite and climbed the same trees as Lydia Jones. They may even have met - they were a similar age - and played together as only the young can without ever bothering to find out the name of their new-found-friend.

Tregunna shuddered as the images of childhood were replaced by ones of Chris Baldwin lying in a pool of seawater, his mask missing and his face exposed to crabs and gulls. He shuddered again and stared out of the car's rear window as they left the park, drove down Sheen Lane and turned right into Stonehill Road.

They stopped outside an impressive detached house with a BMW parked in the driveway. He changed into a protective suit and led a posse of police to the front door. A uniformed constable knocked several times and then turned to Tregunna. He nodded, and a burly officer used a battering ram to gain access.

An L-shaped hallway had a staircase to the right and three doors leading to a kitchen, a downstairs cloakroom and a large, rectangular lounge furnished with both style and elegance. There was a high-backed sofa, a matching armchair in deep maroon leather, and a Persian rug. Against one wall, an oak sideboard was crowded with photographs. As SOCOs began to ferry equipment into the hallway, Tregunna took two of the photographs over to where the sunlight was streaming through patio doors.

One was black and white and faded slightly...the handsome face of a young naval officer, smiling, his cap tilted at an angle. He was leaning on a ship's rail with his back to a calm sea. There was an inscription scrawled in the bottom right hand corner of the photograph:

Home soon. How's my baby boy?

The other photograph, in colour and more recent, was of a graduate with degree in-hand and his mortarboard at the same rakish angle. There was little doubt about the relationship between the two men and they might have been the same person, but for the passage of time.

Even the inscription in the corner of the colour photograph had been written in a similar scrawl:

97

To Mum.
Thanks for Everything.

Both men had the same broad nose, high forehead, crooked smile, and warm eyes and, as he replaced the photographs, Tregunna noted that they were one of the few clues, along with the old fashioned furniture, to suggest this house had belonged to Baldwin's parents. According to background checks, Baldwin had inherited it and Tregunna began to wonder what had happened to them – his parents – and why he continued to live in the family home.

He made his way upstairs.

On the landing, each of the doors was closed.

He opened one and found a family bathroom with white ceramic furniture.

He opened another.

Baldwin's study, shelves groaning under the weight of biographies of world leaders, past and present, and books charting the history of middle-east countries.

Beneath the shelving was a desk strewn with journals headlining conflict-hotspots around the world and, under the journals, was a fifteen-inch laptop.

Tregunna opened the desk's drawer. Its contents were unremarkable: pencils, pens, paper, theatre ticket stubs, a travel brochure for the Greek islands, and an open packet of mints on top of May's issue of *Dive Magazine*. He glanced at a collection of memory sticks labelled Work, Diving, Finance, and Letters, and towards the back of the drawer he found one without a label. He switched the laptop on and slid the memory stick into a USB port. It was empty. Either Baldwin hadn't used it, or whatever was on it had been erased. He switched off the computer, sifted through sheets of notepaper in the wastepaper basket, and then asked a SOCO to bag everything, including the laptop.

The main bedroom, with its double bed, dark colours and lingering fragrance of cologne was, it seemed to Tregunna, the bedroom of a single man. He went into the en-suite and was surprised to see an old toothbrush on the shelf above the sink. Baldwin had been identified, but forensics always appreciated anything that could provide corroborating DNA - toothbrushes being one of the best sources. He pulled an evidence bag from his pocket, deposited the toothbrush and then turned his attention to the wardrobe in the bedroom.

Inside, suits, shirts, and trousers were protected by dry-cleaner's polythene - a bachelor's dream that had Tregunna wondering if *he* would ever be able to afford to have *his* clothes laundered after *she'd* finished taking him to the…

He snorted, tried to smile, and shook his head.

He opened a cupboard above the wardrobe and eased out a flat package wrapped in a counterpane.

Inside were two paintings.

'The love of his life.'

Tregunna spun round and she held out her hand.

'Sue Robinson. Chris's sister.'

'Sorry Guv.' A flustered uniformed Constable was standing at the door. 'She was through before I had time to stop her.'

'No problem.' Tregunna turned to the middle-aged woman. 'Just be careful you don't touch anything.'

She looked ten years older than her brother, with hair that seemed to have a mind of its own and fell about her face in matted tendrils. She wore a smock splattered in paint and fading jeans that did nothing to flatter her ample thighs and bottom.

'She broke his heart,' she said, and took a pack of cigarettes out of her smock pocket. 'Do you mind?'

'This is a crime scene. I'm sorry.' Tregunna held up one of the paintings. 'Yours?'

'I wish I was that talented.'

'They're good?'

'The gallery thought so. The title's on the back.'

Tregunna turned it over.

'Mask of an Angel,' he read, and then turned it back over. She was young, naked, standing in a circle of candles, her slim body twisted in profile - a breast, her buttocks and long, slender legs caught by the flickering light. She was looking over her shoulder, but a mask obscured her face. 'You know her?' he asked.

'No, my brother was always cagey about his love life. I never met her. Seems a long time ago, now. A year. Eighteen months. Time flies. There have been so many over the years they sort of blend into one another. He spent his life being shot at in some distant hell-hole and found it difficult to maintain relationships.'

She pointed at the picture. 'Julian Wyatt. The artist's name's on the canvas, bottom right.'

Tregunna stood the painting on the desk and picked up the other. It could have been the same young woman, but the pose, the location, and a difference in the lighting made that far from certain. She was sitting on a rock, on a beach, and so much of her naked back and long blond hair filled the canvas that Tregunna felt it was almost as a voyeur had used a zoom lens to take a furtive close-up. Her face was turned away but she was holding a mirror at such an angle as to allow the artist to capture her eyes.

'It's good,' Sue Robinson said.

Tregunna sensed she'd admitted it grudgingly.

He turned it over. It was entitled 'The Mermaid' but someone had drawn an arrow between the two words and above them had inserted 'Reluctant'.

'The *Reluctant* Mermaid?' Tregunna asked.

'Yes,' she said. 'I've seen or heard it somewhere before...' She paused. 'No. Sorry. Not sure. Maybe you should check with the gallery. It's in the West End.

Details are on the back. They might be able to give you the address of Wyatt's studio.'

'How do you..?'

'Know all this?'

'I came round one evening, May last year. Chris had just bought them from the gallery and about a week later she dumped him.'

'But you never met her?'

'No.'

'I'll have to keep them.'

'You seem to be taking everything else.' She smiled, but the pain of her loss was evident in her eyes. 'I hope you catch whoever did this. My father was killed in the Falklands. He died before he was able to hold Chris in his arms. My mother brought us up. She died of cancer two years ago. Chris was all I had left. I was very proud of him.'

'And he's lived here all his life?'

'Yes. No. Well, sort of... He left university and lived out of suitcase for years, reporting from the front-line. He brought a flat in London when he started in television and moved back here after mum died.'

'Does he still have the flat?'

'Had. Everything's in the past tense now, isn't it?'

She hesitated and it was clear she was struggling.

'Yes, I think so. He often worked late. It would have been easier, more convenient.'

Again, she hesitated and Tregunna waited for her to gather herself. 'I'm sorry,' he said, 'but I must ask. When was the last time you saw him?'

'The morgue in Truro, the formal identification.'

'I meant...before...'

'About a month ago. A Thursday.'

'That would be...' Tregunna checked. 'May 13th?

101

'I suppose so. Until then, he'd been round for dinner most weeks. My kids adore...' She faltered. 'My kids adored him.'

'But he didn't come for dinner last week?'

'No. He didn't make it. Must have been very busy.'

'And how was he, the last time you saw him?'

'Good. Work was going well. He'd taken over *Ask the Minister* and ratings had shot up.'

'You'll be watching tomorrow?'

'They're going ahead?' She looked down at her trainers. 'Think I'll give it a miss.'

'Any idea why your brother was in Cornwall?'

'Diving? Dived all over the world. A real passion.'

'We don't think he would have gone to Cornwall for the weekend. His club was at Swanage.'

'Oh, shit!' She held her hand over her mouth. 'Shit! Shit! Shit!' She struggled to compose herself. 'Sorry. I've just remembered something one of my girls told me. It didn't make sense at the time.'

'When was this?'

'Last week. Wednesday. My husband was away on business. I was out. I run an art class at the local Comp in the evening. I'd stopped off for a couple of drinks on the way home. The girls were in bed when I got in. The babysitter had taken a call from Chris and told me she'd left a note on the kitchen table. I put the kettle on, checked the girls were ok and went down to watch the late news. I found the note just as I was going to bed.'

'And you still have it?'

'I'm not sure. It could have been thrown out.'

'What did it say?'

'He couldn't come to dinner on Thursday.'

'Why?'

'God, I can't remember. I'll go home and check'

*

102

Jones had looked forward to tea at the Savoy and her arrival seemed perfectly timed...mid-afternoon.

Alexandra was notable by her absence.

'Catching up with her friends,' Lady Emily had said, apologetically, and then rang for tea and scones.

An hour later, Jones was driven to The Travellers and Explorers Club. 'The fire escape door's not alarmed?' she asked the Club Captain.

He sighed heavily - as he had after most of her questions. He'd dismissed any suggestion of impropriety and seemed more anxious about the Club's reputation than the death of one of its most prestigious members. He rejected any suggestion that security needed beefing up, downed his gin and tonic and returned to the bar, leaving Jones to find her way to the basement where the Club's administration was located.

In a cramped office, an attractive young woman, wearing a tight blue sweater, a short skirt and flat shoes, looked up from her computer, beamed, shook her hand warmly, and led her on a tour. On the night D'Ancey was killed, she explained, the main restaurant was closed for minor renovations and the lunchtime restaurant had been opened to cater for the members who'd made reservations. The office staff had clocked off at five-thirty as usual and apart from cooks, waiters and members who were staying overnight, the only other person in the club that evening would have been the night porter.

The tour ended in the dining room where she ordered a coffee for Jones and scribbled her telephone number on a card. She offered to show her the sights. Jones told her she was too busy. The administrator shrugged, told her that if she changed her mind, she'd welcome a call. She smiled, and then went to see if the night porter was available...

Tommy Murphy was dressed in black trousers, white shirt and black waistcoat. His mop of dark hair led Jones to assume that he was a student from Spain, employed for the summer season. But, once he opened his mouth, it wasn't difficult to place him - South London, with a strong hint of Gaelic.

'Dublin, born and bred,' he said. 'Of mixed race - the old man from north of the border.' He smiled broadly. 'How can I help you?' Murphy seemed blessed with the blarney and, Jones reckoned, that would make it more difficult for her to tell whether he was lying.

'So, Geoffrey D'Ancey was *alone* when he arrived?' Jones asked.

'Yes.'

'And went straight to his room?'

'Yes. It's reserved for him.'

'Exclusively?'

'Yes.'

'He didn't use the restaurant or order room service?'

'He asked for a menu.'

'Come on Tommy. Let's make this easy on both of us, shall we? Did he eat?'

'Didn't get a chance.'

She waited, drew breath, struggling to resist the urge to smack his smug face, then asked, 'Did he leave his room?'

She saw a flicker of amusement on Murphy's lips.

'Something I said?'

'No. Sorry.' Murphy hesitated. 'As far as I know, he didn't leave his room until...'

'You find murder funny, Tommy?'

'Of course not. Jesus. Poor sod.'

Jones let it go. 'The fire escape?' she asked. 'Open?'

'Yes, odd that.'

'Panic bar? Located inside?'

'One of the cleaners, maybe, stepping out for a fag.'

'I wasn't born yesterday, Tommy.'

'Well, how else?'

'I'd pinned my hopes on you telling me.'

'It was an accident, wasn't it? The Judge drank too much and toppled from the balcony, right?'

'Was he in the habit of bringing young women back to his room?'

'Not to my knowledge. Against club rules.'

'What other rules did you break for him, Tommy?'

'Come again?'

'Two glasses were found in the room, as well as two sets of prints and DNA profiles. One was female. So, we come back to the central question. Who opened the fire escape door? The Judge? Possibly. Or someone else, doing the Judge a favour, part of a financial arrangement they'd come to?'

'Like I said, could have been...'

'A cleaner? Yes, of course. I'll make a note to remind myself to interview each of them, find out who'd been so careless.'

'Or, one of the other members?'

'Speaking of members...Mr D'Ancey was found with his fly undone. What d'you think? Was he senile? Forgot to zip-up after taking a leak? Did he fall or was he pushed?'

'You can't think I had anything to do with it?'

'When I start turning over stones, it wouldn't surprise me to find you're up to your Irish eyes in all sorts of mischief. We could do this the hard way. I'll take you down the nick, hold you for three days, search your home, and delve into the darkest recesses of your private life.'

'Twas nothing to do with me, honest. I was on duty, yeah, but he came in and went straight to his room. Next thing I know he'd taken a turn for the worse...'

Jones detected a deepening of his accent - a sure sign stress was getting to him. 'It's your choice, Tommy,' she said, 'but make the wrong choice and the consequences will be yours and yours alone.'

She smiled.

'I don't take prisoners, not when I'm trying to find out how someone died. All's fair, you see Tommy. I'll give you five minutes to think about it. I'll be on the terrace, enjoying a well-earned cup of coffee.' She stood, walked over to the stairs, turned and added, 'and don't even think about doing a runner. That would really piss me off.'

Julian Wyatt lived in the loft of a Victorian house near Teddington Lock.

The apartment was, basically, one room, with a small kitchen area, lounge, double bed, and a door leading to a bathroom. Along the north side of the roof, light flooded into the studio through four skylights.

Tregunna had arranged for the artist's details to be processed and H.O.L.M.E.S had thrown up a welcome, but unexpected result. He'd been frisked during a routine stop-and-search and was found to be carrying marijuana that was used, he'd claimed, to ease chronic pain in his right hand.

'S'pose you've come about the wacky-backy?' Wyatt said, inviting Tregunna in.

'I'm investigating the death of Chris Baldwin.'

'Oh, yes, well, yes, saw it on the news, of course. Quite shocking, really. Someone like that. You see him risking his life in some God-awful place, then he goes diving and doesn't come back.'

106

'I found these at his home.' Tregunna showed him the paintings, now housed in large plastic bags. 'Yours, I believe.'

Wyatt used the tips of his fingers to trace the young woman's back as she sat on the rock.

'Talk about the past returning to haunt you...I knew they'd been sold. The gallery sent a cheque. Just didn't expect to see them again.'

'Same girl in both?'

'Yes.'

'And, you know who she is?'

'Yes. Yes, of course.'

'A name would help.'

'Sorry, just a bit of shock after, what, ten years?'

'From the beginning?'

Wyatt walked over to a sofa and perched on one end.

'Her name is Jenny,' he said. 'We met at a gallery in Knightsbridge. She'd just turned sixteen. Looked older. Very pretty. We chatted. She didn't have a clue about art, which was odd...'

'Odd?'

'Why come into an art gallery if you're not interested in art?'

'Perhaps it was raining.'

Wyatt laughed. 'Yes. Do you know, I think it was? I'm sorry, would you like a cup of tea?'

Tregunna pressed him further as they waited for the water to boil.

'We chatted and I asked her if she'd like to sit for me. She wanted to see my work and I brought her here. She wanted to be paid. I was receiving an allowance from my parents at the time - they've always been so supportive - and I'd sold a couple of paintings, so I agreed. To be honest, I saw it as an opportunity to make some serious money. I knew several galleries that would take my work if I got the subject right.'

107

Tregunna looked up from his note pad. 'Right?'

'I specialised in life drawing.'

'Nudes?'

'Yes. She was manna sent.'

Tregunna didn't know one end of a paintbrush from the other, but he looked at one of the paintings more carefully than he had at Baldwin's home. She was sitting on a rock, one leg curled beneath her. She was naked and her skin shimmered like velvet – or so it seemed to his untrained eye. Her long, blond hair had been pulled to one side and her right breast was just visible. Tregunna studied her eyes, reflected in the mirror she was holding, and it seemed to him that they not only smiled, but also mocked and teased at the same time. 'Do you have any more paintings of her?' he asked.

'I'd painted several. I was building a collection for an exhibition. She would come during the day…'

'Here?'

'Yes…oh, I see. The beach? Doesn't exist. I combine images from my imagination, postcards, photographs etcetera.'

'And the mask?'

'Professional prop – one of a dozen I have. My work sold well when I captured the subject's innocence and sexuality without being overtly explicit.'

'The sort of erotica you can hang on your wall and not embarrass your friends?'

'Yes, I suppose you could put it like that.'

'But these two didn't sell for ten years.'

'No. Not sure why.'

'Not explicit enough?'

'Maybe.'

'She looks vulnerable,' Tregunna said.

'It's in the eyes. Wonderful eyes. Expressive. '

'And yours was a professional relationship?'

'I'd pay her as I finished each one.'

'How much?'

'A hundred pounds.'

'The going rate?'

'We had an agreement. If a painting sold, she'd get a percentage. Anyway, after about two months, she turned up on my doorstep and asked if she could stay.'

'Stay? Here? Where was home?'

'No idea.'

'She just turned up?'

'She was distressed. It was obvious something had upset her.'

'And you agreed?'

'Why not? She only stayed a couple of weeks. There was nothing between us. No sex or anything.'

'And you expect me to believe that?'

Tregunna watched telltale blotches invade Wyatt's neck - a lie, embarrassment, or shame - Tregunna wasn't sure. He sat opposite him, cup in one hand, pen poised in the other.

'To be truthful, I'm not interested in sex. Over rated. That's why she felt safe, I suppose.'

'Safe?'

'You don't have a cigarette, do you?'

'Don't. Sorry. Did she say what had upset her?'

'I asked.'

'And?'

'Nothing at first. Then, a week after she'd moved in we were sitting on the floor, propped up against the sofa. We'd had a glass of wine, and she started to cry. I held on to her. Waited. Then she told me...someone had made a big mistake. One he'd pay for.'

'He?'

'Yes.'

'And, that's it?'

'Sobbed her heart out, but never mentioned it again.'

'What about other men?'

'I don't think there was anyone special in her life, no boyfriend, lover. She told me her father tried to rape her when she was ten. He died a few years later. They were renting a council flat somewhere in South London. He came home drunk, fell from the balcony and Jenny ran away.'

'Jenny's surname?'

'I don't know. Don't think she told me. If she did, I can't remember it.' He looked at the portraits. 'Beautiful isn't she?'

'Do you have any that show her face?'

'They're the only ones that survived.'

'Survived?'

Wyatt dropped his head.

'Two weeks after moving in, she attacked me.'

Tregunna put his cup down.

Wyatt lifted his right hand, his cigarette dangling from crippled fingers. 'It's what the wacky-backy's for. This'll be with me for the rest of my life.' He shook his head. 'Crazy woman.'

'Crazy?'

'Twisted, bitter, almost schizo.'

'You didn't see it coming?'

'No. Everything was fine, as far as I was concerned. I'd paint. She'd pose. Loved teasing me. At the end of the day, she'd curl up by the fire, I'd read poetry, and she'd recite a couple of lines. We talked about fine arts, about the artists and their struggle. How dedicated they have to be. Occasionally, she'd turn to me, tears in her eyes, desperation in her voice, like a lost soul swept up in the romance of the story. I'd cuddle her and she'd fall asleep. Sometimes we'd wrap ourselves in the duvet and stay on the sofa all night long. She was like a child really.'

'So, why did she attacked you?'

110

'She wanted more money and was angry when I refused. Well, I couldn't afford...'

'How much more?'

'Five thousand.'

'Five grand?' Tregunna looked askance. 'Where did she expect you to get that sort of money?'

'My parents, I suppose.'

'Did she say why she needed it?'

'No. Said it was her fee. She was insistent...I had to pay for the privilege of seeing her body and of painting her. She accused me of using her. She screamed and became quite hysterical. She took the carving knife and set about every painting in the room. I tried to stop her and she turned on me.'

'The hand?'

'Yes. She stole cash from a jar I kept in the kitchen.'

'Much?'

'Nine hundred quid.'

'A lot of money for a student.'

'My parents used to give me a term's fees and my allowance up front to try to help me manage money. I've never been very good, if I'm honest. Didn't even have a bank account in those early days. Stupid really. Anyway, Jenny left that night and I haven't seen her since.'

He hesitated.

'There's something else. Can't see it in the paintings, but she has a tattoo. A dove...'

Tregunna looked up from his note pad, put his pen down, and said, 'Just below the bikini line?'

'Yes.'

'I'll tell you what,' Tregunna said. 'You draw me a picture of Jenny...'

'It's been ten years...'

'Draw a picture of her face and I'll have a word, see if we can't drop the wacky-backy charges. What do you say?'

111

5

The Flybe flight landed at Newquay on time, ten-past-ten, but the early morning sun had given way to the gloom of yet another wet summer's day. Jones arranged for Tregunna to be dropped off at his digs. She collected the Sebring from the police compound and drove to the Incident Room. Once there, she spent the next five hours on paper work, made several phone calls and tried to assimilate new information that had come in. By four, the waste paper basket was littered with empty take-away cartons and disposable coffee cups and she was asleep, her head resting on folded arms.

Superintendent Hinkson had driven from Truro and had parked behind the station, before stealing into the Incident Room. She was looking at information on the whiteboards when Jones stirred, realised she wasn't alone and stood, shakily, to her feet.

'You've been busy, Inspector.'

'Yes, Ma'am.'

'Unfortunately, so have the press.' Hinkson held a tabloid's front page, its headline unimaginative: *Murder on Beach*. 'The article's speculative, but I'm lunching with the Committee today. They'll expect an update.'

Jones walked over to a whiteboard and explained the significance of the portraits and a sketch of Jenny's tattoo that Julian Wyatt had provided. The relationship, if any, between Chris Baldwin and Jenny had not been established, but the tattoos were noticeably similar. The owner of the art gallery had provided a receipt with Baldwin's name on and told officers that he remembered Baldwin and his *rather striking* female companion.

Sue Robinson, Baldwin's sister, had emailed a recent photograph of him and a transcription of the message he'd left with the babysitter...

*Chris can't come to dinner. He's gone to
Cornwall to see his reluctant mermaid.*

'The message was thrown out, but the bin-men were
on strike and she managed to rescue it.'

'And the 'reluctant mermaid'?'

'If we could identify her...'

'Educated guess?'

'We're assuming that Jenny, the reluctant mermaid,
and the girl behind the mask, are one and the same.'

'No, really?'

Jones felt the blood course up her neck.

Blindingly obvious. She recovered. 'Baldwin's sister
hadn't met her, but said she was the *love of his life* and
the woman who *broke his heart.*'

'Wouldn't stand up to cross-examination, but I've got
enough to keep the Committee quiet.' Hinkson smiled.
'And the weekend?'

'Quiz. Finals tonight. I brought George back with me,
but the trip to London's meant Brenda's had too much
on her plate to nobble Daniel Green. We'll be on the
back foot.'

'Oh ye of feint heart.'

'He has an unfair advantage.'

'Being autistic is an advantage?'

'Having that memory is.'

'Hallo you two.'

Bootsy and Smudge were waiting for her.

'Yes, yes, I know you're hungry, but let me just get
in, for goodness sake.' Jones turned the dead lock and
slipped the security chain...not that they had anything
worth the effort.

113

'Lizzie?'

The cottage was eerily quiet.

'Elizabeth?'

She opened the fridge, took out a can of cat food and scooped the contents into a couple of bowls. She turned to the sink and chased away flies that had set up camp in an unwashed cereal bowl. She ran it under cold water, and then unpacked a carrier bag. As she slipped a frozen meal into the microwave, she found Lizzie's note.

She'd gone into town.

Jones settled on the sofa and was joined by the cats.

She flicked through several channels before settling to watch BBC News.

During the next hour the phone rang twice.

First, Brenda McLeish to remind her that pre-season training started on Monday. Brenda was the team's goalkeeper, captain, and coach, and lived and breathed football. She scared the life out of the referee each week, making her worth half a dozen points before the season had even started.

'You available for the quiz tonight?'

Brenda was also the police team's quiz captain and, again, was probably worth a point or two in the earlier rounds. This year, she'd tried to intimidate *The Nest's* landlord, but he'd threatened to divorce her if she didn't behave.

A second phone call woke Jones up and, with Bootsy and Smudge still nestled on her lap, she muted the TV, cradled the handset to her ear and stared at the ceiling.

'Hallo?'

'Inspector Jones?' It was a woman's voice.

'Who is this?'

'I'm sorry to disturb you at home.'

'How did you get this number?'

'Perhaps I ought to come to see you. It'll be easier that way.'

'Easier?'

'It's my son, Daniel. He wants to talk to you.'

'I'm sorry. Who are you?'

'Mrs Green; Daniel's mother.'

'If this is about the quiz.'

'The quiz?'

'Tonight's final?'

'No, I don't think so. It's about that poor man you found on the beach.'

An hour later, Daniel's mother was sipping tea from a mug that Jones had soaked in bleach for two hours to remove coffee stains.

Short, over-weight and frumpy, Mrs Green looked older than her fifty-two years. Not that she did herself any favours. She'd tied her greying hair in a bunch and fiddled with thick-rimmed glasses that gave her fish-like bulbous eyes. She dabbed her mouth with a handkerchief as she began to explain why she'd come and Jones began to wonder if her mind was – like her appearance - cluttered and confused. But after faltering once or twice Mrs Green soon got into her stride. 'I've been making excuses for my son for thirty-five years. Well, that's not fair...I've had to explain his behaviour...No, that doesn't sound right either... But before you meet him, there are things you should know.'

'Why don't you start at the beginning?'

'Yes. Why not? OK...' She removed her glasses and used her handkerchief to clean them. 'Daniel works at the Passmore Edwards library. You know, the one On-The-Moor, in town. He knows where every book is located, its title and its author. It wouldn't surprise me if he knew the ISBN numbers as well. He has a gift, you see?' She sipped her tea. 'This is cold.'

'Would you like some more?'

115

'Give him any two numbers,' she continued as if she hadn't heard, 'and ask him to add, subtract, multiply or divide them, and he'll give you the answer before you've had chance to draw breath. Mention any word and he'll instantly tell you how many letters there are in it. He can recite poems after one reading. He can recall the detail of bus timetables, times of tides and the phases of the moon on any given date. He watches shipping in and out of the harbour. He goes down to the auction each day and can remember how much fish each boat caught and how much it was worth. He can name every plant, herb and tree in woodland, coastal paths, and around the town.'

'Extraordinary. No wonder we struggle in the pub quiz. But why did you want to see me?'

'His gift comes with a heavy price tag,' Wendy Green continued. 'Early on, teachers realised that he was gifted but was having serious problems relating to other children. He was diagnosed as high-functioning autistic; semantic pragmatic disorder.' She dabbed her mouth and wiped moist eyes. 'He doesn't process language in the same way that we do, especially idiomatic language. For instance, if he heard you say, 'I nearly died when I won a prize at Bingo,' he'd not only be concerned about your welfare, but would also want to know what it was about the prize that had had such an effect on you.'

'But, he holds down a job and his team has swept all before them in the pub quiz.'

'Yes, but he is incapable of learning through social interaction. His teachers would have to move his face so that he looked at them when they spoke to him. He's had to learn everything by heart. *Good morning. How are you?* Everything.'

'Life at school must have been hell.'

'The kids were great at primary school. The teachers told them why Daniel was different and how they could help him. At the Comp, things were a nightmare to start

116

with, but Daniel's ability to remember dates, English Lit quotations, Physic's formulae and theorems earned him a level of acceptance, with kids calling him the 'Nutty Professor'.'

Bootsy yawned, raised himself up, arched his back, dug his claws into Jones's legs, and then jumped heavily onto the floor and left the room. Smudge followed, chasing his brother down the hallway.

'You have cats.' Wendy Green said.

Jones began to wonder if autism was hereditary.

'Daniel fixates,' Wendy Green continued, 'and can become obsessed, to the exclusion of everything else. He's become clinically depressed by events he didn't understand. When my husband left, for instance.'

'Children often blame themselves for the break up of a marriage.'

'Daniel was ten. He didn't speak for five months. On another occasion, he saw live pictures of a shooting at an American school. The next day, he told his Headteacher he was going to bring a gun to school and kill everyone.'

'Oh, my God.'

'It was his way of processing what he'd seen. His way of managing conflicting messages…school is a safe place; school is somewhere people get killed. The two messages didn't make sense to him and he had to find a way of understanding.'

'So, Daniel can be violent?'

'Good gracious me, no. He would never hurt anyone. He's as gentle as a lamb. He reads to kids in the library. He grooms horses at the local stables. He takes Mutley for a walk everyday and feeds him and takes him to the vet when he's sick.'

'And he wants to talk to me?'

'Yes.'

'What about?'

'He hasn't been to work for the last few days. He's withdrawn into his own world. He sits and waits for the news. Local news, national news and the only time his eyes register anything is when they feature the death of the poor man you found washed up on the beach.'

'Does Daniel have information for us?'

'He was walking Mutley when that couple found the body. He stayed to watch.'

'He was taking photographs, wasn't he?'

'Was he?'

'He broke through the police cordon and got close to the body.'

'That might explain why he's been acting up. He says the man was murdered and he keeps saying it, over and over. Murdered. Murdered.'

'When can I see him?'

'You can't. Not yet, at least. He wouldn't be able to cope.'

'What? I sit and wait for you to call? This is a murder enquiry, Mrs Green.'

'I've brought something from him. It's a riddle. He communicates in riddles when he's stressed. I think he's trying to give you a clue.' She handed Jones a note on which Daniel had scrawled:

FH 128

If God intended them to be made of fibre glass…

*

118

When the phone rang just after six, Lizzie was lying on the sofa reading a magazine and Jones was rustling-up a mushroom-and-red-pepper omelette.

'You expecting a call?'

'Leave it,' Jones said. 'If it's work they'd have used my mobile.'

'You said Kate Madison might ring, invite us to dinner.'

'If she does, we're busy.'

Jones came in from the kitchen with an apron round her waist and a tea towel thrown over her shoulder.

'Open this for me?' She handed Lizzie a jar with a screw lid.

Lizzie gripped it, twisted, replaced the lid, and handed it back.

'Thanks,' Jones said.

'Not particularly feminine is it, a vice-like grip?

'Comes with hammering out ditties for twenty years.'

'Ditties? You'll have all the major composers turning in their grave. Ditties?' Lizzie laughed. 'Apron suits you, by the way. You look the part, at least.'

'Cheek.' Jones flicked the tea towel at her. 'The trouble with self-catering,' she said, leaning over and kissing her. 'Is that it wastes valuable time.'

'Let's eat first.'

Jones sighed, picked up the remote control and set the box to record *Ask the Minister*. 'Seriously,' she said, 'if Missy Madison does call, I'd rather we didn't go.'

Lizzie topped up her glass. 'Why?'

'I met her…'

'You said. Taking statements in London. What's she like?'

'Gorgeous.'

'Lydia?'

'Well, she is, but not everyone thinks she's the real deal.'

119

'Dead man's shoes?'

'Chris Baldwin earned his reputation. TV presenters like him are known as The Talent.' Jones puffed out her cheeks and exhaled forcefully. 'Some can be difficult, temperamental.'

'I've met enough of those in my time.'

'Baldwin was different. Popular, knowledgeable, and respected.'

'And Kate hasn't earned her spurs?'

'Yes, something like that,' Jones said. 'Anyway, the dinner invitation...don't you think it's too soon after his father's death to be socialising?'

'That's Stewart's call. Maybe the tonic he needs - to see an old friend. You were at school together, right?'

'No. Summer holidays. I came down to the cottage.'

'Good friends?'

'Until Emma,' Jones said.

'You told me.'

'Not everything.'

'You don't have to do this, Lydia.'

'I do.'

'No, you don't. I'm not interested.'

'It's not as simple as that, unfortunately.'

Jones gazed out at the gathering shadows and shuddered. 'After my parents died, I went to live with my aunt, just over the bridge in Fulham. Once I'd reached my late teens, she used to pack me off to the cottage for the summer holidays. I'd work on the beachfront - anything to earn a bit of pocket money - the fair, local café, selling ice creams. Stewart worked for his father. Film sets, TV studios and magazines, learning the business from the bottom up. I think Richard Lander liked to keep his son's feet firmly on the ground. If Stewart was at home, we'd meet up end of the day, spend time.'

'Close?'

120

'Not like that. More brother, sister.'

'Same University?'

'Stewart went to Oxford. I've never been the sharpest knife…'

'Not true, Detective Inspector.'

'Well, never a high-flyer. Anyway, I was impatient to join up and attended various courses at Hendon.'

'Where you met Emma?'

'No. That was later, during my second year with the Met. Then, I transferred down here.'

'You must specialise in long distance relationships.'

'Yeah.' Jones snorted, tried to smile, then said, 'But I haven't told you the whole story.'

'It's OK, Lydia. Really.'

'I invited Emma down. Took her to meet Stewart. I was trying to impress her with my wealthy friends, I suppose.' Jones's eyes narrowed. 'We couldn't afford much, but we were happy, least I was. That summer, I was sent on another course at Hendon. I left Emma here and, by the time I got back, she'd jacked in her job and moved into Stewart's bed.'

'Oh, God.'

'It gets worse. They were together for six months, Emma hopelessly in love, when he dumped her. She went home to her parents. Two months later, she was dead. Committed suicide.'

'I'm sorry. I had no idea.'

'Why should you? There are a thousand and one things we don't know about each other.'

'But relationships end. It happens all the time.'

'Yes, I know. But you know what? Stewart was 'too busy' to attend Emma's funeral.'

'You went?'

'Of course, but it made me realise how cold-blooded and how bloody ruthless he can be.'

121

'An asset in business. Better to be feared than loved, so they say. It's why so many captains of industry have a reputation for being bastards.'

'But, I'd never seen that side of Stewart. It was as if he'd thrown a switch and erased her from his mind.'

'And you haven't seen him since?'

'No. Well, not until his father's funeral.'

'Come here. You need a cuddle.'

They held on to one another for several minutes until Lizzie said, 'What's that smell?' She sat up and sniffed the air. 'Burnt omelette, Inspector?'

Rita and Henry reached for one another at a particular moment during the show and held hands throughout the rest. They held hands during the journey home on the Tube and stared at their reflections as the train hurtled through the Underground's blackness. And they held hands in the back of the taxi that picked them up at South Wimbledon and took them home.

Not a word passed between them the whole time. Not one, but they both knew it was her.

The day had gone so well, up to then...

Rita had been the first to rise, long before she needed to. She'd been too excited to sleep and was impatient for the day to begin. They'd heard about Chris Baldwin and were shocked and upset.

'A wonderful man,' she'd told the home insurance rep who'd called to collect the monthly premium. 'Sort you could invite into your home, give him a cup of tea and he'd make you feel special. Had lovely eyes. They smiled, even when he was asking difficult questions. He wasn't married you know. Had a flat in London, (so Rita read in a woman's magazine). Moved into his mother's house after she died a few years ago. Bless him. That diving's so dangerous. Can't believe anyone would want to kill him. Must have been an accident. Lovely man.'

Someone phoned from the studios and explained that they were going ahead with the show. 'It's what Chris would have wanted,' the young man had said. 'We're dedicating the programme to his memory.'

Rita wanted to wear a hat until Henry reminded her that it wasn't *a bloody wedding*. They ordered a cab to take them to South Wimbledon station - a special treat they could ill-afford – and Rita spent the journey on the train looking out for suspicious people with suspicious packages.

Henry dozed.

Men!

London was full of tourists. High season was pretty well all year round and Rita watched people stream on and off the train. Noisy children with their friends - girls teasing the boys, boys trying to look cool - bringing the biggest smile to her face. Their Jonathan had been a friendly boy.

It was over-cast, and that helped make the walk to the studios a pleasant one. Against a backdrop of the drone of London's traffic, they hurried along the South Bank, past the Eye and the Festival Hall, and were just in time to join the queue, where they were searched and taken up to hospitality.

Rita took Henry's arm and squeezed until he cried out. He pulled her close, sharing her excitement. They stumbled over each other as they tried to recognise stars smiling at them from photographs lining the wall along the corridor. They were ushered into a canteen where they were offered a drink and a selection of sandwiches.

A young man who, Rita reckoned, couldn't have been more than twenty-three, came in and spoke to them. 'It's been a difficult time for all of us, but it's important that

123

we do the best we can, for Chris's sake. During the show, you'll see someone at the side of the stage telling you when to clap. Please follow his directions. This is live television. We don't get two goes at this. Today's going to be particularly difficult for the show's new host, Kate Madison. I'm sure you'll appreciate how nervous she's going to be. So, please, give her a warm welcome. And finally, as I said, this is live television so no falling asleep or picking your noses.' He waited for the ripple of laughter to die. 'Oh, and please turn your mobile phones off. Enjoy the show.'

When the audience was invited into the amphitheatre, Henry decided he needed to use the loo, and Rita grew impatient as all the best seats were snapped up.

Men!

With everyone settled, they were told that sound and lighting engineers needed to run final tests and producers were checking different camera angles. Whilst they waited the audience were asked to practice clapping. A man stood at the side of the stage and, when he clapped his hands above his head, the audience had to applaud. They tried this several times before it was suggested they gave themselves a big clap. After a few moments, they were asked to be still and quiet and, when the floor managers were ready, the show began.

After the opening music and credits, a man came on and spoke straight into Camera One. He was smartly dressed in a suit and with one of those ties that match the handkerchief in the breast pocket of his jacket.

'Welcome to *Ask the Minister*,' he said. 'As you know, we have had the most dreadful news this week. Chris Baldwin was one of a new breed of reporters and was respected throughout our industry. We've dedicated today's programme to him. May I take this opportunity to express our heartfelt condolences to his family and friends, especially his sister, Susan, who has given her

124

blessing for the show to be aired.' He waited for the gravity of the situation to sink in and then announced, 'This evening's guest is Tom Bond, the Home Office Minister. But first ladies and gentlemen, let me introduce you to our host, Kate Madison.'

The audience applauded enthusiastically and Kate Madison walked across the set, sat down, took a sip of water from a glass on the coffee table and glanced up at the audience. She smiled, nodded and mouthed, 'Thank you.' She turned to Camera Two and spoke confidently into the lens. 'May I offer a warm welcome to everyone here, in the studio, and at home. As well as championing legislation to combat poverty, crime, and extremism in our own country, my special guest is known for his statesmanship, diplomacy and support for those nations less prosperous than ours…'

Thus the show began, without mention of Geoffrey D'Ancey.

Rita and Henry were sitting at the back of the hushed auditorium. From there, it wasn't always easy to hear or see what was going on and they resorted to following the interview on monitors hanging from the ceiling.

Everything seemed to be going well but, for reasons she didn't understand at first, Rita felt uneasy.

The producer seemed to keep the camera trained on Kate Madison and held close-ups for an uncomfortable amount of time.

It was during one particular close-up that Rita and Henry reached out and held hands, but it wasn't until they'd got home and watched a recording that Rita said, 'It's her, isn't it? Whatever she's calling herself these days, it *is* her?'

They sat in silence until the credits.

'Kate Madison,' Henry read. 'Odd name.'

'Sounded like a yank to me. But definitely her.'

'Without a shadow of a doubt.'

'I suppose we ought to be pleased for her.'
'I can't. Not after what she did to our Jon.'

Stewart Lander thought that Kate looked tired as she stooped to avoid the helicopter's rotary blades. But then she had every right to be. She'd carried the show, at very short notice, in very difficult circumstances. He was used to her bubbly personality. It had been one reason he'd been attracted to her. But this was a side he hadn't seen before. She'd been raw, yes...but every successful broadcaster had rough edges, and goofed up and fluffed lines. And that was what she'd become, his experience told him, after only one show – a successful broadcaster. The camera adored her and if this wasn't the start of something big, he'd eat the hat he used when fly-fishing. OK, he reminded himself, he'd used his influence and introduced her to his contacts at ITV after they'd started - what his father had called - their courtship.

He would never forget the evening they'd met for the first time at the Yacht Club, about eighteen months ago.

She'd just returned after a spell in America. They'd spent the evening chatting and he'd asked to see her again. She'd been coy – another of his father's favourite words. But they bumped into one another in London, at the premiere of his latest movie, and it was enough of a coincidence to give them a sense that they were *meant to be*.

She ran across the lawn, threw her arms around his neck, and they kissed, passionately.

He held her close. 'You should be on television more often.'

'You saw me? Was I good?'

126

'Let's get you showered and changed. We'll watch the recording over supper.'

'Don't be mean. Tell me, what did you think?'

He knew she'd want it to be perfect and knew that it wasn't. But he had to give her credit...to have been thrown in at the deep-end like that.

'You want the truth?' he said.

'It was awful, goddam it, wasn't it?'

'I asked if you wanted the truth?'

'Yes. Yes, of course. As long as...'

'You handled things very well.'

She squealed. 'And?'

'That's all I'm prepared to say for now.'

'Stewart.'

'Just be patient. Martha's run a bath, take your time and we'll talk over supper.'

'Scrub my back?'

'I'm meeting with John Hartley.'

'More security?'

'We're a soft target.'

'As long as I can take a pee in private.' She laughed and kissed him on the cheek. 'Missed you.'

About an hour later, she joined him in the sitting room. Gone was the suit, replaced by jeans and a T-shirt. Her urchin-style blond hair was still wet. It was plastered to her head and this served to exaggerate the diminutive dimensions of her head and face, and accentuated the size of her eyes, the fineness of her bone structure and her full, sensual mouth. Lander was in no doubt that she was the most beautiful woman he'd ever seen.

They sat on the sofa and watched the recording until the closing credits. She turned to him, anxious. 'Well, what do you think?'

'A star is born.'

'Really? You're not just saying that?'

'The camera loves you.'

127

'What d'you mean?'

'Some have an affinity with the medium. You have it. Might even be worth arranging a screen test. If what I saw on the small translates to the big, you may find yourself in the movies. But,' he added quickly, 'you'll need to be patient and develop your craft. A star may have been born, but it is a young star and one that might easily burn itself out.'

'But I was good, right?'

'You looked nervous during opening skirmishes with Tom Bond.'

'Oh, you've no idea.'

'But he helped you.'

'What do you mean?'

'He showed qualities that give credence to those who see him as a future leader of the Party. He was sensitive. Sensitive, not patronising. He smiled at you. He eased into his answers without jumping down your throat. He didn't use his considerable experience to put you off balance.'

'How would he have done that?'

'It's the oldest trick in the book. The interviewer asks a question. The politician answers by *asking* a question. This is designed not only to give the politician time to think of an answer, but also to unsettle the interviewer. Some struggle.'

'I asked really probing questions, didn't I?'

'You've obviously learned a lot from Chris Baldwin. You adopted a similar style.'

'I'll develop my own, given time.'

'Yes, but don't ignore the qualities that made him a household name.'

Supper was served on silver platters arranged on a large, rectangular coffee table - cold cuts, followed by champagne-and-strawberry ice cream.

'By the way,' Madison said, 'I met an old friend of yours. Lydia Jones? I'm sure I've seen her somewhere before.'

'She was at the funeral.'

'Couldn't have been there.'

'No, of course not.'

'She's investigating Chris Baldwin's death.'

'Seems it might well have been murder.'

'I know. It's so awful.'

'The news has been full of it.'

'I saw something about our local MP?'

'The Judge?' Lander shook his head. 'Odd how they're linked.'

'Linked?'

'There was an article in today's *Times*. Photographs were found in D'Ancey's room. There's speculation he was involved in an Internet paedophile network.'

'God, how sick's that? But what's that got to do with Chris?'

'Nothing really, I suppose, except that he was going to interview D'Ancey and now they're both dead.'

'Oh, I see.'

They ate silently for a few minutes before Madison said, 'I invited them round for dinner. You don't mind, do you?'

'Them?' Stewart rang for the table to be cleared.

'Lydia and her...'

'Partner. Lizzie. Concert pianist.'

'Gay?'

'S'pose.'

'Well, either she is or she isn't.'

'Wasn't.'

'Did you?'

Lander laughed. 'Lydia? No.'

'Good looking.'

'Doesn't hold a candle to you.'

He hesitated. 'Dinner's not a good idea.'

'Why?'

'Long story. Lydia and I have had our differences.' He pulled her to her feet and said, 'Besides, I can think of much better ways of spending time with the most beautiful woman in the room.'

She giggled. 'What had you in mind?'

'Albert's chilled a fine bottle of champagne. Annie's cut fresh flowers and has arranged them in your room...'

'I hope you don't intend to invite them to the party?'

'Strictly the two of us.'

She kissed him gently, allowing her lips to linger and her perfume to assault his senses. 'Give me half an hour. I need time to unwind.' As she reached the door she turned and said, 'I might invite Lizzie for a canter. The horses need exercising and I'd be interested in meeting her.'

'Does she ride?' he asked. 'I just don't want anything else to happen.'

'Don't worry,' she said, 'I'll look after her.'

The pub was heaving, but the extractor fan was on the blink and the fug of heavy air helped stir echoes of *The Crow's Nest* two hundred years ago. Back then it had been the haunt of Packet ship crews, a whorehouse, and watering hole for petty criminals, smugglers and highwaymen. At least, that was the image the brewery wanted to promote and, with ready money jangling in fewer pockets, Angus McLeish was encouraged to do everything he could to maintain the pub's authenticity. It was a great marketing ploy and, as well as locals who remained loyal all year round, the pub was a magnet for tourists.

The two teams gathered and a rumour spread quickly that Daniel Green wasn't taking part. 'I never touched him.' Brenda McLeish grinned at the opposition and lifted her pint glass. 'You might as well cough up now, the trophy's as good as ours.' She began to milk the applause of customers in the bar, and goaded, 'You've always been a one-man team and we're going to wipe the floor with you.'

Angus McLeish had had enough of his wife's mouth and at six-six and eighteen stone he was the only person in the room big enough and ugly enough to take her on.

'Shut your gob, woman. And sit ye down. Y'makes the place look untidy.'

The pub's regulars cheered and one called for Angus to, 'Give her one.'

'Nah,' he said, 'still picking hairs from me teeth after last night.'

This brought the house down and pantomime reigned as Brenda chased Angus across the lounge bar and into the snug. They returned, arm-in-arm, grinning broadly, and the cabaret ended with an embrace and a slap on Brenda's ample bottom.

Show over, everyone settled down for the main event.

Jones arrived just in time and after deflecting scowls from her teammates she gestured to the barman for a pint and she took her seat.

'Better late than never,' Brenda hissed.

'I fell asleep.'

'Post coital?'

'Watching the news.'

'Yeah, right.'

'I've recorded *Ask the Minister*. We'll catch a rerun on iPlayer in the morning. You're all invited.'

'Not too early.' McLeish saw her husband take hold of a microphone. 'I've got a feeling we're in for a long night.'

131

'Are we ready then, folks?' His voice drifted across the bar and the pub fell silent. 'The first set of questions is about scientific discoveries...'

The evening was a huge success – the free pasties going down well. Late into the competition, and despite sinking several pints, an electrician managed to fix the extractor. The PAWS team beat the police and retained the trophy without the help of Daniel Green.

Most customers had left by twelve-thirty, but a handful stayed, by invitation, to enjoy the landlord's largesse.

Jones stared into her pint. Her head felt heavy, her eyes were scratchy, and her breath was stale.

'Can't believe we lost,' she said.

'We were crap.'

'Yes, George, we were, weren't we.'

She returned to her beer, dropped her face to the rim of the glass and tilted it towards her. She sipped and managed to spill about a mouthful onto the table. She sat - motionless, helpless - and watched the beer run off the edge of the table and onto her lap.

'I'll get a cloth.' Tregunna returned from the bar and handed her a tea towel.

'Thanks. You'd make a wonderful wife.' She dabbed her jeans and tossed the cloth on the table. 'How are things?'

'Marriage counsellor suggested one of them trials.'

'Separation, George,' she said, her words slurred. 'A trial separation.'

'Whatever. Wasn't long before she'd moved in with someone else.'

Jones shook her head. 'Go on, buy us another.'

George was unsteady on his feet. He propped himself up and tried to focus on the artefacts the brewery had bought from a local salvage company.

The relics included an iron cannon, a ship's wheel, two portholes and - most prized of all - a ship's bell.

Jones lifted her head long enough to follow his gaze. 'Look real, don't they?' she said.

'That's 'cause they are,' Angus said.

He poured them each a double brandy and led George back to the table. 'Can ye not see the faces of men and the terror in their eyes as they're lured onto the rocks. Can ye not hear their cries as the waves drag them down, knowing that death was inevitable?'

'Very poetic.' Jones threw back the brandy. 'All I can see at the bottom of my glass are crabs feasting on Chris Baldwin's face. Not a death I'd wish on anyone except your wife when she gets me on that pitch tomorrow.'

'Not sure she'll be in a fit state.' Angus glanced over at Brenda, slumped on her back in the far corner of the bar. Her mouth was open and she was snoring loudly.

'You're a lovely man, Angus,' Jones said.

Tregunna looked up from his brandy. 'I know it's late, Guv.'

'Guv? Oh, for God's sake George it's, I don't know, sometime Saturday morning. Give it a rest.'

'But, I've been thinking...'

Jones lifted her glass, and said to Angus. 'I'm going to need another.'

'It's that gold doubloon we found on him.'

'Yes, George?'

Angus McLeish stood over them and wiped a glass with a tea towel. 'There's always plenty of rumours,' he said. 'Ships wrecked, booty washed ashore. I heard a whisper a few years ago. Someone had found a wreck. If he had a fishing license and dived the wreck each time he went 'fishing', he could have brought up small stuff like coins, jewellery, and ceramics. Then sold it on. As long as he didn't get greedy...'

Jones had fallen asleep.

133

'Could you ask around?' Tregunna said.

'I'll see what I can find out. One of the old timers might know something.' Angus looked at Jones. 'You'd better give Lizzie a ring. Tell her to put a bucket by the bed. I'll get a cab. Can't let one of Falmouth's finest loose on the town drunk and disorderly can we?'

The travelling and the broadcast had exhausted Rita and Henry and they went to bed very soon after they'd finished their mug of hot chocolate. But the shock of seeing Kate Madison – of recognising her - made them restless and it wasn't until dawn that they both fell into a deep sleep.

When they woke, the rain was drizzling down the double-glazing and the clock by the bed was ticking down to eleven-thirty.

Henry struggled out of bed. 'Tea?'

'You're a darling.'

'I'll bring up the papers. We'll prop ourselves up in bed and read through the lot.'

'We can't do that.'

'Why not?'

'It's Saturday. Saturday we go to Sainsbury's.' She smiled. 'Nice idea, reading the paper in bed. Reminds me of when we were younger.'

'Now then, that sort of talk's not good for my ticker.'

'Doctor says it'll do us both the world of good.'

'Not his ticker, is it?' Henry sat on the edge of the bed and pulled on his slippers. 'Well, shall I bring up the papers, or what?'

'Best not, eh? There's always a crowd in Sainsbury's on a Saturday.'

After they had showered and dressed, Henry leafed through the back pages of the paper, checking the test card and the county cricket tables before turning to the rest of the paper.

'Oh, my good God,' he said.

'What is it?'

'Read that.'

Rita brought a chair round to sit alongside him. They read an exposé that filled pages four and five and spent time studying the pictures and diagrams that illustrated the feature.

She looked at him. 'What are we going to do?'

'*The police*,' Henry read out loud, '*are appealing for information that might assist them in their enquiries.*'

'Let's look at it again, calmly.'

They read the article again and looked at each other.

'You think we ought to go to the police?'

'I think so, don't you? If we're right and don't say anything...'

'Shame on you.' Superintendent Hinkson walked into the Incident Room at Falmouth Police Station.

Jones' head was thumping and she felt nauseous. She couldn't remember getting home and had no idea what she'd got up to. Clearly, someone had covered her back, but she wasn't sure how much of last night had reached the Superintendent's ears.

She played it safe. 'Ma'am?'

'The PAWS team, minus Daniel Green, and you still lost.'

'I don't suppose DS George Tregunna's secondment to London to assist an overworked and underpaid DI can be offered in mitigation?'

'No, in a word, Inspector.' Hinkson smiled. 'Floor's all yours.'

'Thank you, Ma'am. I'll start with Chris Baldwin.' She moved over to the paintings propped-up under a whiteboard and realised she needed to give the coffee time to work its magic.

She sat down and invited Tregunna to describe his visit to Baldwin's home, the meeting with his sister, and the subsequent phone call to the art gallery in London.

'Obviously, we need to find Jenny,' Tregunna said. 'I've had her description circulated and the press and TV are running leaders on her today. She's got the same tattoo as Baldwin, same place. Her tattoo's about ten years old. His is fairly recent. May be co-incidence, of course.'

'And the mermaid?' Jones asked.

'No connection so far, other than the paintings were purchased by Chris Baldwin.'

'We know Jenny had posed for them and can assume she's the mermaid,' Hinkson said. 'Anything else?'

'His car's been impounded. We've also removed his computer and other stuff...'

'Stuff?' Hinkson raised an eyebrow. 'Could you be a little more specific, Constable?'

'Contents of his desk and waste paper bin, that sort of stuff Ma'am,' Tregunna said.

Jones winced and held her breath, but Hinkson's broadside didn't materialise.

Seemingly unaware, Tregunna added, 'I passed his toothbrush and razor onto forensics. They'll let us know as soon as they find anything.'

'Thank you, George,' Hinkson said, 'Let's try to be more generous with our information in future, shall we?'

Jones turned to McLeish. 'Dive shops?'

She, too, was nursing a mug of coffee. 'Drawn a blank. No one remembers lending any gear to Baldwin. Nothing from the hotels or guest houses.'

'He must have stayed somewhere.'

'Caravan? Mobile home?' Tregunna suggested.

'Camping?' McLeish added.

'George,' Jones said. 'Check on registered sites.'

'What if he's got friends down this way? Stayed with them?' Hinkson asked.

'They'd have come forward by now, Ma'am.'

'I had an interesting chat with Angus after the quiz on Friday night.' Tregunna glanced at Jones. 'A few of us were having a nightcap and got talking about treasure. Angus said he'd ask around and let me know.'

'Good. Well done, George. Chase him, let me know what he comes up with.' Jones put her cup down, eased herself out of her seat, paced up and down, and then said, 'We now know *one* reason Baldwin was here - his reluctant mermaid. But what was he doing at 40 metres? Why risk diving to that depth? Was it treasure? Spanish treasure? Is that what the doubloon is all about? And why didn't he bring his own gear down?'

'Maybe he left his gear behind because he didn't want anyone to know what he was doing,' McLeish offered.

'I saw a *Dive Magazine* at his home,' Tregunna said. 'Maybe someone advertised, looking for experienced divers?'

'Get back copies and check with the editor. Anything else?' Jones looked round her team. 'No? OK. On Friday afternoon, I had a visit from Daniel Green's mother.'

'You nobbled him.' McLeish punched the air. 'Nice one.'

'We'd left that to you,' Jones said, wanting to move on, the coffee kicking in, at last. 'I swear Wendy Green has the same condition as her son, milder form. Anyway, she reckons that Daniel knows something. Something that's upset him. He hasn't been able to go to work at the library for several days, but he sent us a riddle...'

She pinned Daniel's note on the whiteboard.

FH 128
If God intended them to be made of fibre glass...

'Why not bring him in?' Hinkson asked.

'I'll contact Mrs Green, see how he is.'

'We can't wait forever.'

'With respect, Ma'am, if we push too early, we may lose him completely.'

Jones changed tack.

'I had tea at the Savoy...'

She waited for the catcalls to die down. 'Lady Emily was none too pleased with the revelations linking her husband with organised paedophilia.'

'Not surprised. What about the young woman he was entertaining on the evening he was murdered?' Hinkson asked.

'I spoke to the night porter on duty. Tommy Murphy. A real charmer. At first, he was reluctant to open up, but I managed to persuade him it was in his best interest. He confirmed he'd opened the fire escape to let a woman in. It wasn't the first time he'd performed this task for the Judge. In fact the evening *before* D'Ancey was killed he'd entertained *two* women.'

'Probably what killed him?' McLeish grinned.

Jones frowned at her.

'Tommy Murphy said he'd only known about the first woman when she came downstairs, walked through reception, out the main entrance, and got into a taxi.'

'And the other woman?'

'Later that same evening. Gained access via the fire escape. Young Asian. Left after an hour.'

'Via the fire escape?'

'Yes, Ma'am.'

'But, that was the night *before* D'Ancey was killed?'

'Yes Ma'am. Tommy Murphy's in custody. His home's being turned over. My guess is he'll be helping the Met with their inquiries for some time to come.'

'Did Tommy get a look at D'Ancey's visitor on the night he was killed?'

139

'The light wasn't good, he claims. But, she was tall, with long dark hair and was wearing a three-quarter-length coat. Not much to go on.'

'But he did see her?'

'Probably wouldn't be able to collar her in an identity parade. He watched her get into the lift and waited until it stopped on the sixth floor where D'Ancey had a room. I doubt Tommy Murphy's testimony would stand cross-examination.'

'Half-an-hour later D'Ancey was dead.' Hinkson rummaged through her handbag. 'And she pushed him?'

'All we know is he fell and his fly was undone. The post mortem's confirmed he'd been drinking, but wasn't drunk. Forensics found fingerprints on two glasses and lipstick on one, fingerprints on the balcony door, and traces of make up, perfume and hair on the sofa's antimacassar.' Jones drew breath. 'The lab boys will let us have the results as soon as they can.'

'The Met will keep us up to speed so we can liaise with his family.' Hinkson took out one of her synthetic cigarettes, placed it between her lips and asked, 'Lady Emily wasn't upset or distressed?'

'She was shocked by her husband's involvement in paedophilia, but not his extra curricula.'

'Maybe she's still in shock. Different people react in different ways. Maybe reality's not sunk in, but she seemed in complete control when we told her.'

'Alexandra didn't bother to turn up for our meeting at the Savoy,' Jones said.

'What do we know about the daughter?'

'Not a lot, Ma'am, but she's tall, slim, attractive, and has long dark hair.'

'An interview would seem long overdue, don't you think?' Hinkson took the cigarette from her mouth and used it to emphasise her next point. 'We're looking for a motive. See if she's got an alibi for the evening D'Ancey was killed.'

'His daughter?'

'Motive, Inspector. A DNA sample would be helpful. See if we can match it against swabs taken at the club.'

'But his daughter?'

'Butter wouldn't melt?' Hinkson took a long drag, holding the synthetic smoke in her lungs before exhaling forcefully. 'Perhaps we ought to interview the staff at Bissom Manor. Find out what they make of her.'

Tregunna was staring at the whiteboard when he said, 'The MO's established in both cases. Baldwin rockets to the surface and the Judge is pushed from a balcony after a bit of nooky. But there's no pattern. No link between the two of them.' He was conscious that everyone was listening and the room had fallen silent. 'We know where, and have a good idea how Chris Baldwin died, but we have no idea why?'

'Your point, George?' Jones asked.

'It's just that, all I see when I look at the whiteboard and listen to all the evidence is a woman with long dark hair.'

'Then we'd better run a check on everyone fitting that description.' Hinkson said.

Jones watched the Superintendent walk towards the door and felt a sudden surge of resentment at Hinkson's sarcasm and anger at the stifled laughter coming from several officers.

'What we *do* need...' Hinkson didn't break her stride. '...is conclusive evidence. Something that will stand up in court. We don't even have a prime suspect. Concentrate on Chris Baldwin. He was murdered on our patch. It's our call.'

*

141

The three-storey, grey-stone house that Wendy Green inherited from her grandmother was snuggled between the *Quayside Inn* and *The Chain Locker*. It had a private slipway and views across to Flushing and St. Mawes. On several occasions, well-healed visitors looking for a weekend retreat or holiday home had offered her a small fortune. But, for Wendy Green, the house was a refuge from prying eyes and pointing fingers, and the incessant chatter and cruel gossip. It was in that house - a world of thick stonewalls, small casement windows, and large flagstone floors - that they could go about their daily routine unhurried, unflustered and unimpaired.

She would clean, iron, cook, knit, darn socks and turn collars and the only time she went out was to shop for food, pay the newspaper bill, or collect prescriptions for them both.

When Daniel came home from the library, he'd take Mutley for a walk, same route day in, day out - past the National Maritime museum, along Castle Drive and Cliff Road to Pendennis Point. They'd sit awhile and Daniel would stare out at the sea and at the horizon. After ten minutes, precisely, they would make their way back along Rope Walk and then drop down to the waterfront. Once home, he'd go up to his room, on the top floor at the back of the house, and stare out of the window, watching the daily dramas unfold along the quayside and the harbour.

But, for the past three days, he'd been sitting in his room, staring out of the window, moving only to visit the bathroom, watch updates on news channels, or go to bed. He took his meals in his room, but said nothing, no matter how gently his mother tried to reach him.

*

Jones and McLeish parked at Custom House Quay and walked down a narrow passage to Wendy Green's house where they were ushered in and offered a cup of tea.

'Another time. We've come to see Daniel. Just a few questions.'

'You want me to come up with you?'

'Best if you leave it to us.'

'His room's on the top floor, in the attic.'

They held onto a wooden banister as they climbed the staircase and, near the top, had to duck under a low ceiling. In places, the plaster had cracked and damp had prised it away from the wall.

Jones knocked gently on his door and when Daniel didn't answer, she tried again. She turned to McLeish, shrugged, and then pushed it open.

Oak beams straddled the roof void. A television was fixed to a wall- mounted stand and angled towards a bed. A computer screen and keyboard sat on a small table, the tower underneath. The walls were a dull cream and one was covered with pictures from both cases, cut from newspapers. Daniel was sitting at the window, looking out over the estuary, and rocking gently back and forth, mumbling to himself.

'Daniel?' She couldn't be sure he'd heard her.

She went over and knelt on one knee. 'Hallo, Daniel, I'm Inspector Jones and this is Sergeant McLeish. We're police officers. We've come to talk to you about this.'

She showed him the riddle.

'Can you tell us what it means?'

Nothing.

She cupped his chin in her the palm of her hand and eased his face towards hers. 'Look at me, Daniel.' Their eyes met. 'Can you tell me what this means?' He did not avert his eyes, but continued to stare at her.

'Be careful Guv,' McLeish said.

'Daniel. Your mother says you have something to tell us. Is that right?'

He stared at her then turned to the window. Suddenly, he inhaled and held his breath for several seconds before he slumped forward, raised his head, shook it from side to side, and then stared out of the window.

'Daniel?'

He started to recite something that sounded familiar.

She took hold of his chin and turned him to face her. 'That sounds like a nursery rhyme. What does this mean, Daniel?'

'Three went out; two came back,' he said. 'Three went out; two came back.' His voice grew louder and tears rolled down his face. 'Three went out; two came back.'

'When was this, Daniel?'

'Sunday. Sunday, the sixth. Sunday, sixth of June.'

'What happened?'

'Boat went out. Boat came back. Three people out. Two people back. Three went out. Two came back.'

'Did you recognise any of the people?'

'Harbour lights on at ten past eight.'

'Daniel, what time did the boat go out?'

'Eight minutes to eight.'

'And what time did it return?'

'Sixteen minutes past ten. High tide two minutes past ten.'

'Dark by then,' McLeish offered.

'But the harbour lights were on.' Jones turned back to Daniel and tried to think of questions with a numerical answer. 'Men, women? Daniel?'

He didn't answer.

'How many men?' She tried.

'Three.'

'How many women?'

He looked at her.

144

Jones took his face again. 'Daniel, listen to me. You must tell us everything you know. You can help us find out who murdered Chris Baldwin.'

She held up the riddle.

'What's this? The answer?'

He stared out of the window.

She looked out of the window at the quayside. The estuary was teeming with the summer's influx of craft. Some were anchored against the flow of the current, but most were moored to floating pontoons patrolled by customs officers collecting berthing fees and enforcing regulations.

'Oh, for God's sake.' McLeish muttered.

Jones took her aside. 'How would you distinguish between one boat and another?'

'You're the sailor, Guv.'

'Humour me.'

'Size, shape, colour, class, flag of origin, name.'

'Boats have to be registered, right? FH. Falmouth Harbour.' She turned to Daniel, placed the note he'd written in front of him and pointed at the number 128.

'Is this a boat's registration number?'

He held her gaze for a split second and then turned back to the window.

McLeish was steaming down a cobbled road towards Port Dennis Marina when Jones caught up and grabbed her by the arm.

'What's the rush?'

'We've got our first major breakthrough, Guv.'

'And if we call out the boys in blue?'

'Show of force, Guv.'

145

'Exactly. The quayside will be crawling with them, roads closed and traffic diverted. Customs will launch inflatables and scour the estuary. Uniform will knock on doors and dog handlers will sniff around...then what?'

'We'd find the boat and the lab rats would take it apart...'

'No. We'd attract tourists, locals, press, and TV. And whoever owns the boat used last Sunday would be long gone.'

'God, you're good.' McLeish shook her head.

'Watch and learn.' Jones smiled. 'Softly, softly, catchy monkey.'

'Slowly, slowly...'

'Whatever. I'm right, aren't I?'

'Must be why I'm still a dumb ass Sergeant.'

'That and the mouth on you.' Jones looked across at the hundreds of boats in the estuary, the harbour and the marina. 'Fancy fish and chips and a stroll?'

An hour later, they stood in the Harbour Master's office on Custom House Quay, with registration details of every vessel that had been in and out of the harbour for the past six months including each name, number, country of origin and, most important of all, owner and skipper.

'Softly, softly, eh Guv?' McLeish said. 'All we need to do now is find the bastard.'

It took two hours.

The *Sky Lark* was an opened decked, wooden fishing boat, with a small cabin housing the wheel, compass, sonar, and satellite navigation. It looked fairly old, but appeared seaworthy and the hull, superstructure, and deck looked as if they might have been painted recently.

No one was aboard.

McLeish clambered over a safety railing and lifted the hatch to a small hold in the centre of the deck. It was empty, but reeked of fish.

On both sides of the bow, just above the waterline, the boat's number, FH 128, was stencilled in white alongside its name. Inside the cabin, they found a small brass plaque inscribed:

> If God had intended boats
> To be made of fibreglass
> He'd have grown fibreglass trees.

According to the Harbour Master, *Sky Lark*'s owner, Frank Walker, was local, born and bred, and used to run a boatyard just down from Islington Warf, at the end of a track off Love Lane. For more than thirty years he'd serviced small boats, but the recession had forced him to diversify - taking tourists around the bay and fishing trips. The British Sub-Aqua club used him to ferry divers to wrecks located within three miles of the coast. He had a reputation as an excellent skipper, with a safety record second to none. Taciturn, and reticent, he could be seen most nights in one or other of the harbour-side pubs.

It was tempting - with so much evidence tethered to a mooring – to cordon off the area, impound the *Sky Lark*, let forensics loose, and arrest and interrogate the owner, but they agreed to leave the boat where it was.

Jones called Superintendent Hinkson. 'I'd appreciate your take, Ma'am. I think we ought to tread carefully, set up surveillance, see what gives.'

'Murder unsettles a community like nothing else, but I agree, if we drive them underground we may never find Baldwin's killer. Unless you have already muddied the waters, Frank Walker may be unaware of our interest in his boat. Set up the surveillance. I'm not sure how long we'll be able to afford the extra manpower, but give it twenty-four hours and then pull him in.'

*

Jones knew Lizzie hadn't practiced for a couple of days and, as she got out of the Sebring and stood on the gravel driveway, she could tell she was lost in her music. She was playing a lullaby, light and gentle, and the baby grand sounded as beautiful as ever. It was the only thing Lizzie had purchased when they'd set up home and the outlay, Jones had always assumed, was Lizzie's way of underscoring her commitment. The cottage was home. The flat in London, no more than a bolthole.

Jones pushed open the cottage door, placed a couple of carrier bags on the floor and stood behind her. Lizzie inclined her neck slightly, exposing it, inviting her to massage, or kiss it.

When she'd finished playing, Lizzie got up, folded her arms around Jones's waist, nestled into her chest and whispered, 'Missed you.'

Jones pulled away and strolled over to the window.

'What's up?'

'Read me like a book, don't you?'

'Not that difficult.' Lizzie titled her head.

'I've got to go back up to London this afternoon. I'm sorry. One night, I promise. Plane leaves in an hour.'

'What's so urgent, for God's sake?'

'Geoffrey D'Ancey's death. Charlie phoned.'

'Did he?'

'The TV coverage has produced a good response. An elderly couple say they have important information and the Director of a surveillance company's come forward. A DVD was found on D'Ancey. I need to see it.'

'It's all so important, isn't it, your work?'

Lizzie returned to the keyboard.

Moonlight Sonata.

Hauntingly beautiful. An edge to it.

'Will you be ok?' Jones asked.

'I spend my life travelling the world. You'd think I'd be able to manage for a few days, wouldn't you?'

Terrance Leadbetter had been kept waiting in a room at Scotland Yard for nearly two hours and was really pissed off. If he was honest, he knew it wouldn't be long before the Old Bill came calling. He'd been waiting for the knock on the door since Thursday when the news of Geoffrey D'Ancey's death broke. He'd detailed one of his team to check the CCTV footage and he'd pinpointed the Judge shopping in Regent Street a few days before he died.

'This,' Charlie Hobson began, placing the DVD on the table, 'was found on Mr D'Ancey.'

'His wallet had been stolen,' Leadbetter said. 'We'd caught the incident on CCTV and managed to recover most of his property.'

'Most?'

'Money was missing.'

'Really? Someone looking to make a fast buck?'

'Search me,' Leadbetter shrugged. 'The DVD's copyright. My company should get the credit.'

'Very pubic spirited.' Hobson leaned back in his chair. 'What would you say, DI Jones?'

Jones had hardly had time to draw breath after being met at Gatwick, driven to Scotland Yard, and escorted to the interview room on the thirteenth floor. 'I'd remind Mr Leadbetter that this is a murder inquiry.' She looked up from her notes, hoping neither of them would notice how tired she looked. 'And if he withholds information, we'll take out an injunction, suspend company activities, confiscate computers and run a fine toothcomb over tax returns.' She didn't take her eyes off Leadbetter. 'That's what I would say, Commander, if Mr Leadbetter didn't play ball.'

'Look, I put a lot of time into producing that DVD. Least you can do is give us a bit of publicity.'

Charlie Hobson shifted impatiently on his chair.

'Let's show the Inspector what you're bartering with, shall we?'

Leadbetter opened his laptop and used Google Maps to explain the scope of his company's surveillance and monitoring facilities in London. He switched to HD CCTV coverage of a stretch of Regent Street.

'How long had you known Mr D'Ancey?'

'Several years by reputation, of course, but I only met him that once.'

Hobson produced an image taken from a surveillance camera at the reception in Westminster Hall. D'Ancey's hand was on Leadbetter's shoulder and both seemed to be enjoying one another's company. 'Very cordial.'

'He was impressed by the service we provide.'

'And you'd hope to be rewarded at a later date, no doubt.'

'One good deed.'

They watched CCTV images of Geoffrey D'Ancey walking along Regent's Street. He ducked into an outlet selling theatre tickets, then continued towards Marble Arch. The date and time, to the second, ticked away in the bottom right hand corner of the laptop's screen. One-fifteen. Lunchtime. The House of Commons in recess.

Leadbetter paused the image. 'This is the shop where his wallet was stolen.'

'You have coverage of the incident?'

''Fraid not. Gremlins. Lost the lot.'

Leadbetter smiled and Jones knew he was lying. She glanced at Charlie Hobson. His face was deadpan, but she assumed the lie had registered and he'd follow it up later.

Leadbetter reset the surveillance footage.

'I'll run it again. This time, concentrate on a woman twenty paces behind him.'

They watched.

150

'Run it again,' Jones said.

They watched the rerun.

'It's obvious, isn't it?' Leadbetter was warming to his task. 'The pavement's swarming with people, but she stands out, stopping when he does, following, stopping, following. She's stalking him, for sure.'

She was tall and elegant, and wore large, fashionable sunglasses.

'We can zoom in and enhance the image and then, by using the dimensions of the shop door, we can calculate her height.' Leadbetter paused, took four photographs from a buff folder and slid them across the table. 'The image is good, but her face is obscured by sunglasses. Your police artists might be able to play around with it.'

'So, she's about…?'

'Five ten, give or take. We've also enhanced the label on her handbag.' He passed another image across the table. 'Prada. Exclusive.'

'Knock-off?'

'Possibly. Looks like crocodile skin. If it's kosher, it would've cost a bomb.'

Hobson looked across at Jones, wondering if she had any further questions?

Jones leaned forward. 'How many people have seen the DVD?'

'My technicians downloaded the relevant section of the footage, but they have no idea why I wanted it.'

'Keep it that way.'

'Could be important then?'

'Let me put it this way. You fix the gremlins that mysteriously spirited away the footage inside the shop and let us have it by this evening. You keep everything out of the media and we'll try to forget that you lied to us. You understand?'

*

151

Rita and Henry Harrison were driven from their local police station in Wimbledon. They arrived at Scotland Yard just after midday and were informed that the two officers due to interview them weren't available. They were taken to the canteen for lunch and after lunch they were given a tour of the Black Museum.

Rita stood in front of a gruesome exhibit. 'Crime's a dreadful thing, isn't it?'

'Warped minds, the lot of them.'

After the museum they were shown into an interview room. Several cups of tea (and two trips to the loo) later, Charlie Hobson and Lydia Jones joined them.

Part way through the interview a uniformed officer handed Jones a note. The interview was suspended and the Harrisons were offered more tea. The break stretched to half-an-hour and Hobson and Jones stood in the corridor, trying to make sense of what the Harrisons had told them.

'I want to listen to what we've got so far, before we go back,' Hobson said. 'This could be the breakthrough we've been looking for.' He arranged for the recording to be replayed. They skipped the Harrison's recall of events leading up to their day at the ITV studio, and concentrated on the reason why they'd come forward...

Rita: *The show had just started and the young lady - you know, the one who'd taken over from that nice Mr Baldwin. He was found on that beach.*
Henry: *Don't waffle. Get on with it.*
Rita: *I will if you'd shut up for a minute. Sorry, but it was such a shock seeing her again. Well, actually, we didn't recognise her at first, not definitely, not 'til we watched the recording when we got home.*
Hobson: *Her?*
Rita: *The one who interviewed the guests.*
Henry: *She had a different name when we knew her.*

152

Rita: *Calling herself Kate Madison now.*

Hobson: *What was her name?*

Rita: *Jenny.*

Henry: *Jennifer.*

Rita: *Yes. Jennifer. Jennifer West. We'd fostered for twenty years, you see. Jenny came to stay with us.*

Jones: *So, Social Services will have a record of her?*

Rita: *I suppose so. You can check with them. We had to fill in lots of forms. They're usually very thorough, aren't they?*

Henry: *We read the paper this morning.*

Rita: *We didn't have time yesterday. We were too tired when we got home.*

Henry: *There was an article about that MP who'd been murdered in London. Pushed off a balcony, wasn't he?*

Jones: *The investigation is on going.*

Henry: *Jennifer was very violent.*

Rita: *She attacked our son, Jonathan, with a carving knife. Put him in hospital.*

Jones: *Why?*

Henry: *Jon was a couple of years older. She was very pretty. He had a bit of a crush on her. He told us he'd only wanted a kiss.*

Hobson: *When was this?*

Rita: *She'd been with us for ten weeks, I suppose. She'd just had her fifteenth birthday. She'd had a rough time of it. Run away from home.*

Henry: *Same night her father was killed.*

Hobson: *How did he die?*

Rita: *Don't know. They didn't tell us, but she'd been living rough when The Social picked her up and we took her in.*

Jones: *What happened after she attacked your son?*

Henry: *They put her where she belonged.*

Rita: *A residential home for young offenders. Social Services will know.*

Hobson: *Where's your son now?*

Rita: *Dead.*

Jones: *She killed him?*

Rita: *No. After he came out of hospital he went to agricultural college. But word got round, you know, about what she'd accused him of.*

Henry: *Rape.*

Rita: *He left college after a term and joined the Army.*

Henry: *Afghanistan. His helicopter went down.*

Rita: *He was reported missing.*

Jones: *Missing?*

Henry: *Ten years ago.*

Hobson: *And you haven't heard anything since?*

Henry: *No. But we won't give up hope. Not until we know for sure.*

They stopped the tape, joined the Harrisons back in the interview room and went over what they'd already told them.

Then Charlie Hobson asked them to continue.

'We've come to see you because...' Henry seemed indecisive. 'Well, we just thought...'

'We thought you ought to know she's lying again.'

Hobson looked at Rita. 'Again?'

'She was always lying. She stole money from my purse. Denied it. Lied about where she'd been, who she was seeing.'

'And your son?' Jones asked.

'He didn't try to rape her,' Henry said. 'That was a lie. She attacked him, said she was trying to defend herself.'

'I'm sorry,' Charlie Hobson said, 'but you haven't told us why you've come to see us today.'

154

'Mr Baldwin and Mr D'Ancey, right?' Henry said. 'They were murdered?

'And why do you think she had anything to do with their murder?' Jones asked.

'It's obvious, isn't it? She worked with Mr Baldwin, and that MP was meant to be on the show. I bet if you asked her if she'd killed them, she'd lie, say she had nothing to do with it.'

'Most likely,' Jones wanted to smile, but managed to keep a straight face. Instead, she said, 'There's nothing to suggest she killed anyone.'

'It's just that we know what she's capable of.'

They arranged for an unmarked car to take Rita and Henry home and then sat across the desk from each other until Charlie Hobson rubbed the back of his neck, got up and paced about. 'Waste of time?' he said.

'We've got a name.'

'But it's one hell of a leap from attacking the son, to murdering a senior politician and a TV star.'

Jones showed him the note she'd been handed during the interview. 'Taxi driver dropped off an attractive woman with long dark hair at Belgravia Square.'

'Affluent part of town.'

'Where D'Ancey's wife has an apartment.'

She glanced at the note again. 'There's a list of other journeys by taxi – a reception in Westminster Hall, House of Commons, Regent Street, several from his Club to China Town. The cab company's records show a young Asian woman accompanied him on the night *before* he was murdered. He'd asked the driver to drop her two blocks away from his club.'

'Why?'

155

'Club rules. No over-night guests. But D'Ancey had an arrangement with one of the porters. Tommy Murphy. A man of many talents but no backbone. Sang like a lark once we understood each other.'

'Doesn't rule out Kate Madison.'

'Because she's blonde?' She smiled. 'I wouldn't rule anyone out at this stage.'

The phone rang just as Jones pushed open the door to Lizzie's flat. She hurried into the lounge and picked up the receiver.

'You OK?' Lizzie asked. 'You sound out of breath.'

'I'm fine. You?'

'Keeping your side of the bed warm.'

'I'll be back tomorrow. Make it up to you.'

'So you said. How's Charlie?'

'Lizzie, don't.'

'Cosy dinner for two this evening?'

'If you must know, I'm meeting someone from Social Services in about half-an-hour, and then I'm going to see aunty.'

'Sorry.'

Neither said anything for a while.

'Been busy?' Jones said.

'Exercising the horses.'

'What?'

'Kate called...'

'Stewart's Kate?'

'We had a long chat. She said she'd enjoyed meeting you and invited us to dinner, again. You're in London so it was easy to turn her down, but I won't be able to fob her off for long.'

'A bit inconsiderate, isn't it? Richard Lander died in a riding accident.'

'The horses need exercising.'

'They've got an army of stable lads to do that.'

'I know, but it was fun, 'til I fell off.'

'You did what?'

'Horse reared, but I'm fine, really.'

'God.' Jones bit her tongue. 'So, what are you up to this afternoon?'

'Tea on the lawn and then, if we can get through the media circus, we're going to take her new car for a spin along the coast.'

'New car?'

'Mercedes SL.'

'Circus?'

'BBC, ITV, SKY...Seems everyone wants a piece of her after Friday's show.'

Her mobile clamoured and Kate Madison pulled off the road and stopped the Mercedes in front of a gate barring entrance to a field.

'Sis? It's me,' he said. 'Where are you?'

'What's wrong?'

'We've got a problem. The filth were sniffing about the boat this afternoon, went on deck, lifted the hatch, and looked inside the cabin.'

'Uniform?'

'No.'

'Could have been tourists.'

'Had CID written all over them. They spent a lot of time in the Harbour Master's office, then went and had another look at the boat.'

'Does Frank Walker know?'

'Don't think so. But he's a liability. If he's picked up, he'll drop us both in it.'

'We'll have to make sure he doesn't get the chance.'

'You want me to sort it?'

Madison hesitated. 'Just be careful. OK?'

'Don't worry.'

'You said we should have a contingency if...'

'The balloon goes up?'

'Yes.'

'Not like you to worry, sis.'

'Never had this much to lose.'

'If the filth come calling, let me know immediately.'

Tim Rivers peered at Jones over his reading glasses and leafed through a file on his desk in a drab Social Services office a few streets away from the Elephant and Castle tube station.

'Jennifer West,' Jones said. 'Tell me everything you know about her, no matter how trivial, anything that might help us understand why Geoffrey D'Ancey died.'

Rivers scanned the file, straightened his tie, coughed and raked a slender hand through his hair.

'Jennifer came to our attention twice. The first time, she was reported missing after her father was killed. He fell from the balcony outside their flat in Lewisham.' He read the report. 'Tests showed he'd been drinking, a neighbour saw him clamber onto the safety rail, but didn't see him fall. Jenny was picked up a few months later. She was with her stepbrother when he was arrested after an affray outside a pub.'

'There'll be a record of the court hearing?'

'The charges were dropped. Seemed witnesses had a change of heart.'

'Acute amnesia. Happens all the time.' Jones sighed. 'And the stepbrother's name?'

He checked the notes. 'Peter Brooks.'

'And what happened to him?'

'No idea, but your lot might know something.'

'I'll check our records,' she said. 'So, what happened to Jennifer?'

'She was fifteen, nearly sixteen. She was taken into care and placed with foster parents.' Rivers checked the file. 'Henry and Rita Harrison.'

'I've had the pleasure.'

'Very successful over the years.'

'Until Jennifer West came along.'

'Yes. Soon after her sixteenth birthday, she attacked their son and accused him of trying to rape her. There's a copy of the medical report.' Again, Rivers checked his facts before continuing. 'She stabbed him in the chest. He was lucky. The breast bone deflected the blow and major organs were spared any real damage.'

'Was the accusation investigated?'

'Yes, but nothing was substantiated. It was her word against his, I suppose.' Rivers closed the file, removed his glasses and rubbed the bridge of his nose. 'But, as I remember it, the damage had been done. Mud sticks and the press fuelled the speculation. He was a young man condemned by charges he couldn't defend.'

'Couldn't?'

'No-one would listen. Rita and Henry fostered for a few more years, but Jonathan left home after he was discharged from hospital. After that, who knows?'

'He joined the Army.' Jones paused. 'What happened to Jennifer after the attack?'

'Residential centre. She stayed for a few months, then disappeared.'

'Disappeared?'

'Walked out, back on the streets, we presumed.'

159

'And no-one tried to locate her?'

Rivers looked defensive, as if he was uncomfortable defending another's incompetence.

'Police alerted advice centres, soup kitchens, night shelters...'

'Nothing?

'Nothing.'

'And when did she resurface?'

'About a year later, must have been about seventeen. Arrested for soliciting.' Rivers checked the file. 'She was taken in by Social Services and sent to another residential home, but a few months later...'

'She disappeared?'

'Yes.'

'But, you'll have a photograph?'

'Passport size. It's part of her record.' Rivers handed a file to Jones. 'I've made a copy for you.'

She looked defiant, but dark rings underscored her brilliant blue eyes. She looked like she'd been sleeping rough. Her skin was pale and her mouth was locked in a scowl that exposed stained teeth. Her hair was long, matted, and dirty blonde.

'You worked on the case, back then?'

'Ten years ago? Yes. I was a junior, of course. Colin Povey was head-of-section. Sort of area manager, who'd travel to different centres, checking, advising, and assisting.'

'Colin Povey?'

'Her case officer.' He looked at Jones. 'You know what happened to him?'

'I'd just joined the Met's Homicide Command, a junior, just like you. I was part of the MIT investigating his death.'

'Shocking, it was.'

'Murder usually is.'

'It was murder then?'

'The original investigation was inconclusive but if we reopened it, advances in forensic science might enable us to identify DNA and prints found in the flat.'

'I thought it was odd at the time, you know, a senior social worker making house calls. Normally, care of the elderly, infirm, or anyone needing daily visits is covered by juniors or is outsourced.'

'And, he'd circumvented regulations to accommodate a female friend?'

'Neighbours reported seeing a young girl, teenager, late teens – could have been Jenny - living in the flat for several months. After his death, the tabloids were full of it. I remember, his wife was devastated.'

'Not surprised.'

Rivers shuffled paper around the desk and avoided making eye contact.

'Her photograph was circulated to neighbours,' Jones said. 'Finding her was a priority, but everyone we spoke to said she was much prettier than the photograph.'

'Maybe Colin helped her, gave her money?'

'In return for what, I wonder?'

'Your guess is as good as mine but, if the neighbours were right, she'd obviously recovered her health.'

'But you're sure it was her?' Jones asked.

'Living in the flat? Yes.'

'And Colin Povey fell?'

'From a balcony on the top floor.'

'And, as they scraped him off the tarmac, Jenny West disappeared?'

'Yes.' Rivers stood up and collected a folder from the top of a filing cabinet. 'I came across these. I hadn't seen them before. They're pretty damning, if they're Colin's.'

Jones glanced at the images. 'And you're sure these came from Colin Povey's computer?'

'Yes. At least there's a note to that effect.'

161

She opened her document case and rifled through the file she'd complied on Jenny West. 'Then why weren't they handed over to the investigating officers?'

'No idea.' He smiled weakly. 'Sorry.'

'Yes, of course, you were just a junior.'

'That's uncalled for.'

She ignored his protest.

'Have you seen this before?' She held up a copy of the photograph found in the room at D'Ancey's Club.

'No. No, I don't think so.' He studied it and then matched it against those in Jennifer West's file.

'Good God.'

'Rape. D'Ancey's face in full flush.'

'Can't be sure it's her, but there's no mistaking him.'

Jones paced around the room as anticipation coursed through her. 'Did you catch *Ask the Minister* last night?'

'No.'

'Get your coat. There's something I want you to see.'

After they'd watched the recording of Friday's show, Jones arranged for a car to drop Tim Rivers home and she got back to the flat in time to catch the early evening news.

She was in the shower, when the phone rang.

It was George Tregunna. 'Sorry to disturb you, Guv.'

'What is it, George?'

'Angus called about Friday. You do remember Friday evening, Guv? After the quiz?'

'How did I get home?'

'Angus put you in a taxi.'

'God.'

'Lizzie was waiting on the door step.'

162

'That explains…' Jones hesitated as she recalled the frosty atmosphere over breakfast the following morning: a dull, painful, vague memory. 'And you?'

'Me?'

'You and the wife?'

'Much the same. Digs are the pits.'

'I can imagine.' She hesitated, torn between lending an ear and getting on. 'So, what did Angus have to say?'

'He invited a few old timers into the snug last night. A couple of pints loosened tongues and he couldn't shut them up.'

'And?'

'There are rumour factories all along the coast. Places like Nanjizal and Gwennap Head. Stories of pirates and wreckers and of untold wealth on the seabed…'

'Get to the point, George.'

'It's just that you can understand how easy it would be for someone to be lured into diving a wreck. Maybe that's what Baldwin's doubloon was? A fly to catch the sprat.'

'The sprat to catch the mackerel.'

'Whatever. Anyway, one of the old timers followed Angus back to the bar and had a quiet word. He reckons about two years ago a wreck was found about a mile off shore. Said he overheard a conversation in a pub by the quayside, but didn't get a good look at the men. He told Angus about an antique shop. Has pieces in the window, but nothing that would attract the Old Bill.'

'And the location of this shop?'

'Guv?'

'Call Brenda.'

'But it's gone seven.'

'And you've got better things to do? Afterwards, she'll take you back to *The Nest*. Pie, chips, and a pint. Do you the world of good. Oh, and George, do me a favour…'

'Guv?'

'Ask Uniform to detail a patrol past our cottage. Keep an eye on Lizzie. On the QT.'

'Why's that then, Guv? She at risk?'

'Just do it George. OK?'

'You know,' Charlie Hobson said, 'if you stay away too long, you'll lose your edge.'

They'd driven out of London and through localised flooding caused by a thunderstorm, and were sitting in Hobson's local in Cheam, washing away the taste of the pathologist's report with a pint of Young's Special.

The autopsy had confirmed that D'Ancey's death had been instantaneous. Spikes on the top of the railings had smashed his spine, severed his neck, punctured both lungs, and torn through his kidneys.

A young couple had found him soon after nine when they'd slipped into the garden to escape the drudgery of an ancient relative's birthday bash.

Jones raised her glass. She knew it would be easy to be seduced. Not by Charlie Hobson. She'd moved on a long time ago. But, she had to admit that the resources at the Met's disposal and the quality and intensity of their training were tempting. But home was in Cornwall and when Lizzie wasn't touring there was nowhere else in the world they'd rather be. Their pleasures were simple. A walk along the cliff. Lunch in a pub. Sailing. Sitting in the shade of one the large oaks in the garden and reading the Sunday papers.

She loved to cook for Lizzie.

For Lizzie.

Lizzie.

Lizzie and Kate Madison.

She took out her phone.

'Like I was saying,' Hobson said, 'The longer you leave it…'

'It's not going to happen, Charlie.'

She got up.

'Sorry. Must just make a call.' She walked outside to the beer garden and watched a couple of kids chasing each other, their parents enjoying a few moments respite.

Lizzie answered.

'Where are you?' Jones asked.

'At home.'

'Alone?'

'It's nine o'clock. Of course I'm alone.'

'And you're ok?'

'Lydia? What is it?'

'Nothing. Sorry. I'm tired. I was hoping to get home tonight, but the airport's closed. A storm.'

'Storm?'

'Electrical. Too dangerous to take off. Shut down all flights.' She was unsure how Lizzie would react when she added…'Charlie invited me for a beer.'

'You said you'd be with your aunt.'

'I sat by her bedside for an hour. She's worse. I spoke to her doctor. Seems she may have had another stroke. They're running tests.'

'Hope she pulls through.'

'Thanks.'

'So, how's Charlie?'

'God, why do I feel so guilty?'

'It's about trust, isn't it?' Lizzie said. 'I have to trust you. Believe what you say. What else can I do?'

'Works both ways.'

'Yes, I know.'

Neither said anything for what seemed an age and then Lizzie said, 'Thanks. For telling me about Charlie

'Don't want any secrets. Love you too much.'

165

'Glad to hear it.'

'So, you'll be OK 'til tomorrow?'

'I'm a big girl, Lydia.'

'I could drive back.'

'And get here in the small hours? No thanks. I need my beauty sleep.'

'It's just that…'

'What? What can't wait until tomorrow?'

'I miss you, I suppose.'

'Yes, miss you. Wrap it up and get back as soon as you can. What time does your flight get in?'

'About five-thirty.'

'I'll pick you up.'

'OK.'

'Lydia? Are you sure you're alright?'

'Yes, of course,' she said. 'I'll see you tomorrow. Just take care, ok?'

7

Brenda McLeish opened the morning's briefing.

'OK. Let's have some hush. I know it's Sunday, but think of all those exotic holidays you'll be able to book with the overtime.' She waited for the murmuring to die down. 'Quick update...The DI's back this afternoon. Wants us to re-interview Lady Emily and her daughter. We've identified a boat...'

She pinned a photograph of the *Sky Lark* on one of the whiteboards.

'It's been under surveillance. The owner, one Frank Walker, took a group of divers out yesterday evening, otherwise all's quiet.'

'Won't that compromise forensics?' Asked one of the other detectives. 'Taking divers out?'

'The boat's already had a lick of paint. My guess is, that the lab rats won't find much when it's impounded.'

'Hope surveillance delivers before the money runs out,' Tregunna muttered.

'Too late. It's been withdrawn.'

'But, you said...'

'*Been* under surveillance...past tense.'

'But, we were given twenty-four hours?'

'The manpower was needed elsewhere,' she said, and shrugged. 'You want to tell everyone about our treasure hunt?'

George stayed where he was, hair needed combing, and his jacket was making a bad job of hiding stains on his shirt. 'You'll remember a gold doubloon was found on Chris Baldwin?' He tapped a photograph of the coin. 'We've interviewed the owner of *The Treasure Trove*, a shop on the front. He's bought and sold stuff over the years - coins, pottery, silver rings. He told us he wasn't one to ask too many questions, but he did keep a record of transactions. And guess what? The *Sky Lark's* Frank Walker bought a few gold doubloons a couple of months back.'

'Do we know why?' one of their team asked.

'Sprats and mackerels. Time will tell,' Tregunna said.

'OK...' McLeish waited until she had everyone's attention. 'Today's assignments...' She spent the next ten minutes allocating tasks to officers and support staff, and sent them on their way before cornering Tregunna.

'As sartorially elegant as always, George?' She shook her head, as if close to despair. 'I don't want to keep the aristocracy waiting, but we'll stop off at your digs, find a clean shirt. And, after we've interviewed Milady and her darling daughter, we'll invite Frank Walker for a chat.'

They arrived at Bissom Manor and were shown into the drawing room and offered tea. They were told that there'd be a delay before Lady Emily and Alexandra joined them...they were to make themselves comfortable and use the bell cord if they required anything.

Tregunna had his notepad but couldn't find a pencil.

'I've decided not to unpack my boxes,' he said, 'what with the imminent move to *The Nest*. Problem is, I can't find the simplest things.'

McLeish slipped a pen from a pocket.

'Thanks, Sarge.'

'Not long now.'

'Anything will be better than sharing a bathroom with strangers.' He looked at McLeish and sadness coursed through his eyes. 'Thanks,' he said.

'Yeah.' She smiled. 'Soft as shit, me.'

Lady Emily came in and insisted on being present '...if you're going to interrogate my daughter.'

'As you wish.' McLeish knew she had the option of taking them into custody, placing them in separate cells and interrogating them deep into the night, but couldn't be bothered with the hassle of an enquiry if Lady Emily decided to complain. A light touch, McLeish decided, was the order of the day.

She looked at the two women and wondered how Her Ladyship - beautiful and elegant, with pale unblemished skin - felt every time she looked at her daughter who, apart from being fashionably slim, was the image of her father.

'Let's get the easy questions out of the way first, shall we?' McLeish said, 'It'll give the Constable a chance to warm up his pencil.' She looked at Alexandra. 'Name, date of birth?'

'Sergeant...' Lady Emily took Alexandra's hand. 'You haven't told us why you are here.'

'All murder investigations start with a process of elimination. We whittle away at our list of suspects until we're left with one.'

'And we're both on your list of suspects?'

'Yes, until you can account for your whereabouts on the evening Mr D'Ancey died.'

'And you still think I killed my husband?'

'It matters not a jot what I think. It's simple, really. You'll need to provide an alibi. Both of you. One that's rock solid.'

Lady Emily patted Alexandra's arm, stood up and rang the bell cord. 'I see you're on a mission, Sergeant. And I respect that, but don't get ahead of yourself. This is a difficult time for us, and whilst I'm not going to pretend that my husband's death is a tragedy, he was, nonetheless, my husband.'

A maid appeared at the door.

169

'I need something a little stronger than tea. Take that away and fetch a bottle of brandy – there's a Camus 128 in the cellar. Time we opened it.'

'Lady Emily,' McLeish said. 'Forgive me. I'm confused. You said that your husband's death is not a tragedy. What was it then? Something you expected, welcomed?'

'Planned?' Lady Emily shook her head. 'I'd grown tired of him and had every intention of cutting the financial umbilical. But I didn't kill him.'

McLeish glanced at them - hands interlocked, white knuckled, betraying an anxiety she'd exploit. She looked at Alexandra. 'And what's your reason for getting up in the morning?' She put on her friendly smile. 'A job, for instance?'

'I organise mother's schedule, make appointments, organise transport, and manage the household, hiring and firing where necessary.'

'She's also my companion and confidante.' Lady Emily lifted her head and McLeish recognised the first hint of defiance. 'There are so few people one can trust.'

The maid knocked, entered, and placed a silver tray, four cut glasses and a bottle of brandy on a large coffee table. Alexandra opened the bottle, poured a generous slug for her mother and helped herself before offering up the bottle. They both declined, McLeish anxious to press on.

'So, where were you on the night Mr D'Ancey was murdered?'

'Last Thursday?' Alexandra looked at her mother, who nodded. 'I flew up to London on Monday. We'd attended Richard Lander's funeral in the morning and I caught the three o'clock from Newquay.'

'And where did you stay? The flat in Belgravia?'

'No. My husband stayed there when he was in town. I own another apartment, in Broad Court. It's much more convenient - a short walk to Piccadilly, Regent's Street, and the West End.'

'So, when you went to identify your husband's body, why did you stay at The Savoy?'

'Simple really. I didn't want staff with us and, if we'd stayed at the apartment, we would have had to cater for ourselves. In the circumstances, I preferred to let The Savoy look after us.' She smiled. 'Now, if that is all?'

McLeish ignored her, and looked at her daughter.

'You went to London on Monday?'

'Yes.'

'Why?'

'Why what?'

McLeish noted Alexandra's attitude had shifted, her voice trimmed with suspicion. 'Why did you fly up to London on Monday?'

'I had purchased some jewellery,' Lady Emily said. 'Alexandra went to collect it for me.'

McLeish didn't like her answers being hijacked and turned to the daughter. 'Alexandra. You understand the seriousness of the situation?

'Sergeant...'

'If you'd prefer,' she glowered at Lady Emily, 'we can continue down at the station.' McLeish felt blotches crawling up her neck - something that happened quite often when someone was giving her the run around. 'A cab driver has given us a description of a young woman who had dinner with Mr D'Ancey at a restaurant in China Town. The duty porter at his Club has confirmed that a young woman with long dark hair gained access to the Club via the fire escape and spent time in his room.' She watched Alexandra's scowl falter. 'So, I have to ask myself...was that you, Alexandra? A last supper, or a farewell drink in his room, before you lured him on to the balcony and pushed him overboard?'

'Sergeant, this is intolerable,' Lady Emily stood up.

171

McLeish wished she'd followed her gut instinct and hauled them down to Falmouth nick.

'Were you with your father on the night he died?'

'No.'

'But you were in London?'

'My brother works backstage at the Harold Pinter Theatre. They're presenting a season of Pinter plays. *Death and The Maiden* was shown on the night I was there. The show started at about seven-thirty and ended just after ten. I had a drink with him afterwards and then caught the last train back here.'

'Did you go to the theatre with anyone?'

'A thousand, give or take. A packed house.'

'Anyone specific, a friend who can vouch for you?'

'My brother and the rest of the cast.'

McLeish sighed. 'I'll need your brother's address in London and the train's booking reference.'

Alexandra's eyes shone, defiantly.

'I resent any suggestion that I would lie and implicate my brother.'

'There are those who'd happily sell their granny,' Tregunna muttered.

McLeish glared at him before trying to wrest the initiative and press on with her questions. 'So, you were in London on the night your father was murdered?'

'Yes. I've already said.'

'And, you had dinner with him on the evening he was murdered?'

'No. The evening before.'

'The evening before?'

'Yes.'

'And you went back to his Club?'

Alexandra glanced at Lady Emily, who said, 'You may as well tell them the truth.'

'Would be nice.' McLeish sat forward and Tregunna checked that his pencil was still sharp.

'Let's start by getting the chronology straight, shall we?' Alexandra said, as she sat on the edge of the sofa. 'I saw my father on the night *before* he was murdered. I had dinner with him. Well, it was tea, really. He said he was busy later.'

'Tea, and then back to his Club?'

'Yes.'

'Via the fire escape?'

'God, no. I'm his daughter, not some tart the papers mentioned.' She took a short time to compose herself. 'I've admitted I was at the Club. What more do you want?'

McLeish pursed her lips, her patience wearing thin.

'And after you left the Club, where did you go?'

'Back to the flat in Broad Court.'

'Can anyone vouch for you?'

'No, not really.'

'Sergeant?' Lady Emily sipped her brandy and then rolled the glass slowly between her hands. 'I've suffered enough in the media during the past week. Geoffrey's death was a shock, but we'd drifted apart long ago. Our marriage was a sham masked by a dignified public persona. Geoffrey needed a high profile marriage to accelerate his career and a titled lady was about as good as it gets. I was young when we married, too young. He was attractive and charming and I fell hopelessly in love. Looking back, I was naïve, innocent and probably quite stupid. I'd led a sheltered life and snatched at the chance to escape, much to my parents consternation.'

She smiled at Alexandra and gave her hand another squeeze. 'The media have been particularly vitriolic in their attack on my husband…that ghastly photograph of him raping that young woman and his involvement in child abuse.'

'Allegedly,' McLeish said, wondering where this was going. 'Nothing proven.'

173

'I was not surprised he'd entertained young women. Not that we had an open marriage, but I knew of his infidelity.'

McLeish looked at George Tregunna.

He raised his eyebrows and put down his pad. 'I'm confused,' he said. 'Why did you travel to London to see your father? Why did you have tea with him? Why did you go back to his Club and spend...' He checked his notes. '...at least an hour in his room?'

Alexandra turned to her mother.

'Go ahead, tell them everything.'

'You're sure?'

'Yes.'

'You'll understand, both of you,' Alexandra said, her voice strong, 'that your questions strike at the very heart of our private life and what you're about to hear must not be made public?' She waited for assurances that were not forthcoming. She looked at her mother who raised her hands and shrugged. 'We had afternoon tea and took a taxi to his Club where I gave him a package containing fifty thousand pounds in cash.'

'Cash?' Tregunna said.

'His creditors don't take cheques.' Alexandra turned to McLeish. 'That is why I went to London. No doubt, you'll want to check with Coutts in Canary Wharf. It's a sizable sum, but the bank was happy to oblige. It's not the first time I've withdrawn such a large amount of cash but, in the circumstances, it's likely to be the last.'

She paused, as if considering the implications of what she'd said. She breathed deeply. 'My father patronised an exclusive casino in Soho at least once a week. He'd lost heavily - squandering his own money - and when the losses became unmanageable, he turned to his wife to bail him out. Mother had underwritten his debts on several occasions.'

174

'I'd had enough,' Lady Emily said. 'He'd run up a debt of fifty thousand pounds, told me he'd received death threats and if the money wasn't paid they'd come after us.'

'Has anyone threatened you?'

'No.' She was blunt. 'I'd run out of pity. I'd run out of sympathy and I'd run out of patience. Alexandra went to London to tell my husband two things...the fifty thousand was the last time I'd cover his debts...and to inform him that I'd started divorce proceedings.'

McLeish and Tregunna stopped for coffee and were trying to make up time and avoid congestion when they took a short cut along a minor road and ended up behind a tractor.

On a day like this, they agreed, it was easy to see why so many visitors - Emmets as locals called them - made Cornwall their destination-of-choice. Whether it was the dappled sunlight, hedgerows carpeted by mid-summer blooms, the boats bobbing gently on calm sea, the soft, golden sands, or the romance of the deserted tin mines and jagged cliffs...Cornwall had it in spades.

Tregunna glared at clouds gathering ahead.

'Cornwall. The Graveyard of Ambition...'

He fell silent.

McLeish was not to know that he was thinking of the time he'd told Maureen, his childhood sweetheart, that he wanted to join the police. She'd been so excited, so supportive, so ambitious for him, and for them both. George would apply for promotion, Maureen had declared, and they'd move to London. But Tregunna could never imagine being away from the town where he'd been born and brought up. Besides, he was happy being a Constable. Sadly, ten years into their marriage, it became apparent Maureen wasn't happy being married to one.

'Buried alive.' He shook his head.

'You OK George?'

'Why does everyone keep asking, for God's sake?'

'It's what friends are for, you miserable bugger. Why don't you make yourself useful and phone the guv'nor, tell her about our chat with her Ladyship.'

After what seemed an eternity, the tractor turned off the road and they headed for College Reservoir and picked up the A39. As they skirted Falmouth, they drove through Penryn and took a right down Love Lane. The road petered out and an unmade track led down to Frank Walker's disused boatyard.

A second surveillance team had been deployed and they'd watched the boatyard for twelve hours before being withdrawn. Their tyre tracks were still visible in a coating of overnight rain.

Weeds clambered up the grey block building. Part of the corrugated roof was missing and several windows had been vandalised. The main door was flapping on broken hinges in a wind that had picked up during the drive from the pub.

Above the door, a large sign was hanging from a clutch of rusting nails...

WALKER'S BOATYARD.
REPAIRS AND MAINTENANCE.

They parked at the top of the track and made their way down to the door. Tregunna eased it open and called out. No reply. Inside, the workshop was in darkness. McLeish called out again. No reply.

A single window, part gaping, part boarded, cast a hesitant light through a cluster of cobwebs. A single bench was littered engine parts as though cast aside by a disillusioned engineer who'd toiled to grasp modern economics and had failed.

Dust caked everything.

A door led to the left and McLeish stepped through the debris, pushed it open and called out once more. Silence. The door opened into a large trench. It was, McLeish presumed, a dock into which boats would have been floated, and attached to thick hemp ropes before being hoisted out of the water by the large pulleys she could see bolted to the ceiling. After repairs and a re-fit, they'd be re-floated as good as new.

'Anything?' Tregunna said, examining debris around the workbench.

'No.'

McLeish closed the door to the dock and walked over to another door at the far end of a narrow corridor at the back of the workshop. She turned the handle and pushed. It wedged open against something heavy jammed against it, on the other side. She glanced at a large, dark stain discolouring the wooden floor.

'George, give us a hand, George.'

They prised open the door and stumbled across the body of a man, face down; a knife plunged deep between his shoulder blades.

The floor was awash with blood that had seeped into the floorboard's crevasses and pooled into a crimson lake, speckled by wood-shavings.

The man's face was frozen, his eyes wide, startled, teeth clenched, lips snarling at the betrayal. Blood was mingling with stomach bile that trickled from one corner of his mouth and its sickly stench overpowered any sign of life. Bloodstains on the walls and windows suggested the attack was brutal, too swift to counter, yet sustained enough for him to have suffered. His hands had clawed at the floor and had gouged marks across the grain.

He'd been left to die and had slumped against the door in a final effort to summon help. Tregunna knew it was hopeless, but wanted to be sure. He bent over and placed his cheek close to the man's mouth.

He wasn't breathing.

'Frank Walker, I presume?' Tregunna said.

'Get the lab rats out of their cage.'

'D'you get the feeling they're one step ahead of us?'

'Whatever, they're ruthless enough to take out any weak links. Come on, I need some air.'

They waited for the SOCO to arrive.

Tregunna stood outside by the main door and tried, unsuccessfully, to contact DI Jones.

McLeish strolled down to the jetty, grabbed a few stones and threw them into the water. At that point, she estimated, the river was about a hundred and fifty meters wide. High tide would mask channels deep enough for quite large boats to battle upstream to the ancient port of Penryn. It was high tide and the river was in full flow, ripping past a crumbling jetty, the current strong enough to force yachts to tack and jibe.

In the middle, she noticed a small dinghy inching its way upstream. Its outboard motor was struggling against the tide and a young boy was sitting at the tiller with the hood of his waterproof flapping about his face. He looked miserable and McLeish began to wonder why anyone would be deluded enough to think that messing about in boats was fun, even in the height of summer.

Tregunna joined her. 'Tempted?'

'No. Give me terra firma, anytime.'

McLeish looked towards the marina where yachts, seemingly impatient for wealthy owners to take them for a spin, were moored alongside pontoons that stretched out into water.

Further down the riverbank, half a dozen fishermen were sitting on a wall and seemed to be doing anything - reading, smoking, chatting, or snoozing - rather than keeping an eye on their floats.

'Now, that's what I call a leisure activity,' Tregunna said.

'Fishing?' McLeish muttered, as a SOCO van turned off the road and tumbled down towards the boathouse. 'Its no better than fox hunting or badger baiting in my book.'

By the time Sebastian Coleman joined them, the area had been sealed off. The SOCO's examination was well under way whilst uniformed police held rubberneckers at bay and a local TV crew were preparing to broadcast a live, on-the-spot report.

Coleman was kneeling over the body as McLeish picked her way through the debris towards him.

'You're keeping me busy.'

She noted the irritation in his voice.

'Fortunately, I was in the area - lunch with friends.'

She didn't take the bait.

'At least this is fairly straightforward, Sergeant. Heart failure and loss of blood caused by a single stab wound that appears to have severed the spine and pierced the heart. You will have noted the diving knife buried up to the hilt.' Coleman walked over to the diving equipment stowed neatly on a bench. The outline of a knife was imprinted in a thin layer of dust. 'I think you'll find this is where the knife was housed and this...' He held up a lifejacket. '...is similar to the one that malfunctioned so disastrously during Chris Baldwin's ascent. Ergo...it's likely Frank Walker supplied the full kit. It's no wonder you had no joy at normal dive outlets.'

'Time of death?'

'Core temperature remains relatively static for the first two hours after death, dropping zero point six of a degree each subsequent hour. Current body temperature is twenty-seven degrees, so he's been dead for about eighteen hours.'

'Seven-thirty yesterday evening?'

'More or less.'

'The PM?'

'Will have to wait. It's Sunday. Besides, I have a back-log of cases to attend to.'

'Not all of them part of a murder enquiry.'

He smiled wearily. 'I'll see what I can do, but don't hold your breath.' He stowed his equipment in his bag and left.

'Excuse me, Sarge.'

McLeish turned and found a SOCO grinning broadly at her.

'It's not your birthday by any chance?' He led her to a hatchway. 'You'll need these.' He handed her a pair of latex gloves. 'And this.' He handed her a torch. 'Oh, and when you're done we'll need to take your shoe prints. The place is crawling with different sets.'

'All that dust?'

'Whoever, wasn't too house proud.' He grinned and led them down steps to a cellar beneath the water line.

McLeish played the torch over the walls and plastic walkways SOCO had put on the floor. In the far corner, a tarpaulin had been pulled back, uncovering several buckets. In one, small items of brass, pottery and glass had been carefully wrapped in damp cloth. In another bucket, pieces of timber had begun to dry out, and were discolouring and cracking as seawater evaporated. In a third bucket, two doubloons, submerged in six inches of water, blinked in the torchlight.

'Not exactly treasure to die for, is it?' Tregunna had joined them and was peering over her shoulder.

'That's not all.' The SOCO led them up two flights to a room with a single, unmade bed, a two-ring butane gas stove, a kettle, a microwave, and a small round table with a chair pulled to one side. He lifted a large holdall, placed it on the table and began to empty it.

First out, a *Dive Magazine*, with Chris Baldwin's name scrawled on the top right hand corner of the front cover. 'Probably ordered from his local newsagent and kept under the counter 'til he was home.'

McLeish took it from him and flicked through several pages before she found an advertisement ringed in biro inviting experienced divers to put money into a salvage operation. *Accommodation and dive equipment provided* the advert said. *Interested parties should contact Frank Walker.* His address and telephone number supplied.

The SOCO's grin broadened. He pulled out clothing and a pair of city shoes.

'Baldwin's?' Tregunna said.

'He used a dry suit and would have changed on board *The Sky Lark*. Frank Walker couldn't leave the holdall on the boat, could he? Probably meant to dump it, but didn't get round to it.'

McLeish picked up the shoes by the laces.

'We've been looking for you,' she said, and handed everything back to the SOCO.

'And, finally…' The SOCO led them through to a small, grubby bathroom. 'Toothbrush and shaving gear.'

'New toothbrush?' asked Tregunna.

'Could be.'

McLeish placed an arm round his shoulder and gave him a hug. 'Right, my little ray of sunshine, take everything to that lab of yours and earn your crust.'

*

181

They left the boatyard, drove back to Falmouth, and ordered a ploughman's in the *Chain Locker*.

'If that was Baldwin's stuff,' Tregunna said, 'at least we know where he was staying.'

'I'd wager a year of your salary that's his *stuff* in the holdall.'

'The Dive magazine certainly was.'

'Yeah, but let's not get too excited. Let's wait until the lab rats have done their thing. Get on the blower and update the Guv.'

He tried, but there was still no response.

'She's probably on the plane. I'll try again later.'

Their food arrived.

'You think Walker knew Baldwin was being set up?' Tregunna asked.

'He could have been in from the start, or was paid to keep schtum after Baldwin snuffed it. We'll probably never know but if we assume Walker skippered the boat, he wouldn't have dived. He'd have stayed on deck, and helped divers with their gear. So, we have Baldwin, Walker and one other person on the boat.' McLeish sipped a coke, broke off a portion of cheddar, laced it with chutney and stuffed it into her mouth. 'But we still don't know *why* Baldwin was killed.'

'If they'd found treasure...?'

'And cut him out?'

'Could be.'

'But they'd wait until they'd salvaged most of it, wouldn't they?' McLeish speared a pickled onion with her fork, planted it in her mouth and crushed it between her teeth. After a couple of minutes she said, 'Got a shovel?'

'In for another spot of gardening, am I?'

'Yeah. I've got a feeling there's a lot more to Frank Walker than meets the eye. Start with his home, then his bank. See if his account's been topped up recently. But

182

before you do, go and talk to the young lass accused of not fastening Richard Lander's saddle correctly. See if anyone's bothered to ask for her version of events?'

During the flight, Jones re-examined the evidence accumulated in both cases and it soon became obvious that much of it was circumstantial and would be easy-pickings for any half-decent lawyer.

She studied the Social photograph of Jennifer West and compared it to prints of the two portraits. She reread the Met's report into the death of Colin Povey, and glanced through her interview with Simon Dansk. She skimmed over Tregunna's reported visit to Baldwin's house, but read the babysitter's note several times. She looked at reports from security staff at Madison's flat and CCTV stills provided by Terrance Leadbetter. On the last page of Brenda McLeish's summary of her 'audiences' with Lady Emily and her daughter, she scrawled a note to prompt her to reread Sebastian Coleman's report into Baldwin's death.

The pathologist's autopsy reminded her that she was still waiting for forensics to process samples found at D'Ancey's Club and that she hadn't heard from Met officers who'd checked Alexandra's alibi. She wasn't convinced that Lady Emily's daughter was watching *Death and the Maiden* at the time of her father's demise and, even if she had been, she could have slipped out and walked or taken a taxi to Park Place. It was less than half a mile from the theatre.

None of the evidence so far tied Kate Madison, aka Jennifer West, to Baldwin's death, or came anywhere close to providing a motive. Nor did any of it suggest that Alexandra had killed her father.

As she sipped coffee, Jones had a sinking feeling that both deaths could have been accidents. She'd learned long ago – from Charlie Hobson as it happened - that there were times when, given all the evidence, you had to make a call and stick by it. This wasn't a strategy that relied on a hunch or even - Charlie had said - feminine intuition. It was a calculation based on evidence, hard evidence, that enabled resources to be more effectively deployed and the investigation to focus on making the charges stick.

Trouble was, with hard evidence in such short supply she knew that this was not the time to make the call.

As they made their final approach, she knew she was no closer to joining the dots but felt sure that somewhere in the labyrinth of tales and lies, either Kate Madison, whether she was blond, dark, or had dyed her hair green - or Alexandra D'Ancey - would be her prime suspect.

Newquay airport felt like a portal to a world she called home and, as Jones walked from the plane to the terminal building, she knew that she wouldn't be able to accept Hobson's invitation to move back to London.

Not for any reason.

'Hallo stranger.'

Lizzie was in Arrivals. They kissed and hugged.

'Ouch.'

'You OK?' Jones asked.

'It's my ribs. From the fall. Then, we played squash. Stupid really…'

'We?'

Lizzie smiled. 'Come on.' They walked arm-in-arm, out of the terminal building to the car park.

'Well, don't you two look the darnedest couple of love birds?'

Kate Madison looked up from behind the wheel of her white Mercedes convertible. The roof was down and the red leather interior screamed extravagance. 'Good to see you again, Inspector.' She laughed. 'Jump in. We've decided you and Stewart need to kiss and make up. You're coming for supper. Nothing grand. Just a few drinks and something simple Cook will rustle up.'

Jones looked away as a bizarre sense of nightmare made her head spin and the sands shift beneath her feet. Not only were the girls throwing Stewart and her into the deep-end but - and she had to assume that Madison had no idea that she was a strong contender on a short list of prime suspects.

Couldn't be happening, could it? Jones heard the voice scream in her head.

And yet there she was – Madison - grinning up at her.

'Does Stewart know?' Jones asked.

'Of course, and your car's sitting in the driveway so you can escape any time.'

Madison laughed again, and Jones was struck by the whiteness of her teeth against a light tan. A Great White, she thought, sizing up its prey. Madison tapped the seat next to her and said, 'Jump in. I won't bite.'

As Lizzie climbed in, Jones saw an unmarked car and two men looking at a map. 'Hang on...' She hurried over, spoke to them, slapped the car's roof, and watched them drive off. 'Sorry about that,' she said, as she sat next to Madison. 'They'd sent a car to meet me.'

'But I said I'd pick you up,' Lizzie said.

'Administrative cock up.' She shrugged and realised that this was the closest she'd been to Madison since the interview in London. 'Nice perfume.'

'You like it?' Madison moved closer and offered her neck. 'JOY by Jean Patou. Cost over 400 bucks. The combination of jasmine and rose drives Stewart wild.' She laughed, gunned the car's engine and accelerated into the traffic.

Outwardly, Rosemullion Hall had changed little. The elegant Georgian façade retained its classic symmetry and inside Richard Lander had spent a fortune restoring and refurbishing the entrance hall and main stairway, the reception, living and dining rooms, as well as the kitchen and nine of the bedrooms. He'd bought the house as a wedding present for his bride but, ten years into their marriage, Connie Lander had died after a short battle with cancer.

He'd thrown himself into work, but never really recovered from the shock of losing her and Jones was in no doubt that he would have been looking forward to the day his son was old enough to take on the burden of business.

That day had arrived sooner than either of them could have foreseen.

As they drove through the grand, wrought iron gates at the entrance to the estate, Jones's mobile began to vibrate. She looked at the caller ID and asked Madison to pull over.

'It's my phone. I'll walk from here.' She not only needed to find out what George Tregunna wanted, but she also needed time to get her head together. She was unsure whether supper with a suspect had a precedent. She was also unsure how to play the evening or how Stewart would react after all this time.

'You OK?' Lizzie asked.

'Fine. But I need to take this. You go on in. I'll catch up.'

'Kinda freaked you out, hasn't it, seeing the old place again?' Madison said, as Jones climbed out.

'I was here for the funeral...' *Unlike some*, left unsaid.

She watched the car speed down the driveway, its exhaust amplified by the tunnel of trees. It swerved on the gravel circling the fountain in front of the main door and, from beneath the stone plinth above the pillared entrance, an elderly man made his way down the steps and opened the car door for Lizzie.

The front of the house sulked in shadows cast by enormous Douglas Firs. They were the same trees in which the childhood friends, Lydia Jones and Stewart Lander, had built dens, camped out, scoffed midnight feasts, created a language of their own and inducted new members into their gang with an unworldly oath of allegiance.

At this time of the day, the rear of the house, as she remembered it, would have been bathed in long shadows and the low sun would be flooding the garden with evening light.

She soaked up the silence, savouring the quiet as ghosts of the past played out before her: Stewart, a homemade wooden sword slashing the air, warding off demons, defending their castle and their stash of food; tomboy Jones abandoning her shield as imaginary enemies approached, and hauling up the rope ladder just in time. Happy days. Days of innocence. Days before Stewart's mother died, Emma's suicide, and before Richard Lander's horse reared.

She called George Tregunna and he told her about Frank Walker and *the stuff* they'd found at the boatyard.

'And you've handed everything over to the lab?'

'Yes, Guv.'

'Chase them.'

'Yes, Guv.'

187

'Lady Emily's daughter?'

'Yes, Guv?'

'Tell me exactly what she said about the days leading up to her father's murder.'

He did.

'And you believed her?'

'Sounded pretty convincing.'

Jones snorted. 'She would, wouldn't she...mummy's little angel. Anything else?'

'We're convinced Baldwin believed he was diving for treasure.'

'And Walker was in on it from the start?'

'Probably.'

'Makes sense. Thanks, George.'

She cut the call and looked up.

Lizzie was walking briskly towards her.

'Someone's dying to meet you,' she said.

'Lizzie. Can we talk?'

'Lydia. Come on. Be brave.'

In one of those moments when resistance seems futile and, if she'd stood her ground, things could have spun out of control, Jones allowed Lizzie to lead her to the foot of the steps at the front door.

'Good evening, Ma'am,' the old man said, 'Welcome to Rosemullion.'

'Albert?' Jones said, wide eyed.

Madison stood beside Albert. 'He's been here for, what? Forever, I'd guess. What do you say, Albert?'

'I've been fortunate to serve this family for many years, Miss.'

'You betcha.' She slapped him on the shoulder as she walked to the door. 'Come on Lizzie, the champagne's getting warm.'

She waited for Albert to open the front door and disappeared inside. Lizzie glanced at Jones, shrugged, turned and followed.

188

'Lydia?' The old man shuffled towards her, his hand outstretched. 'Forgive me. I didn't recognise you.'

'It's been a long time, Albert.'

'And such tragic times of late.' His eyes were dark and moist. 'You're a police officer?'

'Yes. Why? Are you OK?'

'I just wondered if I might have a quiet word?'

'Something wrong?'

'It's just that…a few days before his terrible accident, Mr Richard confided in me and I think you might be interested in what he had to say.' He looked away as the large oak door opened. 'But not here, not now…'

'We'll meet in town. De Wynn's?'

'Yes.'

Jones looked towards the front door and saw Stewart Lander accompanied by a tall, well-built man wearing a sharp suit and sunglasses.

'Lydia.'

'Stewart.'

'Good of you to come.'

'Not that either of us had much option.'

'It's been a long time.'

'The house is much as I remember it.'

'It's been restored sympathetically.'

'You've done well.'

'Come on in. I have some excellent Bordeaux.'

'I'm afraid I won't be able to stay long. I've got a full day ahead of me.'

'Let's try not to disappoint the girls. They've worked hard to arrange this evening.' Lander turned to the man in sunglasses. 'Thank you, John. I don't think we need worry too much about DI Jones. I'll see you at the briefing at nine tomorrow morning.'

'Sir.' He looked at Jones. 'Inspector.' He turned, and walked down the steps and down the drive, towards the gated entrance.

'John Hartley,' Lander said. 'Head of Security.'

'Doubles as your helicopter pilot.'

'And my body guard.'

'Sign of the times, eh?'

'I'm afraid so. Come on, let's see where the girls have got to.'

Jones followed him across a huge foyer, along a wide corridor and into the library where they found Lizzie, alone, studying several small oil paintings - hunting scene, hounds and horses, fox on the run.

Stewart took her hand. 'Come on. Let's leave Lydia to reacquaint herself with the old girl whilst I take you on a tour.'

Jones watched them disappear, back towards the grand entrance, knowing that Lizzie had played in many great houses and she'd approve of the restoration. She made her way to the drawing room, selected a single-malt from one of four decanters, and poured a generous slug into a cut glass tumbler. She stood before the grand fireplace and, as she looked at the portrait of Connie Lander above the mantle piece, she recalled that first Christmas at Rosemullion. It was a few months after her parents had died in a car crash and despite their intrinsic sadness, she found herself smiling at the memories...

She'd hung her stocking alongside Stewart's and had felt the warmth of the fire. Whilst she'd known the chimney was big enough, she'd wondered how Santa would survive the flames. It had snowed the night before and the estate had been bathed in a magical light. They'd tobogganed down the hill that tumbled towards the stables and paddocks.

It had been fun but in the quiet of the night the awful wretchedness of her new status – an orphan – made sleep difficult and tears a frequent visitor.

Richard Lander had collected her from her school in Putney and told her about her parent's accident.

He'd sorted things…Her aunt became legal guardian. The cottage was transferred to a trust fund that was to mature when Jones reached eighteen. In the meantime, it was rented out and accrued a tidy sum that saw her through her training and probationary years.

In those early days, holidays were spent away from London with the Landers. Stewart was like a brother and Richard and Connie Lander had offered her the support of their family at a time when she'd needed it most.

She raised her glass in silent salute to the old man's wife, just as Lizzie and Stewart came through the French doors.

'Kate not with us yet?' Lander asked.

'Probably putting on her face.'

'Well, I'm sure she'll be down soon.'

They stood, awkwardly, for a few moments until Stewart said, 'Kate tells me you met at the studios?'

'Investigating the death of Chris Baldwin.'

'Great tragedy. A real talent. I'd kept an eye on his early career, opened a few doors.' He fell silent, briefly, and then shook his head. 'How's it going?'

'The investigation? We're getting warmer.'

'Playing things close to your chest?'

'Takes time.'

Madison stood in the doorway. 'What, still no closer to solving the mystery, Inspector?'

She welcomed Stewart's arm and kissed him on the cheek. 'My apologies, disappearing like that. I hate it when people keep me waiting.' She smiled, seemingly self-conscious. Her voice had altered, slightly. Gone was the strident mid-Atlantic and in its place was a more pleasant and rounded tone. Estuarial, Jones remembered thinking when they'd met in London…estuarial, with just a touch of mid-Atlantic.

'Come on Lizzie,' Madison said, 'Let's go and chase supper.'

Lander poured himself a drink and offered Jones a refill. She declined, but decided to take the fight to her host. 'She's very beautiful,' she said.

'A breath of fresh air.'

Lander stood with his back to the fireplace.

'Father took a shine to her - the daughter he never had, I suppose. They walked together. She made him laugh. I'd forgotten how much he used to laugh before mother died.' He snorted. 'They played chess in his study...'

'Kate?'

He laughed. 'Yes. He'd let her win.' He exhaled, forcefully. 'They rode together for hours on end.'

'She was with him when he died?'

'Yes. Well, no.'

'Was, or wasn't?'

'He'd ridden ahead. She found him.'

'I see.'

There was an awkward silence.

'Where did you meet? How well do you know her?'

'Lydia, if this...' He faltered, as if searching for words. 'I don't like being interrogated in my own home.'

'Simple questions from someone who has your best interests at heart - where did you meet her and how well do you know her?'

'She's been vetted. Father ran background checks on women I dated.'

'A lot at stake. His fortune. His son.'

'The old man wanted to protect me.'

'And she checked out?'

'Lydia? Is there something you're not telling me?'

'Sorry. This evening, you and me standing here just like old times – difficult for us both, I'm sure.'

'Yes.' He recharged his glass, smiled and seemed to relax. 'We met at a Yacht Club party. The Chairman was celebrating the delivery of his latest Elan.'

'Lotus?'

Lander laughed. 'Powerboat.'

'And who said we're in the middle of a recession?'

He appeared not have heard. 'The Yacht Club was heaving,' he said. 'Members, plus a few folk from the British Sub Aqua Club. And there she was, standing on the veranda, looking at the boats moored in the Marina. A vision of loveliness.'

'She's very beautiful.'

'So you keep saying.'

'Love at first sight?'

'Lydia, why do you have to make everything sound like a cross-examination?

'I'm sorry. It's been a long day and I'm tired.' She looked into Lander's eyes, knowing she'd need to build bridges before bringing him in.

'You two OK?' Madison came in, stood beside Lander, and slipped an arm round his waist.

'I was just telling Lydia how we met.'

'Oh, do tell...' Lizzie stood beside Jones and slipped her hand behind her back in a mirror image of their hosts. 'Was it love at first sight? I bet it was.'

'Sounds like you two rehearsed this?' Lander snorted. 'I'm not sure how Kate felt, but for me...' He broke away, walked across the room and placed both hands on the back of a Jacobean fireside chair. 'She was on the veranda. The BSAC Dive Officer introduced us.' He held out his hand and Madison took it and stood beside him. 'He said you were special. And he was right.'

'It was cold.' Madison smiled. 'February.'

'I mumbled something banal.' Lander smiled. 'Even took my jacket off.'

'You were very gallant.' She pulled him close to her and looked into his eyes.

'Next thing you know,' he said, 'we're getting along like a house on fire.'

'How long before?'

'Lizzie?' Jones glared at her.

'I was only going to ask how long it was before they knew it was serious.'

'And you guys?' Madison titled her head to one side, lifted her eyebrows.

'A week?' Lizzie looked at Jones.

'Three days.'

'I travel light.' Lizzie smiled.

A maid knocked and the spell was broken.

Supper was ready.

They strolled into the dining room.

Jones felt distant.

Her mind was staging an unwelcome slide show of images she'd studied of Chris Baldwin's face and she hoped Lizzie would cover for her as the evening dragged on.

The meal, like the conversation, was varied and light. As they ate grouse and asparagus soup, Stewart regaled them with childhood adventures he'd shared with Jones.

Lizzie's tales of travel, concerts, and the outrageous behaviour of fellow musicians, were complemented by fillet steak in a shallot and truffle sauce, new potatoes and salad.

A rhubarb and gooseberry syllabub sprinkled with grated chocolate, served to soothe Madison's thwarted ambition to ride her own horse at Badminton.

Jones managed to avoid saying anything of substance and when Albert brought brandy to the table she hoped its arrival spelt the beginning of the end of the evening.

Madison poured herself a generous slug, then looked across the table, saluted and said, 'You haven't answered my question, Inspector.'

'Kate, I don't think…' Lander said.

'But she hasn't told us if they've got anyone in the frame for Baldwin's murder.'

'Kate.'

'It's OK,' Jones said, 'As I told Stewart earlier, we're making progress.'

'You'll be making an arrest soon?'

'The investigation's entering its final stages. We're waiting for forensics.' Jones stared at Madison a second too long. She cursed wordlessly and blamed herself for allowing her to get to her when she was vulnerable.

Madison took another sip of brandy. 'I'm sure I know you from somewhere, Inspector.'

'So you said.'

'No, seriously...' Her words slurred slightly and she held her glass up and used it to point at Jones. 'You were much younger...'

'Kate. That's enough,' Lander said. He cushioned the reprimand with a smile. 'Perhaps Lizzie would play for us?'

Madison's brandy glass slipped from her fingers and shattered on the parquet floor. 'Jesus wept.' She looked mortified and held her hand to her mouth. 'God, I'm so sorry...'

Jones pushed back her chair, collected another glass from the sideboard and, as she recharged Madison's, she heard Lizzie say, 'You wanted me to play something?'

'Before you do,' Madison said. She struggled to her feet, stood behind Stewart and threw her arms around his neck. He patted her forearm, but his message was too subtle for her. She kissed him clumsily on the cheek and said, 'Let's tell our friends our good news, shall we?'

'Kate, I...'

'We've fixed a date for our wedding.' She looked at Lizzie. 'And I'd like you to be my maid of honour.'

'Oh, I'm sure you'll have closer friends...'

'Well, if we're going to celebrate,' Stewart said, 'I'll ask Albert to fetch champagne and get someone to clear up the mess.' He walked across the room and through the double doors.

'I'm sorry,' Madison said, looking across the table at Lizzie. 'I didn't mean to embarrass you. I'd love you to be there on the big day.' She hesitated. 'You are happy for Stewart, aren't you? Both of you?'

'Stewart's father...' Lizzie's voice sounded calm, reassuring. 'His death was a great shock for those closest to him - for everyone who knew him. It's only a week since the funeral, but if he was here, I'm sure he'd be the first to congratulate you.'

'Oh, he'd already given us his blessing.'

Madison had fallen asleep soon after Lizzie started to play and they left her curled up on the Chesterfield.

They were standing outside the front door.

'It was good of you to come,' Stewart said. 'I'm sorry about Kate, she's...'

'Had a long day.' Lizzie smiled.

'Yes. Yes, I suppose so. Good night.' He kissed her on the cheek, and then turned to Jones. 'Good night, Lydia.'

She took his hand. 'Good night, Stewart. Sleep tight.'

The Sebring fired into life and Lizzie eased it down the driveway and out of the gates. Half a mile from the cottage, she pulled off the road, parked in front of five-bar gate and turned off the engine.

'You mind telling me what that was all about?'

'Sorry?'

'You seemed...God...I don't know...I've had a great time with Kate during the last few days. We've ridden together, walked, sketched, played squash.'

'Did you shower together?'

'Did we what?'

'After squash, did you shower together?'

'Yes, well...not together, but...'

'She was naked?'

'Lydia.'

'You saw her naked?'

'Of course I did.'

Jones stared ahead, silent, wrestling with just how to unravel the puzzle for Lizzie. 'You trust me?' she said.

'What do you mean, do I trust you? We've been through this. I said, didn't I?'

'How much do you know about me?'

'Enough.'

'And how much do you know about Kate?'

'Very little, I suppose.'

'And Stewart? How much do you think he really knows about his fiancée?'

'Lydia, what are you trying to say?'

Jones knew she had no idea and felt it was probably just as well. She decided to tell her...

They sat in darkness as Jones outlined the evidence they'd gathered, collated, crosschecked and confirmed. She included Jennifer West's tragic and sordid early life, but didn't mention Walker's death or the discoveries at his boatyard.

'She's one of two in the frame,' Jones said. 'And, if she's guilty, God knows how unstable she is.'

'But I saw nothing of that,' Lizzie said.

'I need you to come to the station in the morning.'

'Oh, for God's sake.'

'I asked if you trusted me?' Jones hesitated, her smile weak. 'I appreciate that this is pushing the limits of that trust, but I'll explain everything, I promise. I can only ask that you keep faith with me.'

'I love you. You know I do. And, I do trust you. But, I can't believe what I'm hearing.'

197

Jones looked at her, detesting aspects of her work that brought Lizzie such pain and anguish.

'Kate Madison may have been responsible for several murders and what you saw in the changing room could prove crucial in any case we bring against her.'

8

George Tregunna couldn't sleep. Shards of hair were lodged under his collar and irritating the hell out of him. He still couldn't bring himself to look at his shorn locks in the mirror for longer than a nanosecond. Brenda McLeish had struck again. She'd taken him to a friend who'd opened up her salon without hesitation - anything, she'd explained to McLeish, to get out of the house and away from 'my slob of a husband.'

The only time she did show any impatience was after she'd finished Tregunna's nails and given him a face massage. Twice she had to repeat a regenerative regime she'd designed for him - which creams he should use at night, how he should apply an undereye lotion, how to wash his hair once then apply a conditioner, then wash again after letting the conditioner do its thing.

She cut his hair and explained how he'd have to use *styling products* to maintain his new image. And, yes, she'd assured him more than once, he *was* still young enough to carry it off if he did so with confidence and dressed accordingly.

Next stop? A return to the boutique owned by another of McLeish's friends. She'd opened just for them and the last of last season's stock had been set aside for him to trawl through. It had taken an hour and a half – including a break for coffee and sandwiches - before he'd been bullied into taking home a jacket, several shirts, three pairs of trousers, a pair of designer jeans, two pairs of shoes, a casual suit, and a selection of belts and ties - all mix-and-match and colour coordinated. Any clothes left at his digs were collected and sent to the dry-cleaners. They'd be ready on Friday and would do for work but, McLeish warned him, if she saw him wearing any of his 'old clobber' off duty he'd be in serious shit.

At five, he nipped across the landing buoyed by the thought that this would be the last time he'd have to share a bathroom. He was also thankful he was first to use it - before anyone else got up. He'd been to *The Crow's Nest* to check if the brewery had agreed to his tenancy, but Angus had waited until Tregunna had demolished a shepherd's pie before he'd confirmed the arrangement.

He locked the bathroom door, wiped the grime stains from the rim of the bath, set the taps flowing, sat on the toilet and skimmed through a copy of *Cosmopolitan*. A few moments later, he put the magazine down after he realised that it may well have been thumbed by everyone who'd visited the bathroom over several years.

The bath was shallow and he washed quickly, then doused what remained of his hair with water trickling from a hose connected to the taps. He didn't recognise the man in the mirror as he shaved. His nose seemed smaller, his eyes brighter, his hair...*Christ, my hair.* He stood in front of the mirror, took the top off a can of styling moose, shook it and squirted a golf-ball-sized blob on his palm, and tried to remember what to do.

One of the other tenants banged on the door and demanded to know how long he'd be. 'As long as it takes.' He smiled and applied the moose.

'Hurry up, for fuck's sake. I need a crap.'

He combed his hair and tweaked his quiff. There was another bang on the door. He gathered up his toiletries and took one final look in the mirror, adjusted a stray strand of cropped hair, and nodded at his reflection. *The name's Bond.*

It was six-fifteen.

He hesitated, very briefly, at the foot of steps leading to the entrance to Falmouth's police headquarters, then took them, two at a time. There was a lightness in his step and uniformed officers, who were chatting with the duty Sergeant, applauded as he pushed open the double doors into reception.

'Nice one, George.'

'Nailed a trolley-dolly, clocking up all them airmiles to London and back?'

He bowed and smiled. It was approval of sorts and his first hurdle. On the third floor, he ducked into the gent's, checked his hair and his new shirt and jacket, and smiled at his reflection. 'Stuff 'em.'

He went into the Incident Room and poured himself a coffee but as he waited for it to cool he suddenly realised that they'd missed an opportunity - potential witnesses – and that if he moved quickly he might catch them before they went home...

The sun was struggling to break over the hills and a heavy mist rose from the mirror-still water as he parked down stream. He couldn't see them and was about to head back to the station when he heard a muttered curse beyond a line of poplar trees.

'Morning.' Tregunna crouched between two anglers, downstream from Frank Walker's boatyard.

He showed them his warrant card.

'We've got our licence.' One growled.

'All legal, like.'

Tregunna looked along the towpath.

There was a sign...

NO FISHING.
NO DIGGING FOR BAIT.

'Been a good night?' he asked.

'Not bad.' The growler pulled up a keep-net full of squirming fish and eels. 'Want one? Take back to the missus.'

'No thanks,' Tregunna said. 'She prefers cold tongue and grouse these days.' It fell on deaf, disinterested ears. 'Fish here most nights, do you?'

'During the season. Be too cold later in the year.'

'And what time do you set up?'

'Oh, I don't know. Depends, really. 'Bout six, six-thirty, give or take, wouldn't you say, Joe?'

'There or there abouts, Tom.' He turned to Tregunna. 'Why? What's this all about?'

'Murder in the boatyard across the water.'

'I heard there'd been a commotion,' Tom said.

'Saturday evening? You were here?'

'Early on like, but not after sunset. Packed and went as soon as it got dark.'

'Make us sound like ruddy vampires.' Joe laughed as his rod dipped and float sunk beneath the water. 'Excuse me. One for the pot.' He reeled in his catch, but it was too small and he threw it back.

'Either of you know Frank Walker?'

'No, not really. Fallen on hard times, I heard. Decent enough chap, folk do say.'

'He was stabbed on Saturday evening, around seven or seven-thirty. Did either of you see or hear anything?'

'See anything?'

'Hear anything?'

'Someone acting suspiciously? Or, an argument? A car? Anything that might help us?'

Tom looked at Joe. They propped their rods against the trunk of a tree, packed their gear, then took each of the fish from the keep-net, slapped its head on a rock and stored it in a large cool box.

'Sun's up, Constable,' Tom said. 'If you want to ask any more of questions, you'd best be buying breakfast.'

*

202

They left the cottage at six and drove into Falmouth. In the Incident Room, Jones watched as Lizzie studied the evidence displayed on whiteboards. She'd arranged for them to be alone and had asked Lizzie to concentrate on images gathered during the investigation: CCTV of Kate Madison in Regent Street; the photograph from Social Services; digital photographs of a girl being raped by Geoffrey D'Ancey; more CCTV stills of Alexandra D'Ancey, taken by security cameras at Lady Emily's apartment; stills of Kate Madison at the Lander flat in St James's Square; Chris Baldwin's tattoo and the portraits recovered from his house.

Lizzie took her time and then said, 'These are two different women.' She looked at Jones. 'You're not going to help me, are you?'

'They're both suspects.'

'OK.' Lizzie exhaled. 'This is Kate.' She pointed at several different images. 'The other woman's taller...' She spoke out loud, as if to help her untangle ideas. 'The passport photo is Kate. Looks ghastly doesn't she? She's had a makeover since - teeth, eyebrow shaping, eyelash extensions and, maybe, collagen injections to enhance the pout.'

'Expensive.'

'It's not a crime to make the most of what you've got. But you're right. Where did she have the work done and how did she afford it?'

'America?'

'Why not?' Lizzie shrugged, as if resigned. 'It's not a crime is it, putting yourself in the shop window? She's taken a new name, new identity. So what? Followed to its logical conclusion, Norma Jean would have been in the dock alongside countless other showbiz stars. And who hasn't had a nip or tuck here and there?'

Lizzie took down two photographs - the passport and of the rape - and held them alongside the portraits.

'This could be Kate,' she said. 'Similar eyes, intense blue. The hair could be a wig, or a stage prop.'

'Or a disguise.'

'But, *could be* is not enough is it?' Lizzie seemed to be confused. 'Why did you ask if I'd seen her naked?'

'She has a tattoo.' Jones walked to the whiteboard and tapped the photograph. 'Same as Chris Baldwin's, in the same place, just below the bikini line.'

'Doesn't mean she killed him.'

'But it ties them together.'

'No it doesn't. Beside, her relationship with Baldwin is not a secret. She just didn't want Stewart to know the true extent of it.'

'Why? Got something to hide?'

'I don't know. Some men can't cope. Too immature.' Lizzie shook her head. 'I saw her naked, but I didn't check her out...well, I didn't get close enough to see if she had a tattoo.'

'You're quite sure?'

'Lydia.'

'Well?'

'I'm not going to dignify that.' Lizzie folded her arms and turned away.

There was a knock on the door and one of the officers gathered outside told Jones they were waiting to start the briefing...'The one due at seven-thirty, Guv.'

Jones gave him short shrift and closed the door.

Lizzie was standing with her hands on her hips.

'For what it's worth Inspector, you have a problem... masses of evidence but no proof. It's all circumstantial.'

There was another knock and the door opened. It was Brenda McLeish, George Tregunna hovering behind.

McLeish grinned. 'Sorry, Guv, but the lab-rats' report has just come through - the D'Ancey crime scene DNA and photos.'

Jones opened her jacket and handed a sandwich bag containing fragments of glass to McLeish. 'Fingerprints, DNA, run a comparison. My prints are on it. Make sure they know.' She shut the door.

Lizzie was standing, mouth open, eyes wide. 'Jesus, Lydia. You must have been watching her all evening and when Kate dropped her brandy glass, you didn't hesitate, did you?' She shook her head as though she was unable to reconcile what she'd just seen with the woman she'd fallen in love with. 'Yours is a very sad world, Lydia.'

'Not pretty, is it?' Jones tried to take in her arms, but Lizzie recoiled. 'I couldn't bear it, if anything happened to you.'

'To me?'

'Oh, for God's sake, if I'm right and she gets wind of what's happening, you could be next.'

'Why? Why would she want to harm me?'

'To get at me, to throw me off the scent, divert attention. I don't know.'

'And if you're wrong?' Lizzie broke away.

'I'm not prepared to take that risk.'

Lizzie looked at her, eyes ablaze. 'I hope to God you know what you're doing.'

Stewart Lander stood at her bedside.

Her face was calm and relaxed, her lips tickled by a smile. Her long, graceful neck rested gently on a pillow and a cream silk sheet covered her naked body from the waist down. She was beautiful - he had to admit.

He looked down at a card he held between thumb and forefinger. His name was scrawled beneath his father's name and the Company's. He put it back in his waistcoat pocket.

She stirred and opened her eyes. She giggled, pulled the sheet up and snuggled down into the luxury of her bed. 'That's not fair.'

'Fresh juice, mango, toast, and coffee.' He put the tray down at the foot of the bed, walked over to the window, drew the curtains, and looked at the countryside and towards the cliffs and the sea. The sun was shining, but there was a hint of white horses far out in the bay. 'It's a beautiful day,' he said, and turned round.

'What time is it?'

'Eight.'

'What have you got planned?'

'I'm meeting with John Hartley. Run a check over the security.'

'More security?' She yawned.

'I just want to make sure we've done all we can, the world the way it is.' He poured her a coffee. 'I'm going into town. Albert's asked to be dropped at the shopping centre. He'll be out for most of the morning. Would you like us to wait for you?'

'No, you go ahead. I'll go in later. Run a few errands. Perhaps we could meet up for lunch?'

'I can't. I'm going to London. The movie's in the cutting room and they want me to check the latest edit.' He hesitated. 'Later this afternoon, I'm going to RAF Benson, near Oxford. I've contacted an old friend to arrange a training course.'

'Training...'

'I need to learn how to ditch the helicopter if there's a mechanical failure or birds get sucked into the engine.'

'Ditch? In the sea? What for real?'

'Flight simulator. We ditch, wait for the helicopter to sink and, when the blades stop, we surface and swim to safety. Least, that's the theory. Military practice for it all the time.'

206

'Jesus, Stewart, you sure know how to scare the crap out of me.'

'One of the few remaining bits of paper I need to get my licence. John's overseeing my progress.'

'Boys with their toys, eh?'

'He'll move on once the security upgrade's in place.'

Kate sat up and stretched, and let the sheet fall from her shoulders. 'Then I'll have you all to myself.'

'There'll always be someone watching my back. It's something I'll have to get used to.'

'I should have my own bodyguard.'

'A woman.'

'Don't trust me?'

He didn't respond.

'I'd never be unfaithful. You know that don't you?'

He exhaled forcefully. 'Did you know Chris Baldwin was down in Cornwall last week?'

'God no. Why would you think that?'

'He may have mentioned it at the studios when you were prepping his last show. Hoping to see you, maybe?'

'We worked together, that's all. He was history long before…'

She folded her arms and pouted like a small child - an exaggerated protest, he thought, and one she punctuated with a flash of her eyes and a smile. 'You really have nothing to worry about,' she said.

'It's just…' He managed to crack a smile, but it was heavy going and Lydia Jones's question…*How well do you know her?*…was baying in his head. He pulled the name card from his waistcoat pocket. 'Recognise this?'

She sat up, took the card, studied it, turned it over and handed it back to him.

'No. Why, should I?'

'It was found in your bedside cabinet.'

'What?'

207

'Routine checks my father had in place, whenever...'

'Whenever someone new came on the scene?'

'I have a lot to lose.'

She sat up. 'Lot to lose? Jesus...' She hesitated, shook her head in disbelief, and then looked up at him, her eyes narrowing. 'And? Did I check out?'

'You wouldn't be here if they'd found anything.' He stood silently and watched her; trying to imagine what turmoil the card had induced.

'Stewart?' She hesitated again. 'I don't know what to say. My privacy's been violated.'

'So, you do recognise it?'

'No. No, for God's sake, I said, didn't I?'

'Greenwich Park, ten years ago? You were lying on a bench. We chatted. I gave you that card after I'd written my name and mobile number on it. I said I wanted to see you again and asked you to contact me.'

'Greenwich Park?'

'You told me your name was Jenny?'

'Stewart...' She lent forward and clasped her knees.

She was struggling, he guessed, with images from the past, and debating whether to come clean or lie.

He wasn't sure what he wanted to hear.

She threw off the cover, got out of bed and draped a silk robe over her shoulders. 'I need some space. I'm not sure how I feel. We'll talk about this later.'

'No,' he said. 'We'll talk now.'

She stood, her back towards him, lifted her head, sighed heavily, and then turned, tears in her eyes.

'What can I say? I'm sorry. I'm truly sorry. I meant no harm. I just wanted us to be together because that's what we both wanted, not because of some schoolgirl crush that mushroomed into something of an infatuation. There...yes, I admit it,' she cried, 'I've carried that card everywhere. Look at its condition. Crumpled, dog-eared.

It's meant so much to me, so much more than you could ever imagine.'

'Then why lie? Why not just tell me the truth?'

She stood before him, make-up streaking her face. She placed a hand alongside his cheek.

'Because I was afraid.'

'Afraid?'

'Afraid I'd lose you. Afraid that you'd think I'm no better than a scheming little tart. Whereas,' she said, smoothing his hair from his brow, 'nothing could be further from the truth. I love you and I want to spend the rest of my life with you.'

The station was abuzz with speculation...there had been, so rumour broadcast, a significant development in the investigation and a TAG or Armed Response Unit was about to be deployed. The day shift spilled into the Incident Room and fresh coffee and bacon sandwiches were made available - the night shift grabbing a share before leaving.

'Butty, George?' McLeish asked.

'No, thanks. I've eaten enough to keep an army on the march for at least a month.' He took his coffee and sat behind his desk.

'You look like shit.'

'Been up since five.'

'Another early bird...' McLeish nodded towards a closed door. 'DI's been in with the Super since seven-thirty.'

'Was that Lizzie being escorted from the building?'

'Yeah.'

'What's that all about?'

'Search me.'

They sat for several minutes.

Tregunna discarded his coffee after a few sips and McLeish tucked into a bacon butty.

'I look like shit...' Tregunna watched grease trickle down McLeish's chin. 'For good reason...Double egg, chips, beans, tomatoes, mushrooms, black pudding...' He recalled the plate of forbidden fruit. 'Three rashers of back, two slices of Mother's pride, and the largest mug this side of a chimp's tea party.'

'All in the line of duty, I suppose?' Hinkson said.

No one had noticed that the Superintendent and Jones were standing by the door, watching the floorshow.

Hinkson turned to Tregunna. 'George, apart from the full-English, what's your excuse for looking like shit?'

'Sorry, Ma'am. It's been another long night, but I do have eyewitnesses who saw things at the boatyard...'

'Things?'

'Approximate time for the attack on Frank Walker, a description of the assailant and the car he used.'

'I'm all ears.'

Tregunna flipped open his notebook and read back information provided by the two anglers over breakfast.

They'd given him a description of a tall, heavily built man who'd parked outside the entrance to the boathouse at about seven-thirty. He had the hood of his jacket over his head and was driving a dark green or dark blue pick-up. He went inside and came out ten minutes later.'

'Did they hear anything?'

'Anything, Ma'am?'

'A fight. An argument?'

'Don't think so. Not sure.'

'Go back and ask. Good work, George. Just hope your stomach will forgive you.' Hinkson lifted her chin. 'DI Jones?'

'Thank you, Ma'am. We've just had confirmation that Lady Emily's daughter was, as she maintained, at the theatre when her father took a turn for the worse. That doesn't rule Alexandra out, but the Super and I have agreed to concentrate efforts and resources on Kate Madison.'

There was, she detected, a murmur of support for this. She was grateful. She was feeling vulnerable after crossing swords with Hinkson who'd rounded on her for not arresting Frank Walker sooner. She'd tried to fight her corner and had reminded the Superintendent that the surveillance had been withdrawn too early, but Hinkson hadn't been prepared to countenance any excuses.

Jones turned to McLeish and Tregunna. 'Locate the car and its owner, but don't do anything until you've checked with me. If we come heavy handed, we could blow it.' She looked at the earnest faces of the officers gathered in the room. 'Everything's in place. We'll move tomorrow afternoon. You've all worked bloody hard to get this far, but it's essential you keep your mouths shut - tight as a duck's proverbial.' She allowed the levity to underline the seriousness of the situation. 'Brenda and George will manage the boys in blue.'

'My favourite colour,' McLeish said.

'I'll handle Stewart Lander and Missy Madison.'

Albert sat at a table by one of the large windows at the back of De Wynn's. From there he could not only enjoy the warmth of the sun and watch the plethora of boats scurrying about the estuary, but could also watch out for DI Jones. He'd ordered a pot of his favourite brew and a round of toast, unsalted butter and locally produced, homemade strawberry jam.

211

De Wynn's had opened in 1780 and had maintained a reputation for service and quality. Tables were draped in white cotton and staff were, invariably, rushed off their feet from nine in the morning until closing time at five.

For Albert, the tearoom meant much more than tea and scones or Duchy Pie. Born and bred on a farm just outside the town, his mother would take him there on the way back from Monday's Market-on-the-Moor. He did his courting in De Wynn's over buttered crumpet and brought Alice there nearly thirty years ago to celebrate their appointment as Cook and Butler to Richard Lander. And, it was there that he'd introduced a young Stewart Lander to the delights of Thunder and Lightning with treacle and ice cream.

After about ten minutes, he saw Jones hurrying from a police car and rose to greet her. 'It's good to see you again, Miss. I've ordered your favourite.'

'Granny Nunn's Bread Pudding? Albert, you spoil me.' She would have enjoyed indulging the old man, but time was precious. Stewart Lander had been tailed since he dropped Albert at the shopping centre and it was only a matter of time before he'd finish his meeting and take the helicopter to London.

She dabbed her mouth with a paper napkin. 'You have some information for me?'

Albert took two envelopes from the inside pocket of his jacket. 'I thought you might be interested in these.' He opened one, took out several photographs, and laid them on the tablecloth. It looked as though a zoom lens had been used to photograph Kate Madison and Chris Baldwin as they walked along a footpath. In another, they were embracing outside a bookstore. In a third, they were sitting at the window of a coffee bar. There was another as they left the bar and one that captured them in another embrace, but this time - it seemed to Jones - the body language suggested more than affection.

'How did you come by these?'

'We've spent many happy years at Rosemullion. Mr Richard has been...' He took a deep breath, his face etched with the pain '...had been a model employer. His wedding present to us was a cottage on the estate at a peppercorn rent. Our children were born there and, to all intents and purposes, were part of the Lander family.'

'I remember it well.'

'Yes, yes, of course. Happy days.'

'But?'

'Mr Stewart was about ten when his mother died. It was a shock to us all, as you'd imagine. She was so young. Mr Richard threw himself into his television and film work and...' Albert hesitated, clearly upset...'And, at the time of his death, he was one of the richest people in England.'

'And Stewart will inherit everything.'

'Everything.' Albert agreed, pausing to wipe his eyes. His hands shook slightly as he poured another tea and he seemed unable to disguise the bitterness in his voice. 'Then Mr Stewart met Miss Madison. She moved into the west wing and began to lord it over us 'downstairs'. One would expect some changes, of course, but she's the most perplexing of people. She can be charming, with the most radiant of smiles and those beautiful eyes. It's easy to see why Stewart is so enamoured of her.'

'And is he?'

'Besotted. Infatuated. Head-over-heels. One might even say *madly* in love.'

'An interesting choice of word, but it might explain why Stewart's view is somewhat different to yours.'

'He seems oblivious to the effect she's having on the household.'

'Charming one moment...'

'Disrespectful, discourteous and dismissive. She has an edge. I'd put that down to being an American.'

213

'She's not. Born in London, on the wrong side of the tracks. I just don't understand why Richard didn't see through her.'

Albert sipped his tea. 'As you'd imagine, Mr Richard did all he could to make her feel welcome.'

'Have there been many gold diggers?'

'A few, but measures have always been in place to protect Mr Stewart and the family fortune.'

'Measures?'

'Whenever a new young lady came on the scene, Mr Richard engaged the services of a private investigator.'

'He had Kate Madison followed?'

'On this occasion? No, only background information. Mr Richard's anonymity assured at all times, of course.'

'Stewart knew. He told me last night, just before we had dinner.'

'Ah, yes…I don't think he knows everything, but he may have to after what I'm about to tell you.'

'Go on.'

'Mr Stewart met Miss Madison at the Yacht Club in February last year. Once his father realised she was more than a passing fancy, I was asked to contact the private investigator.'

'And?'

'He drew a blank. Nothing before her arrival from the USA in January last year.'

'I have a colleague in Scotland Yard who's liaising with counterparts in Los Angeles.' Jones made a mental note to make sure Hobson had passed on Jennifer West's Social Service records – including her photograph - to the LAPD.

'We'd retained the services of the private investigator and, in May, Miss Madison met Mr Baldwin…' Albert tapped the photographs.

'She'd had an affair with him before she took up with Stewart.'

'Really? I didn't know.' Albert paused, as if needing to assimilate this information. 'Anyway, photographs were taken, transcripts of telephone conversations, an account of times they spent together, where they went, and so on.'

'What did Richard Lander do?'

'He confronted her. She told him that they'd worked together in London, but their relationship was nothing more than friendship. She was committed to Stewart and would not be seeing anyone else.'

'And he believed her?'

'He was, I suppose - as we all were to start with - caught up in the romance of it all. She made Mr Stewart happy. She was young, bursting with energy, attractive, and it's not beyond the realms of possibility that Mr Richard saw something of his wife in her. Perhaps he *wanted* to see Miss Connie in her.'

Albert opened the second envelope and dealt another set of photographs across the table.

Jones glanced at them. 'These have been taken more recently?'

'Yes.'

'Then he must have come down this way more than once? Maybe several times over the past few months?'

'It's possible.'

Jones realised that a pattern was emerging. Baldwin would front *Ask the Minister* on Friday evening, take the train down to see Kate Madison - the train would explain the BMW in the driveway outside his house – and return to London in time to prep the next show. Jones began to wonder how often they saw each other in London and how they'd kept things quiet and away from prying eyes. Baldwin's flat, the love nest, perhaps? She also began to wonder *why* Madison had kept Baldwin dangling and how many hoops she'd made him jump through before she severed their association for good.

'Sorry, go on.'

'It wasn't long before Miss Madison's conduct and demeanour altered and the household grew restless and resentful. Mr Richard was also having misgivings. She was spending more and more time in London and had started to use the flat in St James's as if it was her own. She opened a charge account and was running up large bills - designer clothes and other extravagances.' Albert drained the dregs of tea from the pot. 'About a month ago, Mr Richard engaged the private investigator again.'

'Did he say why?'

'No, and the investigator had nothing to report until one evening when he phoned. We met and...' Albert tapped the photographs.

'And you passed them on to Richard?'

'Of course.'

'And what did he do?'

Albert took an A4 piece of paper from the breast pocket of his jacket. He unfolded it and used notes he'd made as a prompt. 'These photographs were taken on the 14th and 15th of May, and delivered to us on the 17th. I remember. They had just finished dinner. They'd been celebrating Mr Stewart's engagement to Miss Madison.'

'Did Stewart see them?'

'No, it was all a bit cloak and dagger, to be honest, but Mr Richard wanted to be sure before...'

He wiped his eyes on his napkin and checked his note once more.

'On Saturday 21st May, Mr Stewart left on a business trip to London. On Sunday 22nd, Mr Richard confronted Miss Madison again.' Albert dropped his head, breathed deeply, and then looked up at Jones. 'By midday on Monday 23rd, Mr Richard was dead.'

*

216

'What *is* it,' McLeish muttered, as they drove through the town, towards the harbour, 'about spending all night on a river bank, ripping out the insides of a defenceless creature's mouth, then clubbing it to death on the nearest rock?'

'I'm thinking of giving it a go.'

'You must be joking. You're depressed as it is.'

'Give me time to think, work out what I want to do with my life. Get things into perspective.'

'You need to get laid, George. First, second and last. Works wonders.'

'Been there.'

Forensics had ruled out the surveillance team's tyre tracks, but another set, found in the lane leading to Frank Walker's boatyard, matched the description of a vehicle seen by the two anglers. Tregunna had been back to interview them and they'd told him that it was, actually, an old four-by-four, possibly dark green. The wind was up that evening, so seeing someone in a hood up wasn't something they thought strange. They didn't take much notice when he arrived and couldn't remember exactly when he left. They also told Tregunna that they hadn't seen anyone else, but agreed that someone could have got there before they'd set up camp on the river's edge.

DVLA had compiled a list of cars: make, age, colour and location. Traffic police eliminated most, using drive-by surveillance, and that left half a dozen to be checked out.

So far, they'd drawn a blank.

The refurbished BSAC clubhouse was their next port of call, but they stopped at the *Maenheere Hotel*, went inside, and ordered two rounds of sausage sandwiches and coffee. They sat at a table by a large sash window, from where they could keep an eye on the target vehicle.

'Club's got a great location,' McLeish said. 'Right on the water's edge.'

217

'A cinch for Frank Walker to come alongside, tie up, load the Sky Lark and be off.'

'I don't think this is where he picked up Baldwin. There'd be too many people around. I think he came here, loaded the dive gear, then collected Baldwin from the boatyard and motored to Custom House Quay, where he picked up the killer.'

'But before they cast off, Walker should have radioed the Harbour Master and whoever was on duty would have seen three men...Walker, Baldwin, and the killer.'

'Not if the killer was invisible.'

'Invisible?'

'Oh, come on George, I don't know. Pretending to fix something in the wheelhouse, out of sight?' She took a lump out of her sandwich. 'Then the diesels kicked-in and Baldwin had embarked on his final journey.'

'You're enjoying this, aren't you?'

'The butty?'

Tregunna looked at her.

'Exercises my vivid imagination,' she said.

'Go on then, what happened next.'

'A mile out, isolated in an ocean of choppy, cold, dark, murky water, they dropped the anchor. Baldwin was unhappy with the quality and condition of his diving gear - particularly the life jacket - but with Kate Madison back on shore...'

'And the treasure.'

'Missy Madison, plus treasure - irresistible.' McLeish sipped a coffee. 'The killer carried a pneumatic hammer connected to his aqualung. That's a hammer with a force of three thousand psi. But Baldwin wouldn't have been suspicious. Hammers are often used for treasure hunting. After about fifteen minutes on the sea bed the killer used it to smash Baldwin's mask, then slipped off his weight belt and inflated his life jacket.'

'A fucking nightmare.'

218

'We were lucky.'

'Lucky?'

'He could have drifted past Land's End and be on his way to South America, but the tide and currents brought the body ashore at Pendennis.'

'Where a young couple found him.'

'Yes.' McLeish laughed. 'They'd been away for a dirty weekend and went home to a blaze of publicity. That'll take some explaining.'

'Serves 'em right.'

They finished the sandwiches, drank their coffee and Tregunna screwed up his napkin and tossed it into an ashtray. 'She must be pretty special.'

'Missy Madison? Yes, makes you wonder why Chris Baldwin was so obsessed with this particular bit of skirt? Why a man who's prepared to put his life on the line falls for such an airhead. I found it difficult to reconcile, at first, but then I remembered that most men think with their dicks.'

Tregunna snorted. 'Yeah.'

He sat in silence for a moment, as if reflecting on his own susceptibility. 'She's very beautiful.'

'Skin deep.'

'As it turns out.'

'Hey, up.' McLeish nodded towards a man who'd come out of the clubhouse. They watched him open the Defender, take something out and go back inside. 'Show time.'

'The Guv said we should be careful, not to spook anyone. Softly, softly…'

'Not my style, but under the circumstances…you think I should call her?'

'Best.'

McLeish did, but Jones wasn't picking up.

'Come on, bit of initiative never hurt.'

They walked over the road and across a small car park set aside, so a large notice read, 'For Committee Members'. There was only one car. A single-cab pick-up that had seen better days, its steel wheels and bonatti-grey bodywork caked in mud.

They walked round it, trying to look casual, glancing through windows and trying out door handles. They checked the registration against one provided by DVLC and went inside the clubhouse. It was busy. There were twenty or so members sitting at tables and enjoying the subsidised food, whilst half-a-dozen others stood at the bar, probably swapping exaggerated tales of their diving adventures.

The bartender dipped his hands in the sink below the counter to wash a few glasses. 'Members?'

'Any club that would have me as a member...' McLeish did her best with the Groucho Marks impression but it fell on stony ground.

'Eh?'

'Where's your D O?'

'Tony? Probably up to his armpits in slag.'

'Slag?'

'He's renovating a miner's cottage along the coast somewhere.'

'So, that wasn't him loading the rust bucket in the car park?'

'Could be. Compressor's playing up. Needs fixing before tonight's dive.'

'You dive at night?'

'Best time to see the more bizarre members of our underwater world, especially lobsters, crab, and other crustaceans. Did you know...'

McLeish lent forward, her face inches from his. 'The D O? I wouldn't want to miss him.'

The bartender looked away in time to see a heavy-set, muscular man saunter in from a side door.

220

His face looked as if thunder was rumbling in his head and he scowled at members who greeted him over their chicken and chips.

'Tony. You got a minute?' The bartender waved a tea towel in the air. 'There's a couple here want to talk to you about the club.'

'Hope they're not wasting my time,' he said, without looking towards the bar. He scanned through notices on a board and tore a couple down. 'Tell them, if they're not going to take this seriously, to go take a fucking dance class. Right now, they can give me a hand with the fucking compressor.' He turned and left through the same door, McLeish and Tregunna close behind.

They watched him drop the tail of the pick up.

'Can we help?' McLeish asked.

'What and ruin your designer gear?' He looked at her. 'You were here a couple of nights ago, right? Cop, asking questions about that celeb who croaked it?'

'I wished I had a memory like yours.'

'So, this ain't about the club?'

'Nah, sorry.'

'But you'll let us have that lifejacket when you've finished with it?'

'I hadn't forgotten, for your museum, right?'

'Yeah.'

'My Superintendent found it odd that you weren't interested in Chris Baldwin's little accident.'

'She should get out more. Now, you going to give me a hand with this or what?'

Tregunna took the other end of the compressor and helped lift it into the back of the Defender.

The D O jumped into the cab, rummaged through a pocket in the dash and threw a couple of leaflets towards them. 'In case you change your mind and decide to join.'

'Thank you,' McLeish said. 'Sorry, didn't catch your name.'

221

'Be in there, under Dive Officer.'

He started the engine, but she lent in and turned it off.

'I haven't finished with you, sweetheart,' she said. 'See, I take everything seriously, especially murder.'

'Murder? Do me a favour. I told you...accidents happen.'

'Not to someone as experienced as Mr Baldwin.'

'At forty metres? Could happen to anyone.'

'So he was out of his depth?' McLeish tilted her head to one side.

'Now, you're taking the piss.'

'Tell me, darling, where were you on Saturday the fourth, through to the small hours of Sunday the fifth?'

'Tucked up in bed. Where else would I be?'

'Forty metres?'

'Do me a favour.' He turned the ignition key, and crunched the lever into first gear. 'I'm busy. Anything else, you know where to find me.'

They stood to one side. He accelerated towards the exit where he stopped, took out his mobile, made a call, and then swung into a gap in the heavy traffic.

McLeish flicked through the leaflet and found his name listed just below the Chairman's. 'We taking Tony Simpkiss seriously, George?'

'I'll get out my shovel.'

'Yes, do.' She put the leaflets into an evidence bag. 'Drop these off with the lab rats, and tell them to run any fingerprints through the database. Then, I want you to check if press releases mentioned that Baldwin dived to forty meters?'

'And, you?'

'Me? The Guv'nor and I have a date.'

*

222

They were sitting in an unmarked car, waiting for Stewart Lander to finish his meeting.

'George seems happier,' Jones said.

'Likes gardening.' McLeish looked at her.

'Any luck?'

'Not yet. Tony Simpkiss has gone to ground. Got an old cottage he's renovating. Maybe he's hold-up there.'

'Where?'

'Don't know. Sorry, Guv. Missed that one. I'll get George to check.' McLeish hesitated. 'There was one thing Simpkiss let slip.'

Jones looked at her, waiting. 'Well?'

'He knew Baldwin reached forty metres.'

'That was on a strictly need-to-know basis.'

'And nothing to that effect was mentioned in any of the press releases. I checked.'

'Shit.' Jones looked at McLeish. 'Find him, ASAP. There's only one way he'd know how deep Baldwin dived...' She drummed her fingers on the steering wheel. 'If he is Madison's oppo, there could be at least two murders down to him.'

'I'll give George a bell and see if he's had a result.'

'Let me know as soon as he's located Simpkiss.'

'Yes, Guv.'

They sat in silence for - what seemed to Jones - like an eternity before McLeish said, 'Had anything back from forensics?'

'I've asked them to make the clothes and shoes a priority, but you know what they're like?'

'Yeah.'

As Jones looked across at Fox House, McLeish read her mind. 'Reckon he's slipped out the gent's window?'

Jones smiled. 'Solicitor? Third floor?'

'Yeah. Been in there...' McLeish checked her watch. '...just over half-an-hour. Car's the silver Rolls, parked on the quay.'

223

'Well, I can't wait any longer. Keep the chauffeur company.'

Jones walked to the side entrance of Fox House, but had to step aside and wait as a gaggle of office workers spilled onto the street.

McLeish made her way over to the Rolls and, before the chauffeur had time to look up from his *Daily Mirror,* she'd opened the passenger door and slid beside him.

'Don't mind me.' She flashed her warrant card. 'Finished with the sports page?'

'My guv'nor's not going to like this.'

'Just relax and let's enjoy our time together, shall we? You don't have a fag I could cadge, do you?'

Jones took the stairs to the suite of offices on the third floor from where Stewart Lander's solicitor plied his trade. A receptionist with the widest grin this side of the River Fal greeted her...

'Good afternoon. How can I help you?'

Jones walked over to the window and looked across the estuary and out to the sea. 'Nice view.'

The receptionist took another call and passed it on. 'Do you have an appointment?'

'I presume Mr Lander won't be long?'

'Perhaps I could I help you?'

Jones glanced down the corridor and saw a tall, well-built man, with close-cropped hair and sunglasses leaning against the wall. Sunglasses, she thought. John Hartley, Lander's bodyguard, cum security expert, cum helicopter pilot.

She sat down, picked up a back copy of *The Tatler,* and watched the receptionist punch a pre-dial. Someone must have responded immediately and a short, grey-haired man in his late fifties bumbled his way into reception, anxious eyes fixed on Jones, his voice high-pitched and breathless.

'Can I...' *wheeze.* '...help you?'

224

'You should get some new magazines. Feels more like a dentist's waiting room.' Jones showed her warrant card. 'I'd be awfully grateful if you'd let Stewart Lander know he has a visitor.'

'Look, I'm not sure what this is all about, but you can't...'

'It's OK Ralph.' Lander walked along the corridor, closely followed by John Hartley. 'Detective Inspector Jones is not known for her tact or civility. What is it, Lydia? What do you want?'

'A quiet word.' She turned to the solicitor. 'Is there a room we could use?'

'I'll buy a coffee.' Lander took hold of her forearm and led her to the stairs.

'I wouldn't stray far from your offices, Ralph,' Jones called at the foot of the first flight. 'Your services may yet be required.'

She followed Lander out of Fox House, across the car park, and past the Rolls.

McLeish waved languorously. The chauffeur smiled weakly and shrugged his shoulders.

'This had better be good, Lydia. That was an important meeting.'

'Sorting out your prenup?'

'None of your business.'

Jones stopped abruptly. 'Call off the gorilla.'

Lander nodded at Hartley and he stood to one side.

They crossed to a table outside the *Quayside Inn* and, after a waitress had taken their order, Lander said, 'I've a helicopter to London in an hour.'

'Postpone it.'

'Can't do that.'

'Couple of hours should be enough.'

'You want to tell me what this is about?'

Jones stared across the estuary. The sun disappeared behind clouds mushrooming from the west. Her mood was tempered by a sudden sense of loss. It had crept up on her from nowhere and, like the clouds, it had sent a chill running through her as if she was experiencing his pain before she twisted the knife.

'How well d'you know Kate?'

'Oh, for God's sake, you're not still…'

'Your private investigator didn't find anything when he checked her background. No records, no addresses, no family…nothing, until Kate Madison flew from LA and touched down at Heathrow. Didn't that ring any alarm bells? Why didn't you persuade your father to dig deeper? Were you afraid of what you might find?'

'We all have a history.'

'Just answer the question.'

'You're enjoying this, aren't you?'

'I make no apology for doing my job. So? Kate? How well do you know her?'

'Sorry, I'm not going to play this game. Not 'til you tell me what's going on.'

'OK. We'll do it the hard way.' She flipped open her mobile, dialled a pre-set and the Rolls eased forward, swung round and drew up in front of them. McLeish climbed out and led John Hartley to the unmarked car.

'You're arresting me?' Lander asked.

'No, but we need to go somewhere quiet. You won't want anyone else to hear what I've got to say.'

*

226

Lizzie was sitting at the piano when she heard the car pull into the drive. She sighed and closed the fallboard. Through the window she saw the Mercedes shudder to a halt behind the Sebring.

She glanced round at the phone resting on the arm of the sofa. She was indecisive, momentarily, and by the time she'd grabbed it and started to dial, Kate Madison had slammed the car door and was making her way down the path.

She replaced the phone in its cradle and waited.

Madison rapped on the front door with an urgency and force that startled Lizzie. The sound reverberated, unsettling the tranquillity.

Madison struck the door again, three times, more urgent, demanding.

Lizzie took a breath, tidied her hair, glanced in the mirror over the fireplace and opened the door.

'Kate? What a lovely surprise.'

Lizzie lent forward and kissed her on the cheek, but Madison brushed past her and stepped into the centre of the small lounge. 'I should have called, I know. But, I was passing.'

Lizzie could see she was nervous and she wondered if Madison's antenna was tuned to the same frequency and had picked up on her own apprehension?

'You OK?' Lizzie asked.

'Me? Yes, why wouldn't I be?'

'Tea?'

'What?'

'Tea.'

'Yes. Yes.'

'Here, sit down.' Lizzie picked the phone off the sofa and placed it on its cradle on a side table by the wall. 'You sure you're ok?'

'Yes.'

227

Lizzie retreated to the kitchen, filled the kettle and, as she switched it on, she was surprised to find Madison standing behind her. She smiled at her. 'I meant what I said. It's lovely to see you.'

'I was in the area. I...'

She seemed preoccupied and Lizzie used the lull to open a tin of biscuits and offer them. Madison took one and bit into it, seemingly distracted.

'I hope,' Madison said, 'that I didn't disgrace myself the other evening?'

'God, no. What makes you think..?'

'Falling asleep. Not exactly recommended in the *Good Hostess Guide,* is it?'

Lizzie laughed and took cups down from a cupboard above the work surface. 'If I had a pound for every time I let my hair down.'

'Just wanted it to be perfect, you know? It's been such a difficult time, especially for Stewart.'

'You were with him, weren't you?'

'Richard? Yes. It was awful.'

'Was he wearing a riding hat?'

'Lizzie, you're beginning to sound like Lydia. Of course he was wearing a hat.' She sounded defensive, her words, Lizzie realised, tinged with anger.

'Sorry. It's an occupational hazard...living with a cop.' Lizzie tried to laugh. 'Sugar?'

'What?'

'In your tea.' She poured hot water into cups.

'Has she said anything to you?' Madison asked.

'Who?'

'Lydia, of course.'

'Lydia?'

'About the investigation into Chris Baldwin's death.'

'No. Why would she? We don't talk shop. Well, try not too.'

'It's just...'

'Shall we sit outside? It's such a lovely day?'

Lizzie led her through the lounge, out the back door to the garden and placed the tray on a grubby, wooden picnic table.

'It's just…'

'Another biscuit?'

'What? No.' Madison hesitated, sipped her tea, and said, 'Lizzie, I need to talk to you.'

'Sounds ominous.'

'Stewart…' She seemed unsure. 'We've had words.'

'Words?'

'An argument. Well, not really an argument. God, I don't' know. We'd met before, ten years ago. He didn't remember or recognise me.'

'Long time ago.'

'It was late afternoon and I was on my way home from school. We'd had a careers talk – young cop from the Met, would you believe. I didn't want to go home and stopped off in Greenwich Park. I was lying on a bench when Stewart found me…'

'Found you?'

'You know…he was walking past. Anyway, he stopped, we chatted and he gave me a name card. Asked me to get in touch. I promised I would and kept the card. I've had it all these years. He found it. Accused me of lying.'

'Lying?'

'Well, I'm not sure what he thought, to be honest. At dinner the other night I was so happy - you know, telling you about the wedding…'

'It was a fun evening.'

Lizzie watched Madison scrunch her serviette.

'It was the way Lydia looked at me just before you played. I'd asked about the investigation and she said something about *waiting for forensics* before they could

229

make an arrest. She stared at me for ages. Made me feel guilty just by looking at me.'

'Probably nothing.'

'What do you mean, probably? She's said something, hasn't she?' The pitch of her voice had fallen.

It was as though the air had turned cold and all Lizzie could muster was, 'Lydia? About what?'

'I knew it. She *has* been talking to you, hasn't she? She thinks I had something to do with Chris Baldwin's death?'

'Now you're being paranoid.'

'No.' Madison stood up and threw the serviette on the table. 'No, I'm not. Stewart's had a private detective snooping around, going through my personal stuff.'

'What?' Lizzie didn't know what else to say and felt isolated suddenly, cut off, in the garden, in the middle of nowhere, staring across a table at someone who may, if Jones was right, have murdered several people. She felt lightheaded, dreaming, a nightmare over which - like all nightmares - she had no control.

They drove out of town, through Penryn and down Love Lane to Frank Walker's boatyard, where Jones and Lander got out of the Rolls and walked to the jetty. McLeish and Hartley followed in the unmarked car, got out and stood nearby.

'You know that I'm investigating the murders of Chris Baldwin and Geoffrey D'Ancey...'

'An arrest is imminent. You said, during dinner.' He shrugged, and lifted empty hands. 'That's it? You disrupt an important meeting, delay my flight to London, and drive me all the way out here to tell me what I already know?'

'Enquiries have uncovered two more deaths that may, at the very least, be categorised as suspicious. Two men who, like our friend the Judge, discovered the meaning of terminal velocity the hard way.' Jones paused. 'A fifth man was found here, inside the boathouse, with a knife buried in his back.'

She looked at Lander. His face was locked in anger, his jaw muscles were working overtime and his mouth was small and pinched. He shook his head and turned to watch high tide surge past the jetty. 'And what's this got to do with me or my fiancée?'

The time wasn't right, not quite. Instead, she said, 'I asked you how well you knew Kate?'

'How well do you have to know someone before you're allowed to fall in love? What was it? Three days? Three whole days before you shacked up with Lizzie?'

'I'm not worth a fortune.'

'This is not about Kate, is it? It's about us, you and me. About Emma. About her suicide. Payback for something I had no control over. This, DI Lydia-big-shot-Jones, is retribution and I don't intend to put up with this charade any longer. You were right. My solicitor's services will be required.' Lander took out his mobile.

'I intend to search your home.'

'Oh, for Christ's sake.'

'Before you make that call, hear me out.' Jones held up her hands like a ham actor in an old western, hoping to buy time, knowing the respite would only delay his torment. 'Kate's real name is Jennifer West.'

'Jennifer?'

'She didn't tell you, did she?'

'Why should she?'

'It's part of being in love. No secrets.'

'So, Lizzie tells you everything, does she? Who she's screwing on tour?'

'Oh, come on. You can do better than that.'

'Don't be naïve. I know the people in the industry. I work with them. I see what they get up to.'

Jones smiled. She managed to hold the smile for few seconds before it faltered. She tried to dismiss fleeting images of Lizzie with another woman, or man. The spell fragmented when she heard Stewart Lander say, 'People change their name for all sorts of reasons.'

'Yes,' she said. 'To escape prosecution for one.' She could see he was struggling. It was a good sign, a sign she was pressing the right buttons.

'Actually, Inspector,' he said. 'I did know.' He took a name card out of his waistcoat pocket and handed it to her.

She flipped it over and, despite its condition, could make out Stewart's name and a contact number scrawled beneath the name of his father's Company.

'You must have made quite an impression.'

'A randy twenty-one year old,' he said, 'looking to score. Sport, nothing more.'

'You gave her your number.'

'I was on my way to see my parents and had cut through Greenwich Park. She was lying on a bench. Just left school, so she said. She was quite stunning, even then.'

'You said you'd like to see her again?'

'Yes. You know, like you do. Thought nothing of it.' He was quiet, managed a chuckle. It sounded hollow. 'She lied about her age.'

'Didn't we all?'

'She told me she had a modelling contract, had her eye on Hollywood. *I will marry well*, she said.' He dropped his head into his hands.

'And when she explained why she still had the card and why she'd kept it hidden, you believed her?'

'She told me she was afraid that I'd think the meeting at the Yacht Club was a set up, and she just *happened* to be at the film premiere.'

'I asked if you believed her?'

'Yes, yes of course. What else am I to think?'

'Clawing her way into your affections may have cost at least two people their lives.'

'Your mind's made up then?'

'The evidence stacks up. You want me to run through it again?'

Lander shook his head. 'I don't believe it.'

'We think Jennifer West left for LA when she was sixteen. And, when she returned to the UK, it was Kate Madison who touched down at Heathrow.'

'And Baldwin? D'Ancey?'

'We haven't linked them formerly, but evidence points that way. I'm sorry.'

'Oh, you will be, Inspector. Make no mistake...' He turned on her, his fists clenched. McLeish stubbed out her cigarette and John Hartley looked wired to intervene.

Jones held up her hand to keep them both at bay.

'We'll want to check her passport. My guess is it's a forgery. Even if she claims Madison's a stage name, her passport should have her birth name the letters *aka* and her assumed name.'

'If you're so fucking certain...' He turned and moved away. His language was deteriorating, a sure sign that frustration was beginning to overwhelm him. '...If you're so certain, why are we here, on a riverbank? Why aren't we in an interview room somewhere, with you, your Sergeant...me confessing I'd known all along, my lawyer advising no comment? Could it be that the great DI doesn't have a case?'

He spun round and McLeish and Hartley took several steps forward, Jones putting them on hold again.

'You think I'm stupid? Do you think I'd let Kate into my life if I thought she'd killed someone?'

'She's had help.'

'Help? An accomplice? A whole fucking army?'

Jones waited - resolution soaked by compassion.

'I'd hoped you'd cooperate, maybe help us eliminate her from our enquiries, provide the alibi she's going to need. I'd hoped we'd come to an understanding and sort this out between us. I misjudged things. I'm sorry. We'll continue down at the station. I'll arrange for a search warrant.'

'You've just accused the woman I love of murder. How did you expect me to react?'

'Let's sit down.'

She walked over to the top step of the jetty, waited for Lander to join her and spent twenty minutes outlining much of the evidence the CPS would submit to local Magistrates. By the time she had finished, he'd crumbled, shoulders sagging, chin on chest, his head rocking gently from side to side. Jones put a hand on his shoulder and Lander lifted his head, tears dammed in his eyes.

'In my heart,' he said, his voice cold, 'I know you're wrong. Kate may be many things, but she's not capable of murder.'

She hadn't told him about Albert.

His father's murder would keep.

'SOCO are on stand-by,' she said. 'We'll do this by the book. A warrant.'

'I'll want to be present.'

'It would be better if Kate wasn't, but that's your call. The rest of the household should be kept in the dark, if only to keep things out of the media.'

'You have it all worked out, don't you?'

'Pretty much.'

Lander paced, his breathing laboured, then turned and stabbed a finger at her. 'If you're wrong about Kate - and I believe you are - you must know that I *will* destroy you?'

Albert was the only member of the household who knew what was happening. He'd told Jones that Madison had insisted on private quarters. Until they were married, she'd reasoned, her reputation was important. Oddly, Jones thought as Albert led the way to her bedroom, they'd fallen for it. She knew that parents could be hypocritical when it came to their offspring's sexual odyssey and maybe, just maybe, Richard Lander had seen it as a sign of Madison's sincerity, her commitment. For all Jones knew, he may even have considered it quaint, a throwback to the days of propriety and chastity.

Chastity? Jenny West? Chaste? It was all Jones could do not to laugh out loud, but then, just as suddenly, she felt angry with Stewart and his father for being so stupid. Madison got her way and the suite was refurbished, money no object.

She might have needed her own space, but Jones placed a bet with herself it wasn't because she wanted to preserve her modesty. Madison had something to hide...

They concentrated on two rooms.

Madison's bedroom, with its sofa, two arm chairs, a writing desk, super-king bed, and a balcony overlooking meadows sweeping down to cliffs and the sea - and her bathroom with an en suite and a separate walk-in closet. The closet, Albert had explained, doubled as a panic room.

Anything SOCO disturbed, was replaced as they'd found it. Digital photographs were used to make sure the alignment was exact. Clothing presented a particularly difficult challenge because seams couldn't be ripped, or fabric left crumpled or folded incorrectly. The medicine cabinet in the bathroom was emptied, each item replaced on the same shelf, in the same place. They removed the floor of the wardrobe and screwed it back. They picked the lock on her writing desk, searched it, and then replaced and relocked each of the drawers.

When one of the SOCOs asked McLeish what they were looking for she'd shrugged, raised it with Jones and got a terse, 'I'll know when I see it.'

After an hour, they'd found nothing and were about to shut up shop when they started on a pair of antique Chinese bedside cabinets. Like many pieces of furniture of that age and provenance, secrecy was a high priority. It took fifteen minutes to work out how compartments interlocked and another ten to extricate each drawer until, towards the back, they found a plastic wallet.

'Guv?' McLeish emptied the contents onto a white cotton sheet and stepped back whilst Jones examined them.

After a few moments, Jones sighed. 'We're done here.'

'You OK?'

'Clear the room. I need to talk to Stewart, alone.'

'We still on for this afternoon?'

'Yes.' Jones hesitated. 'Put everyone on standby. Clear the building.'

'You want me to stay?'

'Yes. I'll interview Madison informally, and then crank it up, caution her. I don't want the clock to start ticking before we've had a chance to get under her skin.' Jones shrugged the tension from her shoulders. 'Where's George?'

'Back at base, coordinating the search for Simpkiss.'

'Hasn't located the place he's renovating?'

'Not yet.'

'He can't have disappeared.' She felt uneasy. 'Tell George to get over to my cottage. I need someone I can trust with Lizzie's life.'

'You serious, Guv?'

'Probably overkill. But, if Missy's history's anything to go by, and with Simpkiss on the loose, I can't take any chances. Draft in Andy Thompson to assist.'

'Does it have to be Handy Andy, Guv? Only, he and George don't exactly…'

'Yeah, I know, but everyone else is involved here.'

'And Lizzie?'

'I'll square it with her. Now, go and tell Mr Lander I'd like to see him.'

McLeish saw John Hartley outside the drawing room. She nodded and he opened the door. She found Stewart Lander with his back to the fireplace and a glass of whisky in his hand.

'DI Jones requests the pleasure.'

'Does she?'

'If you don't mind.'

Lander's laugh sounded derisive, but he didn't say anything. Instead, he shook his head, placed his glass on the mantelpiece and left the room.

'Stewart.'

Jones looked across at John Hartley.

Lander nodded, Hartley left, and Jones led him to a seat beneath the bay window.

'We've found a California driving licence and four passports.'

'Four?'

Jones held up a plastic evidence bag.

'Jennifer West…her first, I'd guess, and the one she used to travel to the States. In this, she's calling herself

Alison Fairweather. Long blond hair cascading over her shoulders, doll like, wouldn't you say? It's the same as the photo on her driving licence. And this is one you will recognise. Kate Madison.'

She gave Lander time to study them.

'Doesn't prove anything.'

'No, in itself, it doesn't, you're right. But why would anyone want, or need, four passports, each in a different name? How did she get them? And who supplied them? A lot of unanswered questions, don't you think?'

'They don't prove a thing.' Lander pointed at her, and rolled his hand into a fist. 'You know it as well as I do.' His composure was crumbling. His gestures had become exaggerated and threatening. His pale skin was suffused bright pink and his mouth was locked in a snarl, spittle seeping from the corners.

Jones stood her ground. 'The fourth passport looks new. It's in the name of Zoe Radclyffe.' She held up an evidence bag. 'Expensive looking wig.'

Lander stared at it, but didn't say anything.

'Checked your bank accounts recently?' Jones said. 'She has access to your money, doesn't she...all those expense accounts in West End shops. Or has she been salting it away over time? Looks like she's planning to do a runner.'

'And, what does your crystal ball tell you, Inspector? Before or after the wedding?'

Jones shrugged. 'Your guess is as good as mine, but I'd say she'd want to go the whole nine yards, wouldn't you? Just in case she changes her mind and decides to settle down with you and be the dutiful wife?'

They sat in silence, Jones allowing Lander to soak up the reality of what was painfully obvious and hoping he'd calm down. She tried to keep her voice as neutral as possible, but knew what she was about to say would be more distressing than anything so far, for both of them.

'There's one thing I haven't told you.'

'What could be worse?' Lander's face was a mixture of anger and resignation. 'It's not every day I find out the woman I love has lived rough, been a whore, stabbed two people, and thinks nothing of using her beauty and sexual magnetism to lure men to their death.' He looked at Jones, the pain stamped across his face. 'What is this? What's happening? Is this payback time?'

'I told you, this has nothing to do with Emma.'

'But you're enjoying it, aren't you?' He stood up and started pacing about the room. 'Have you finished?' He stopped suddenly, slumped onto the sofa, grabbed a cushion and hugged it.

'Your father...' Jones tried to stay calm.

'Oh, God, no.'

'He confronted Kate on the evening before he died. She'd met Chris Baldwin. He wanted to be sure she wasn't two timing you again.'

'Again?'

'She was Baldwin's lover when you met at the Yacht Club. You're father hired an investigator...'

'To run the background checks. Always did.'

'A different one, with a brief to find out if she was lying about Baldwin.' Jones was unsure if Lander was listening. She slid photographs from an envelope and placed them in front of him. 'The investigator took these photographs of Kate and Baldwin about a week before your father died. She'd told Richard she was having nothing more to do with Baldwin. But he was persistent, came down several times, tried to persuade her to marry him. His infatuation led to his death. The skipper who took him on his final dive was stabbed two days ago.'

'She was with my father when he died.' He began to rock against the cushion, shaking his head slowly and staring across the room towards bright sun that steamed through the window. 'You'll be arresting her today?'

239

'Bringing her in for questioning, under caution.'

'I'll be able to see her?'

'Not immediately. Not if we detain her. She'll be informed of her rights and, if she asks us to contact you, you'll be notified. You might like to get your legal team out of bed. She'll be entitled to representation as soon as the clock starts. We'll hold her for twenty-four hours and then, if the Superintendent agrees, that'll be extended to forty-eight.' She waited, not wanting to sound trite. 'I'm truly sorry, Stewart. If there is anything I can do?'

'I think you've done more than enough, don't you?' His mobile rang. He discarded the cushion and wiped his eyes. He flipped open the mobile, checked the caller ID, gulped in air and brushing hair off his forehead. 'Hi.' He turned his back on Jones but didn't lower his voice. 'Where are you?' He was quiet again, listening. 'No, nothing's wrong. Had to reschedule my trip, that's all. Something's come up. It would help if you could come home. I'll explain when I see you.' He listened again, then said, 'I love you.' He took his time closing the phone, then replaced it in his shirt pocket, slipped both hands between his knees and began to rock gently.

'Where is she?' Jones asked.

He looked up at her, and she could see a mixture of fear and contempt in his eyes.

'With Lizzie.'

The sun disappeared behind thunderclouds billowing from the west and Lizzie suggested they move inside. She was glad to have the chance to relieve some of the tension in her body, but knew she had to keep Madison talking. She needed to keep her focused on her favourite subjects (herself, her fiancé, and life after their wedding) but knew they'd have to return, eventually, to Madison's most pressing concern: the inconvenient truth that DI Lydia Jones was gunning for her.

Madison followed her into the kitchen, placed the tray on the work surface and dropped the cups into the washing up bowl. 'Thanks.'

'Can't beat tea and biscuits,' Lizzie said.

'I meant, for listening.'

'Isn't that what friends are for?'

'Does that mean you'll be there, at the wedding?'

'And why wouldn't I be?' Lizzie said and wished she hadn't.

'*Am* I a suspect?'

'I told you...'

'Yes. No pillow talk. I get it.' Madison wavered, but there was anger in her eyes. 'Sorry,' she said.

'You're here, aren't you? They haven't locked you away from us, thrown away the key?'

'Us?'

'A risk to society, and all that?' Lizzie forced a smile. 'Listen,' she said, and took Madison's hands, 'this isn't a game that cops play. If you were a suspect, they'd either have you under surveillance or you'd be cooling your heels in a cell down at the station.' She looked around. 'And do you see any burly officers in bulletproof vests hiding in bushes?'

Kate shook her head and for the first time Lizzie thought she saw a sad and vulnerable little girl trying to make sense of it all.

'Yes, you're right, I suppose,' Madison said, and hugged her. 'Thank you.'

'It's a pity you've brought your car.' Lizzie held her close, wondering what to do next, hoping she'd take the non-too subtle hint and leave. 'I'd offer you something stronger.'

Madison tightened her grip and then pulled away. 'I need a tissue and a pee.'

'But not necessarily in that order?' Lizzie smiled, compassion getting the better of her. She ran a hand over Madison's cropped hair and shuddered involuntarily as images she'd seen in the Incident Room flooded back. 'Top of the stairs, second left.'

Lizzie heard the bathroom door close and, as the bolt slid across, she hurried across to the sofa and grabbed the phone. As she waited, she looked out of the window at the first drops of rain and heard thunder rumbling in the distance. Crows circled overhead, some settling in a large tree, sensing the storm was about to break, others, on the wing, chasing down a meal.

'It's me,' she said. 'She's here. Kate. Yes, Kate, for God's sake. In the bathroom.' She listened. 'What? Why?' She looked through the window at an unmarked car in the lane at the top of the drive. 'They're here. Jesus Christ, Lydia, what's going on?'

She didn't hear her come down the stairs. 'What are you doing?' Madison stood, mobile in hand.

'What?'

'Who are you calling?'

'What do you mean, who am I calling?'

'And I thought you were my friend.'

'I was just…' Lizzie replaced the phone and glanced through the window and up the driveway.

'Looks like you've got company,' Madison said. She opened the cottage door, walked a few paces up the driveway, made a brief phone call, turned, retraced her steps, lent forward, kissed Lizzie on the cheek and whispered, 'Goodbye, my friend.'

*

Jones had spoken with DC Andy Thompson but that hadn't stopped him grumbling long before they got into an unmarked car. He was resentful. *I'm not a fucking baby-sitting service,* he'd told Tregunna, and *not only that* he'd been half-an-hour from the end of a shift and had already bought a twelve-pack in preparation for a close-season friendly on SKY that afternoon. Tregunna had waited until the rant finished and then reiterated the DI's instructions to stay vigilant, maintain radio silence, but leave channels open.

They'd driven out of town, along coastal roads and down narrow lanes, silent throughout the journey. They slowed as they approached the low, dry-stone wall that enclosed the cottage.

'This is it,' Tregunna said. He slowed to a halt. 'Two cars in the driveway. And two women. One getting into a Merc, the other standing at the door.'

'Jesus,' Thompson muttered. 'I'll have to get my eyes tested. I've got double vision. Both fucking gorgeous.' He sniggered.

Tregunna shook his head. 'Wait until the Merc's out of the way, then park behind the Sebring.'

'She expecting us?'

'DI said she'd phone her.'

They watched the Mercedes back up the drive and, as it neared the gate, Tregunna jumped out, beckoned it onto the road and had to move quickly out of the way as its wheels screamed for purchase and the car accelerated down the lane. Thompson eased the squad car through the gate and along the drive as Tregunna closed the gate.

Lizzie was standing in the doorway, her face locked in a scowl that George would be able use to strip the wallpaper in his room at *The Crows Nest*.

She managed to drag humour from somewhere.

'Hope you like prison food?'

'Nice motor,' Thompson said. He circled the Sebring and kicked a back tyre.

'It's a kit car.'

'And you built it, yeah?'

'Do I look like a mechanic to you, Constable?'

'So, who..?'

'The DI's father.' She took clothing off the washing line and carried it inside.

'Would be nice to know,' Thompson said when she was out of earshot, 'why we've been asked to babysit the dyke DI's bit of skirt.' He grinned.

'You're not man enough to say that to her face.'

'Love to be a fly on the wall when they...'

Tregunna shook his head, but couldn't muster the energy to combat Thompson's cesspit of a mind.

'Word is, she's on someone's hit list.'

'Oh, great.'

'Relax,' Tregunna said. 'If she was really at risk, do you think the DI would trust you with her safety? Come on, let's get cracking.'

Lizzie reappeared at the door. 'I've put the kettle on.'

'Thanks. We'll be in as soon as we've swept outside.'

'You're here to protect me, not tidy up.'

'No, I meant...'

'I know what you meant, Constable, but I'm not good at being cooped up in my own home. You'll forgive me if I amuse myself at your expense.'

She went back inside.

Tregunna noticed Thompson giving her the once over and thumped him on the arm.

'Shit! What the fuck?'

'Concentrate,' Tregunna said. 'Ogling's not on the agenda. Keeping her alive is.' He sent him off to check the rear of the house and the back garden, and caught up with him five minutes later. 'OK. The perimeter seems secure. What do you think?'

'Fucking sieve's got fewer holes.' Thompson shook his head and looked at the dry-stone, perimeter wall. 'Fucking Shetland pony could hop over that. Why the fuck didn't they just stick her in a cell for the night and let the rest of us get on with our lives?'

'Watch your mouth.' Tregunna moved close enough to smell Thompson's body odour. 'You wouldn't want to give the impression that all coppers are foul-mouthed pricks, would you?'

White vans brought SOCO and uniformed police to the Hall and the staff were told that the Hall had to be evacuated for a few hours so that John Hartley could carry out safety and security checks. They were taken out of a side entrance, loaded into a coach with blacked out windows, then driven out of the main gates, past the paparazzi, and taken to a local community centre where they were offered a choice of snack and drink.

Jones stood in the near empty house.

The air was cold. The stone was cold.

She wondered if Stewart would ever forgive her. She shuddered. *'Someone's walking over your grave,'* her father would have said.

Brenda McLeish escorted Stewart Lander across the lawn to a gravelled area where a table had been prepared on a terrace above a flight of steps leading down to the formal gardens. They stood and waited for Jones to join them. When she did, she checked the contents of a large hamper on the table. A few moments later, they heard the Rolls crushing gravel as it swept into the drive.

'Stay here,' Jones said, and went to greet her.

'Lydia?' Madison got out of the car and hurried to the front door. 'What are you doing here? Where's Stewart?'

'Waiting in the garden.'

'Waiting?'

Madison walked past her and into the house, leaving Jones in her wake.

She caught up with her in the drawing room.

'It's about time we talked.'

'Talked?'

'Informally. Help with our enquiries. Perhaps a stroll in the garden? I need some air. After you.' Jones stood aside and waved her through to the rear of the house. 'Stewart asked to be present. You don't mind?'

'Mind? Why should I mind?'

Jones opened the French windows, stepped into the garden and tried to clear her head, knowing that such a high-risk strategy could go either way. She'd been given the green light after explaining to Hinkson that she needed to rattle Madison - the supreme liar for whom normal interrogation would be a walk in the park. She needed to see if she could get Madison to react...before she was arrested, cautioned, brought in for questioning, and the clock started ticking.

The sun was high and fierce in the June sky and the estate rolled gently away towards the vast sweep of the bay and the steep cliffs that dominated the shoreline.

Jones led Madison to the picnic table. Stewart Lander was standing alongside McLeish, his back towards them.

As soon as she saw him, Madison ran, calling out his name and, as he turned, she threw herself into his arms.

He held her, looking over his shoulder at Jones.

'What's happening?' Madison had noticed uniformed police searching a copse, partially hidden by a circle of tress and thick bushes, a hundred metres from the house.

'They're looking for clues,' Jones said.

'Clues?'

'It's where Stewart's father was killed.'

246

'She's well aware of that,' Lander said. 'They've been over that ground a thousand times.'

'We've reopened the case.'

'Reopened? Why?'

'I asked them to.'

'I don't understand. I was there when it happened.' Madison looked confused. 'It was an accident.'

'He fell. Broke his neck,' Lander said, his voice edged with anxiety. 'The Coroner's inquest. You must have read the report, Inspector. Accidental death. Kate gave evidence. Don't you believe her?'

Jones remained calm. She turned to Madison. 'Please, follow me?' She led them to the copse. Behind trees, and hidden from the house, was a large outcrop of rock that had been cordoned off. 'This is where he fell?'

'Oh, Lydia, do we have to do this?'

Jones called over one of the police officers and asked him to lie down.

'It *was* an accident,' Lander said.

'Yes, of course.' Jones stood over the officer, but her question was directed at Madison. 'You'd been riding for about an hour and were returning to the house?'

'Yes.'

'You arrived together?'

'Yes. Well, no. I was a few minutes behind.'

'So, you'd challenged him to a race, finishing here?'

'Not exactly a race.'

'And his horse was startled by something?'

'I suppose so. I didn't actually see him fall.'

'But when you caught up, he was lying here?' Jones looked down at the officer.

'Yes. Well, I can't be sure if that was exactly where he fell.' Madison looked at Jones, her body language defiant.

Jones offered a hand to the officer on the floor.

'Thanks, Guv. I can manage.'

He got to his feet, dusted down his uniform and re-joined others overseeing the SOCOs.

She turned to Madison and smiled. 'We may decide to exhume Mr Lander's body.'

'Why?' Madison's face flushed, her eyes snapping from Lander to the ground.

Jones crouched and rubbed her hand where the police officer's head had rested. 'I don't think he fell off his horse. I think he dismounted, he was knocked to the ground, and his killer smashed his head on a rock.'

'Killer? You mean he was murdered?' Lander said.

'But that's impossible. I didn't see anyone.' Madison hesitated. 'But, that's awful. Why would anyone?'

'That's what's been puzzling me. Why would anyone want to harm the old man?' Jones shrugged, raising her hands skywards, as though the mystery was impossible to unravel. She looked at Madison, searching for traces of panic. 'Then I realised the answer was here all the time, staring me in the face.' She took Madison's arm, led her across the open ground and up the steps to the picnic table. She waited for the others to catch up then turned and said, 'to think, Kate, in time, all this will be yours. The wealth, the servants, and the house.'

'That's none of your business,' Lander said.

Jones ignored him. She opened the hamper and took out a bottle of champagne. 'Fine wine and delicacies like these will be your staple diet. Caviar from the Caspian Sea, eaten with a silver spoon. Fresh strawberries served on the finest china. Tables draped in linen.' She smiled at her. 'A life of luxury, never wanting for anything, the world at your feet. It's what you want, isn't it?'

'Inspector?' Lander threatened.

'It's OK, Stewart,' Madison said. There was an edge to her voice and traces of anger and exasperation. 'I will have it all, as you say, when we are married.'

Jones noticed a change in Lander's demeanour and although she couldn't be certain she guessed he could be recalculating the cost of their forthcoming nuptials. She put the bottle of champagne back in the hamper and said, 'But, my dearest Jenny, it's not going to happen, is it? It *is* Jennifer, isn't it? Jennifer West?'

'Lydia?' Madison appeared calm, but a slight tremor in her left hand seemed to suggest otherwise. 'Why are you doing this? What's happening? I don't understand.'

'Remember Colin, Jennifer? Colin Povey. Set you up in a flat in London? Photographed Geoffrey D'Ancey as he raped you?'

Madison didn't flinch. 'Colin was a dear friend, a father figure. He looked after me, cared for me. I was devastated by his death.'

'You pushed him.'

'No. I'd moved out. Went to stay with a friend.'

'Yes, we know all about Julian Wyatt, the artist in the attic. We have two paintings of you. They're the only ones to survive the night you destroyed the other canvasses and turned the knife on Julian.'

'I'm sorry, Lydia, I'm not sure where this is going, who you've been talking to, or what you've been told, but I stayed with Julian for a couple of weeks before he lent me the money to buy a ticket to the States.'

'You see Jenny, if you'd stopped at the murder of your father, Colin Povey and Geoffrey D'Ancey, all of whom abused you in one way or another, there would be those who'd have some sympathy, might even applaud you. All three men would have got what they deserved - their 'just deserts'. But you couldn't stop, could you, not with the big prize in sight, all this wealth, this luxury?'

'Inspector?' Lander said.

'My father was drunk,' Madison said. 'He fell. Can't say I was sorry, but I had nothing to do with his death.'

'You're right, of course. Prosecution's going to have a hard time selling that one and the CPS may decide there's not enough evidence to proceed in the Colin Povey case.'

'I don't have to listen to this,' Madison said.

''Fraid you do.'

'Stewart, I want a lawyer.'

'I agree. This has gone far enough.'

Lander took Madison by the arm.

They turned, as if intent on leaving, but Madison stopped dead in her tracks when Jones said, 'You'll remember Jonathan Harrison?'

'Jonathan?' She turned around.

'You stabbed him.'

'That was ten years ago.'

'Stabbed him in the chest and accused him of rape.'

'Because he *did* try to rape me, for Christ's sake!'

'An adolescent crush. All he wanted was a kiss.' Jones smiled, and changed tack. 'We've spoken to the stable girl who took the flack for not securing Richard's bridle. She says it was very secure.'

'Well, she would, wouldn't she?'

'She says he was wearing a hat.'

'He was.'

'One like this?'

Jones put her hand in the hamper and pulled out a riding hat secured in a plastic bag. 'It's a new range. Very fashionable. Bright colours.' She rapped it with her knuckles. 'Plastic? Polycarbonate, maybe? Super strong. We've found Richard's DNA, but someone got careless, thought they'd wiped it clean, but missed a thumbprint. It's not yours. We're checking the national database…'

'I shouted out for help. Someone came, one of the groundsmen, I think. He took Richard's hat off and gave him the kiss of life.'

'He'd stopped breathing?' Lander asked.

250

'I guess. Why else would he..?'

'You should've left him where he was,' Lander said, 'and waited until the ambulance arrived.'

Jones didn't take her eyes off Madison. 'But why would anyone want to wipe fingerprints from the riding hat?' She turned to McLeish. 'Sergeant, get Uniform to re-interview any staff who came to help Miss Madison and get on to the ambulance crew.'

'Yes, Guv.'

Jones reached into the hamper. 'We found these.' She pulled out the pair of city shoes. 'You recognise them? No? Jam-packed with Chris Baldwin's DNA.' She tilted her head. 'For argument's sake, let's say Baldwin hid behind that tree over there.'

'Baldwin?'

'Someone else, then? Your stepbrother?'

'My stepbrother?'

'Peter Brooks?'

'Peter?'

'Arrested outside a nightclub?'

'Ten years ago. Sent down, for all I know.'

'Whether it was Baldwin or Brooks, it's only a matter of time before SOCO finish working their magic.'

'Why the hell would I want to kill the old man?'

'Oh, that's easy...' Jones waved her arm in an arc that encompassed the house and the estate. 'He was about to advise Stewart to dump you.'

'Stewart, tell her just how crazy this is.'

'Inspector?'

'No,' Jones said, 'you're right. We should do this by the book. Sergeant,' She turned to McLeish. 'Perhaps you'd do the honours?'

McLeish stepped forward.

'Wait,' Lander said, 'there must be something you're not telling us?'

251

'Look, what would I gain by murdering someone?' Madison pleaded. 'Do I look like someone who'd resort to murder?'

'You're extraordinarily beautiful, Jenny.'

'Stop calling me that.'

'Alison, then? I get confused, all these names. Which one went to see Mr D'Ancey? Was it Kate? No matter, we have forensic evidence and if any of it matches your DNA...'

Madison laughed, shook her head. 'I don't deny visiting Geoffrey. We'd had a drink together at the Ritz. I wanted to get under the skin of the man I was scheduled to interview. I didn't feel I'd gleaned enough information and when he invited me back to his Club, I went.'

'In disguise?'

'Yes, I wore a wig.'

'Used the fire escape?'

'Being discreet. It's called professionalism.'

Jones had heard enough. She nodded at McLeish, who said, 'Jennifer West, I'm arresting you on suspicion of the murder of...'

Madison turned and ran.

McLeish looked at Jones.

'All yours, Sergeant.'

'You have the right to remain silent,' McLeish called, and gave chase.

Madison crossed the lawn outside the drawing room, stopped, pulled her mobile and hit a preset.

They heard her muttering... *Come on. Come on...* and then a brief mixture of anger and expletives before she snapped the phone shut and ran through the open French windows. She stopped, her escape cut off by uniformed officers.

'Jennifer West...' McLeish was struggling for breath. 'You do not have to say anything, but it may harm your defence if you fail...'

'Listen. You're making a terrible mistake.'

'Won't wash, Jennifer. Game's up.' Jones rested against the doorframe. 'Read her the riot act and take her away.'

Tregunna and Thompson had taken shifts, one sitting in an armchair in the lounge listening to the cries of crows and leaves rustling in the breeze, whilst the other crashed out on the sofa, patrolled the garden, or read a magazine. Occasionally, a car would pass, its approach causing heightened anxiety that only abated once the noise of the engine had faded.

Thompson had missed the match, the rabbit's food the DI's skirt had dished-up was playing havoc with his stomach and he found watching the garden grow about as exciting as paint drying. When Lizzie served lunch - more rabbit's food - he'd scraped it under a bush and, after she'd gone upstairs to rest, Tregunna watched him rummage through cupboards in the kitchen until he found a packet of crisps.

The afternoon dragged and Tregunna found himself watching Thompson, asleep on the sofa, his body hanging off the edge, his breathing punctuated by snuffles and snorts. He wasn't surprised that he'd been unable to find a woman desperate enough to live with him. There again, he mused, neither had he, as it turned out.

At five-forty he heard the creak of floorboards, the rush of a shower and the gentle lilt of her voice. He prodded Thompson's backside with his foot and told him to get a fire started while he checked outside.

Bright sunlight had given way to the cool of the evening and Tregunna shivered, stretched, and yawned, gulping down air scented by rose and honeysuckle. The arrest must have happened by now, he assumed, and he checked his personal radio for messages. He wondered if the double shift would be rewarded by time in-lieu? He was due a couple of days, at least, he reasoned, putting himself on the line like this. A couple of days would give him time to get his rooms at *The Nest* sorted. Then he realised he was beginning to think like Thompson and that any time spent in the company of Handy Andy's was detrimental. He smiled, stretched again, and glanced at the bushes, trees and the dry-stone wall. He turned and walked up the path, his footfalls sending a swarm of startled crows screeching into the air.

He reached inside his jacket and wondered what it must be like to carry a firearm? A couple of years back, he'd volunteered to train with members of a tactical response team. He'd been complimented for his *cool head* during the course. Easy to be cool, he'd thought at the time, firing at a static target, and when the final selection was made, and he wasn't chosen, he was quietly relieved. Each time he'd held and fired a gun he'd felt queasy – God knows how he would have felt with a real gun in his hand, real ammunition, in a real situation.

He heard footsteps behind him and spun round to find Lizzie wrapped in an overlarge, white-cotton bathrobe. 'What the hell?' he said. 'Inside. Get inside. Move!' He crouched low, scanned the garden in a wide arc and backed into the cottage. 'Andy,' he said, as he closed the door, sliding bolts top and bottom. 'Thompson!' He turned and glared at Lizzie. 'Stay away from the windows.'

The fire smoking and spitting, drawing air from the room and strength from firelighters packed beneath. The floorboards above creaked and Tregunna hurried to the foot of the stairs.

He paused, conscious of his breathing - laboured, short, and shallow – and, as he began to climb the stairs, he felt the sensation of sweat trickling down his neck and between his thighs.

'Thompson.' His voice strangled. 'Thompson?'

A door at the top of the stairs opened and Handy Andy appeared, struggling with his zip.

'What the..?' Tregunna said.

'What?' Thompson shrugged.

'Where the fuck have you been?'

'Taking a piss, for Christ's sake. What? Now, there's a law against taking a piss?'

Tregunna lent against the wall, threw his head back, breathed out heavily and led Thompson down the stairs.

'I'd like to practise.' Lizzie stood in the kitchen doorway, her shoulder-length hair stark against her white bathrobe. 'The piano?' She glanced at the baby grand nestling in the bay window. 'I must practise. And, please can we open a window and get some fresh air into the place?'

They'd reached the foot of the stairs and Thompson looked at Tregunna, unwilling to take responsibility for any breach in security.

'Sorry ma'am,' Tregunna said. 'But, opening the window's more than my job's worth.'

'I can't practice?'

'I'll get shot if the DI finds out. Sound travels, like a calling card.'

'Very poetic, Constable, although you should try not to mix your metaphors.'

'Ma'am?'

Lizzie smiled. 'You leave DI Jones to me. I need to practice. Twenty minutes. Half-an-hour, tops.'

She sat at the piano, lifted the fallboard, and sat for a few moments before she began a series of scales and arpeggios.

Tregunna and Thompson listened for several minutes before Tregunna's communicator crackled into life.

He snatched it from his lapel. 'Yes? Sorry? What did you say? Yes, Guv...Miss James? Practising, Guv. The piano? Yes, Guv. She's only just...What's that?' He signalled to Thompson, thumbs up. 'Yes, Guv? The news? I'll switch it on. Hang about.' He picked up the remote and pointed it at the television. 'The Super, Guv? Got it. With that Commander from London?'

Lizzie stopped playing. 'Commander Hobson.' She sighed. 'Here, give me that.' Tregunna handed over his personal communicator and she spoke to Jones. 'How's it been?' she said. 'A blast, what else? I'm fine, thank you for asking. The sofa will probably need fumigating. Don't ask. Yes, they've been terrific. No, I'm not being sarcastic. Look, I'm sorry, I appreciate why you...' She shrugged off a smile. 'Yes, me too.' She handed Tregunna the communicator.

He listened intently. 'Yes, Guv. Yes. OK, got that.' He switched it off and looked at Lizzie. 'We've orders to stand down. They're sending a car. You can practice all you want.'

'And open the window?'

'As wide as you like. Here let me.' He lent over the piano, unhooked the latch, and said, 'Thompson, get the front door.'

Andy Thompson released the bolts, pushed the door wide open, then sat on the sofa and switched on the TV.

The newscast had switched to a suicide bombing in Baghdad but, scrolling across the bottom of the screen, the telescript read...

Police have arrested a woman in connection with the murders of MP Geoffrey D'Ancey, and ITV's Chris Baldwin.

Lizzie turned back to the keyboard and started to play a polka - dance music that should have filled the cottage with joy but, as her rendition increased in tempo, her spirits plummeted and her fingers hammered at the keys. She was struggling with the celebration of Kate's arrest. The arrest of someone she'd thought of as a friend...a friend who was about to spend the night behind bars. She struck the final chords, stopped playing, got up and went into the kitchen.

Tregunna looked across at Thompson, shrugged and mouthed. 'I'll go.'

He stood in the doorframe and watched her fill the kettle.

'I suppose you'll want a cup of tea?' she asked, but her question went unanswered as an explosion ripped through the air and shotgun pellets hit Andy Thompson, tearing part of his shoulder, neck and face away, and throwing him across the lounge.

He landed heavily, spread-eagled across the sofa, blood pouring from his wounds.

Tregunna turned to see the silhouette of a large man filling the frame of the front door but, before he had time to react, a second blast slammed into his gut, forcing him to crumple and fall backwards. He fell at Lizzie's feet.

The man stepped forward, his face in shadow, the stench of shotgun fire hanging in the air.

'Fucking amateurs,' he said, surveying his handiwork as he broke the shotgun and rearmed. 'Sent fucking amateurs to look after you darling.'

Lizzie knelt by Tregunna.

'What the fuck d'you think you're playing at?'

'We need to stop the bleeding...'

He grabbed her arm and hauled her to her feet. 'Don't fuck with me lady.' He circled her, snarling into her neck. 'Do what I say or I'll crush each of those delicate little fingers.'

'You won't get away with this,' she said, her voice clear and strong, her heart pounding against her chest. 'Every police force in Britain will be looking for you.'

'That's why you're not only my insurance, but also my trump card.'

'I don't understand.'

'Don't you?' He moved behind her and, as he nestled his face into her hair, he whispered, 'we're going on a trip, you and me. And when we're holed up and out of harm's way, I'm going to contact Detective Inspector Jones and have a cosy chat, see if I can persuade her to drop the charges against my sister.'

'Your sister?'

'Drop the charges...' His whisper gave way as he turned and stepped over Andy Thompson's motionless body. 'Or I'll blow your fucking head off!'

'You don't think anyone's going to listen to you, do you? God, you must be stupid. If she's innocent, why..?'

'Shut the fuck up. Just shut the fuck up.' He planted the muzzle of the shotgun against her forehead.

'Jesus!' She pushed the shotgun to one side and dabbed the burn mark on her forehead.

'That'll leave a lasting impression.' He smirked.

'Kill me and you'll have nothing to bargain with.'

'Only if they know you're dead. How long d'you think they'll keep looking for you? Days? Weeks? How long before you're no longer a priority, before resources have to be diverted?' He hunched his shoulders and opened his arms, inviting an answer.

'You don't get it, do you?' Lizzie said. 'Nobody's going to release Kate just like that, even with me to bargain with. That's not how it works.'

'It does, you know. Witnesses change their minds. Evidence doesn't stack up. She'll get bail and it'll be at least six months before a trial. Plenty of time to arrange a dismissal without prejudice.' He raised the shotgun and Lizzie flinched, convinced he was about to strike her. Instead, he said, calmly, 'and all the time, you'll be hidden away, waiting for your girlfriend to sort it out. And she will you know? She'll do exactly as I ask. It'll be difficult for her, but love will find a way. We're both romantics at heart, see, the DI and me. We believe in overcoming the odds, in finding a way to make things work. Now...' His voice turned into something akin to a snarl. 'Don't fuck with me. Just do as you're told and we'll do just fine.' He stepped away. 'Lose the robe.'

'Oh, for God's sake.'

'The robe.'

'I'm naked.'

'And?'

She looked at Tregunna and Thompson.

'At least let me see if I can help them?'

'Listen, Florence fucking Nightingale. Lose the robe. Now!'

She loosened the belt and the bathrobe slipped from her shoulders. She gathered it in both hands and held it behind her back.

'Nice.' He nodded, staring at her breasts. 'Very nice. Once we've settled in and had time to get to know each other, we'll have some fun, you and me. Something for us both to look forward to.'

He held up a hand, motioning a twirl and, as she spun around he nodded again and pursed his lips. She spun once more, slowly this time and, during the floorshow, she moved the bathrobe from behind to cover her front, allowing him a clear sight of her back, legs and bottom.

He smiled, grabbed a handbag from a small side table and held it up. 'Yours?'

'What do you think?'

'Mobile?'

'Yes.'

'Take it out. Leave it with me.' He waited until she'd passed it to him. 'Now...upstairs, get dressed, and pack. Nothing special. You won't be needing much where you're going.' He turned his back and used the butt of the shotgun to smash the telephone junction box nestling beneath the eaves outside the front door. It took him several attempts, each one more urgent and powerful but, when satisfied they wouldn't be disturbed, he leant the shotgun against the sofa, turned and grinned. 'What are you waiting for? Upstairs, now!'

She gathered her robe and clutched her handbag to her chest. She ran to the bedroom and threw the robe and handbag on the bed. She took a suitcase from the top of the wardrobe and placed it on a chair in the corner. As she pulled open two drawers and selected several items of underwear, her mind screamed retribution, but her anger threatened to render her useless. 'Stay calm,' she muttered several times. 'Stay calm.'

She didn't hear him come up the stairs and it wasn't until she heard him say, 'that an invitation?' that she turned to face him.

'You shouldn't bend down like that,' he said. 'Not fair, teasing me.'

'Teasing you is the last thing I have on my mind, right now.'

He laughed. 'Good to see you've got some fight left in you, but don't try anything stupid.'

She glanced at her handbag on the bed. 'D'you mind? I've got my period, need a few minutes in the bathroom.'

He picked the handbag up, and stood to one side of the door to the en suite. 'Sort yourself out. But, don't do anything stupid. I'll be right here, outside the door.'

He pushed the handbag into her gut and she winced, winded slightly, and doubled over.

She slumped against the doorframe, slipped her hand inside the handbag, and closed her fist round the pepper spray. 'Oh, and by the way,' she said, and dropped the handbag, raised the canister, aimed at his face, and pressed. Nothing happened.

He snatched her wrist and tried to prise the canister out of her hand. She tightened her grip, pulled him slightly off balance, and then rammed her knee into his groin, wrenched her hand free and pushed him towards the top of the stairs.

He stood up, his face creased in agony. 'I'm going to make you wish you'd never been born.'

She forced her thumb under the flip top safety catch but, as she pointed the spray at him, his fist slammed into her face. She dropped the canister and staggered backwards. The pain was unlike anything she'd known and blood was pouring from her nose and a split lip.

He knelt down, picked up the canister, and aimed it at her.

She saw his thumb press down on the trigger. Instinctively, she screwed up her eyes and turned her face away but, as she did, an explosion fractured the air and shotgun pellets hit him between the shoulder blades, snapping his head backwards.

He groaned, blood spilling from his mouth.

He dropped the canister and sank to his knees, his eyes still locked on her.

She kicked the canister away and as she picked it up, she heard him moan, drag in air, and haul himself upright. She stepped away from him, her thumb poised under the safety catch. She pointed the canister harmlessly across the bed, pressed the nozzle and watched the spray hit the wall. She turned, levelled the spray and fired.

He screamed and his hands grabbed at his eyes. She lifted the canister again, but as she moved towards him there was a second explosion. She felt searing pain near her right temple and was thrown backwards onto the bed. She managed to prop herself up for a few brief moments – time enough to see him lying face down with the back of his head a mass of blood and tissue – before she collapsed.

Kate Madison was taken to Truro where the Custody Sergeant asked her preliminary questions - name, date of birth, address, occupation – and arranged for mug shots to be taken, as well as finger and palm prints, blood, urine and saliva samples. He explained her rights and asked if she'd like to see the duty solicitor? She told him her fiancé would be arranging her legal representation.

The Sergeant explained that she'd be detained until formal interviews had taken place, after which she'd be charged and taken before Magistrates or released on bail pending further enquiries.

Throughout, Madison remained calm, self-assured, and confident - like an old lag, the Sergeant would tell his mates later – like she'd known that whatever she'd said could be used in court.

'This is,' she said, as the process continued, 'a terrible injustice. I am innocent and have complete faith in due process. I'm confident that when *all* the facts are known it will be obvious the police have acted hastily. I would like to speak with my fiancé, Mr Stewart Lander.'

Finally, she was escorted to a cell.

*

The police club laid on food, but most involved in the investigation decided to retire to *The Crow's Nest*, where Angus McLeish was offering free drinks. They watched the news and cheered when Superintendent Hinkson, in Plymouth, and Charlie Hobson, in London, appeared on the screen.

Several were on their third pint when Jones joined them. She acknowledged the applause and catcalls, and took a charged glass from the bar and toasted everyone. The celebrations continued with a spontaneous rendition of *Why Was She Born So Beautiful* as Jones clambered onto a table and tried to restore order. She failed and turned to Brenda McLeish for assistance.

McLeish stood on a chair, put her hands on her hips and scowled, making things worse. 'Right...' She raised her fist. 'Shut the fuck up, or I'll call the police.' This greeted by ribald suggestions that Angus should '*See to her.*' and '*Take her in hand.*'

'OK, that's enough. Thank you,' Jones called.

She waited and when she was sure she wouldn't be interrupted, she chose to single out the efforts of civilian staff and uniformed officers who'd worked above-and-beyond. This was greeted by enthusiastic applause. She then highlighted the contribution made by Tregunna and McLeish.

McLeish lifted Jones's arm in the air as if she was the victor at the end of a particularly brutal boxing match.

'Well done everyone,' Jones said. 'Enjoy the rest of the evening.'

She took McLeish outside, the air fresh and cool, the sun sitting on the horizon out at sea.

'Tony Simpkiss?'

'Checked the clubhouse and his flat in Falmouth. No show.'

'The place he's renovating?'

'We've flagged up a warning – armed and dangerous - and Traffic's been alerted. They're combing the area, visiting known haunts, interviewing club members and friends.'

'We should have picked him up earlier.'

'We hadn't connected all the dots, remember?'

Jones was quiet, queasiness in her gut.

'Keep me posted.'

'Lizzie OK?' McLeish asked.

'I've told George and Andy to stand down.'

'Want me to look in on her?'

'No, she'd only accuse me of mothering her.'

'You did what you thought best. Just because nothing happened.'

Jones's mobile rang. She listened, face draining.

'Guv?' McLeish said.

Jones held up her hand.

'Shots?'

'Guv?'

Again she held up her hand, still intent on the call, then slumped against an unmarked police car.

'Oh, my God.'

Jones cut the call.

'Guv?'

'The cottage. Now.'

They had to pull over twice as ambulances, travelling in the opposite direction, negotiated the lane leading to the cottage. McLeish was silent, unsure whether to turn round and give chase. Jones stared at hedgerows, her mouth locked in grim resignation. When they got to the cottage, the road had been cordoned off and Uniform were directing traffic.

They were waved through, parked in the lane, and made their way down the path in time to see ambulance crew pushing two trolleys onto the grass and around the Sebring and an unmarked police car. Jones stopped the first trolley, looked down at the red blanket that covered the body. She hesitated. Her hands were trembling and her breath was shallow and rapid. She took the corner of the blanket and pulled it back.

Andy Thompson.

She dropped her head and felt a mixture of relief and sadness - guilt playing havoc, threatening to sabotage her composure and render her useless. She examined his wounds, and stroked his forehead - one of the few areas of his face still intact – and muttered an apology.

She stepped aside and paramedics pushed the trolley towards an ambulance parked at an angle across the lane. She didn't move as the second trolley was wheeled into place. She looked down at the blanket, felt her whole body shudder and nausea catch in the back of her throat. She blinked, unable to resist the tears and unable to stop her face from crumbling. She pulled back the blanket.

It was a face she didn't recognise.

McLeish stood alongside her.

'Tony Simpkiss, Guv.'

Jones gulped in air and allowed tears to flow.

A paramedic eased the blanket back and began to push the trolley towards the ambulance.

'Wait,' Jones said. 'Where are the others?'

'On their way to the Royal Cornwall, in Truro. We were on another call out. Arrived after they'd been dispatched.'

'And their condition?'

'No idea. Best call the hospital. Probably not arrived yet, but I can radio in if you want?'

'No. No. Thanks. We'll sort things here.' She turned to McLeish. 'You don't have a tissue, do you?'

265

McLeish didn't, but one of the paramedics handed her a couple of large swabs. 'Thanks.' She walked towards the cottage, sidestepped the Sebring, and glanced at the blood coagulating on its bonnet. She blew her nose, wiped her eyes, and gulped in more air. She got to the front door and ducked under mangled metal and trailing telephone wires and stepped inside.

It was cool. Cold. There was a cloying stench of blood. The sofa was a patchwork of stain and fabric and there was a splatter pattern on the wall behind it. A crimson pool had blackened the carpet and the piano's fallboard had been lifted to expose white keys flecked and smeared.

SOCO were poring over the lounge and kitchen, and Truro's DCI Bannerman was sitting at the bottom of the stairs. He didn't get up. Jones sat beside him.

'What happened?' she asked.

9

The vigil lasted all night, Jones restless in a chair beside her bed. Any sleep she managed was punctuated by phone calls from colleagues and a visit by investigators from the Independent Police Complaints Commission.

She'd expected the IPPC to be straining on the leash. They'd be waiting for Lizzie to regain consciousness and would want to know her version of events. Firearms had been fired and it was standard procedure for all such incidents to be investigated. Standard procedure that didn't make it any easier and, if Lizzie had fired a shot and killed a man, she'd probably be arrested and charged with murder.

Yes, yes, the argument raged inside Jones's head, even if it was self-defence, Lizzie would still be arrested, charged, then probably released on bail pending further enquiries and a submission to the CPS.

Murder. Manslaughter at best.

The sun rose at five. She took a breather, went into the corridor and got a cup of coffee from a vending machine. She didn't see Lizzie's doctor go into her room but, when he dropped several files on the floor as he came out, she turned and smiled weakly. 'Hope you're not a surgeon?'

'Consultant. She's in good hands.'

'How is she?'

'It's odd, isn't it,' he said, 'that violence comes into our lives on a daily basis, on TV, on the news and yet most of us walk away largely unscathed? Some people experience it first hand, but remain unaffected. Others are not so lucky and suffer a range of disorders including post-traumatic stress.'

'I asked how she is. I didn't come here for a lecture.'

'You don't appreciate what's happened here, do you? Miss James may have witnessed death at close quarters and may have turned a gun on the killer.'

'But, she's OK?'

'Her injuries are superficial. Your ballistics people will be able to give you chapter and verse, but I'd say if she'd been standing any nearer the top of the stairs she'd have been hit several times. As it is, two gunshot pellets grazed the right side of her head. That, and a cut to the lip and bruising round the nose, should heal in no time. She'll be allowed home this evening, but she'll need monitoring round the clock. Is there someone...?'

'You're looking at her.'

'Then you must understand...unless she's very lucky she'll suffer nightmares, flashbacks, insomnia...'

'OK. I get the picture.'

Jones saw DCI Matthew Bannerman walking along the corridor. He was wearing a sharp suit and looked freshly scrubbed. He nodded at her and waited for the doctor to leave. 'How is she?'

'They've sedated her.'

'She told you what happened?' he asked.

'No.'

'I've been asked to lead the investigation.'

'So, I gathered.'

'We've taken gunshot-residue and ferrozine swabs from everyone involved,' Bannerman said, 'including Lizzie. Samples are already with the lab. Results will take time.'

'And when the squad car arrived?'

'They found Andy Thompson slumped against the sofa and Tregunna spread-eagled over the bonnet of your car. Lizzie was unconscious on the bed. The assailant was on the bedroom floor. He'd been shot, twice.'

'Do we know who shot him?'

'Not yet.'

'Or what weapon was used?'

'Shotgun.' He consulted his notepad. 'He probably shot both officers, but we won't know anything for sure until Lizzie regains consciousness...' Bannerman paused. 'There'll have to be an IPCC investigation.'

'Yeah.'

'They'll also be interested in this.' He took an evidence bag containing the pepper spray canister from his jacket. 'Yours?'

'No.'

'Lizzie's?'

'Yes.' She hesitated. 'Excuse me,' she said, 'I need to get back.'

'We'll talk later.'

Jones turned and went into Lizzie's room.

She was propped up on a mountain of pillows, and was asleep. Jones pulled up a chair, sat next to her, stroked her arm, and then took her hand. 'Hi,' she said, quietly, not knowing what else to say.

At eight, Jones drove to Police Headquarters, Lemon Street.

'Lawyers are with Madison,' McLeish said.

'Plural?'

'Two, probably more waiting in the wings.'

'There are times...' Jones shook her head.

'You sure you're up for this, Guv?' McLeish handed her a coffee.

'Wouldn't miss it for the world.'

'How is she?'

'Lizzie's sleeping.'

'But she's..?'

'Yes. Thanks. Let's get on with it, shall we?'

They'd scheduled the interview for eight-thirty.

A uniformed WPC stood at the door as Madison and her lawyers were shown into the room and steered towards a formica-topped, dark green table. A recorder and CCTV camera were primed and, with the formalities out of the way, Jones said, 'Good morning Miss West, I trust you slept well?'

'I'd like to speak to my fiancé.' Madison said, quietly.

'He's been informed of your detention. Said he had a few things to sort out, but would be here as soon as he could.'

Jones opened a file, introduced McLeish and, for the record, reviewed the circumstances relating to the deaths of D'Ancey and Baldwin. She invited Madison to clarify or confirm what she'd heard, but her lawyers advised that their client would not, at this stage, be making any comment.

Jones then outlined the evidence the prosecution would present and included the probable outcomes of on-going forensic tests and police enquiries.

Then, she handed over to Brenda McLeish, sat back and sipped her coffee.

McLeish chose her words carefully. 'Last night, there was an incident involving police officers and two members of the public. Shots were fired.'

'How dreadful. I didn't know. I was here, of course. Food's awful, by the way.'

'One of the men shot dead was...' McLeish consulted her notebook. 'Tony Simpkiss. You know him?'

'No. I don't think so. Name doesn't ring a bell.'

McLeish took a photograph from an envelope and slid it across the table. 'He's the Dive Officer at the British Sub-Aqua Club in Falmouth.'

Madison looked at the photograph of a corpse lying in the morgue and traced his face with her fingertips.

'Yes. Yes, I remember,' she said. 'At the Yacht Club, the night I met my fiancé. In fact, he introduced us. I assumed he was a friend of Stewart's.'

'And you haven't spoken to him since?'

'No. Looks as if he must have suffered terribly.'

'Shot, twice.'

'My God.'

'Sergeant...' One of the lawyers – an attractive woman in a sharp suit and hair piled in a bun – put her hand on Madison's forearm and said, 'If you're trying to shock my client, to distress or torment her, I'd advise against...'

McLeish didn't give her a chance to finish. 'Your copy,' she said, sliding the photograph across the table. 'Pretty isn't, it? Distressing? Shocking? I'd agree. But only for those who give a shit. Your client has already told us that she'd only met him once, fleetingly. You don't honestly think she'd be tormented after such a brief acquaintance, do you?' McLeish smiled, held her gaze, and then looked at Madison. 'Well?'

Madison shook her head and pushed the photograph across the table. 'Sorry, can't help you.' She smiled and tilted her head to one side, challenging her.

'So, this isn't your stepbrother?' McLeish showed her the photograph again.

'I told you, I've no idea where he is.'

McLeish knew she was lying. She'd seen it often enough - each fabrication betrayed by a slight, almost imperceptible, hesitation. She looked at Jones who'd scribbled something on her notepad and had handed it to an officer at the door. McLeish waited until she'd sat down again, then smiled at Madison.

'How well do you know Lizzie James?'

'We're good friends.' Madison sat forward, her eyes wide, mouth open. 'Oh, my God, you're not telling me Lizzie was involved in the shooting? She's not..?'

271

'She's in hospital.'

'But she's..?'

McLeish looked at Jones.

Jones opened a file.

'Tell me about Chris Baldwin.'

'Inspector.' It was one of the lawyers. 'My client asked after her friend, Lizzie James. The least you could do…'

'When we met in London…'

'Inspector?' Her lawyer looked at Madison who rolled her eyes.

'When we met in London you lied to me, twice,' Jones said. 'I asked if you'd met Chris Baldwin.' She pushed photographs across the table. 'Taken by a private detective. That's you and Baldwin. Very cosy. Intimate, I'd say. Richard Lander confronted you and the next day he was dead.'

Again, the lawyer intervened. 'A coincidence.'

'I loved the old man,' Madison said. 'He was decent, caring. I had to put up with the crap about protecting Stewart and the family fortune, but I told him Baldwin was history. He believed me. Why the hell would I kill him? Makes no sense at all.' She crossed her legs and turned away from Jones.

'You also told me that you'd flown to London on the evening of Sunday 6th June, in your private helicopter.'

Madison looked into her lap, interlocking her fingers. 'I was mistaken,' she said, and turned to face them.

'Kate?' The other lawyer was a squat, round faced, bald man in his late fifties.

Madison ignored him. 'Well, not really mistaken, more confused. Flights back and forth tend to blur after a while.'

'And now it's all as clear as mud?' McLeish lent forward.

'I was scheduled to fly back to London. I had some research to do, but the flight was delayed by a technical glitch. Our chauffeur took me into Falmouth at about seven-thirty in the evening.'

'To catch the train?'

'Yes, but it wasn't due for an hour. I'd felt nauseous for a few days, first thing in the morning.' She looked directly at McLeish as if trying to play the woman-to-woman card. 'You know. Thought I might be pregnant. I decided to find a chemist. Stewart would have been thrilled.' She hesitated. 'No luck, I'm afraid.'

'What? Finding a chemist?'

'It was Sunday,' Madison said, 'but eventually we tracked one down. Bought a testing kit. False alarm. Must try harder.'

'You told Mr Lander?'

'Stewart had a lot on his mind. I didn't see the point.'

Jones sensed Madison was gaining confidence, relaxing, and hoped it wouldn't be too long before her guard slipped.

'Had you met Frank Walker before that evening?'

'Frank Walker?'

'This is you?'

Jones handed her one of the photographs Daniel Green had taken from his attic window, and passed a copy to the lawyers. Madison was on Packet Quays, standing at the top of steps leading to the *Sky Lark*. 'It's digital and places you on the quayside at seven forty-five. The boat's owner, Mr Walker, was knifed to death last Saturday.'

'Inspector, I really must insist,' her lawyer said. 'Two and two making five. Your mathematics would be laughed out of court.'

Jones looked at Madison. 'Mr Walker?'

'I saw something on the news. Dreadful.'

'Another coincidence, I suppose?'

273

'Of course. I'm really sorry to disappoint you, but I'd wandered down to the quayside. It's quite beautiful down there, and relaxing, you know - the cool air off the sea, the boats scuttling around the estuary. I'd stopped, soaked up some late evening sun. I was excited about being pregnant, about being a mother. It was a very special moment.' She looked at the photograph. 'I'm sorry about...what did you say his name was?'

'The photograph was taken the evening Chris Baldwin went diving, hoping to find treasure. Hoping, maybe, to win your heart. Three men went out that evening, but only two returned.'

'What can I say?'

'You can start by telling us when Zoe Radclyffe is going to do a bunk, taking the family jewels with her?'

'Zoe?'

'Please, don't bother. I've heard enough of your lies.'

'Inspector.'

'I need the bathroom,' Madison said.

'We're not done.'

'I need to pee, for Christ's sake.'

Jones signalled to the technical team. 'Interview suspended at eight forty-seven.' She nodded at the WPC. 'The officer will accompany you.'

'And we'd like time with our client.'

'Half-an-hour.'

Jones waited for the door to close, got up, stretched and paced about the room. 'She's lying.'

'Of course she is,' said McLeish, 'but we've got fuck-all. She'll walk if we're not careful. I'll put a bomb under the lab rats.' She got up. 'I need a pee now.'

Ten minutes later, they were standing by a vending machine along the corridor from the interview room when an officer handed Jones a couple of A4 sheets. She skimmed them, cursed under her breath, screwed up one of the sheets and threw it into a waste paper bin.

'Guv?'

'Tony Simpkiss doesn't have a record.' She smiled. 'Peter Brooks, on the other hand, has a charge sheet as thick as your skin.'

'But nothing that ties him to Madison?'

'Nope.'

'What about DNA?'

'If they're stepbrother and stepsister, they won't share a father, or mother. I'll run it past the boys at the lab, but don't hold your breath.'

Hinkson had watched the interview and agreed to a full extension. 'Court's booked for Friday afternoon. We'll refuse police bail, of course, and request she's remanded in custody to give us time to secure the evidence. We can but pray the hearing will be chaired by a JP or a District Judge, and not a lay Magistrate.'

'You'd better have a word with the CPS. Warn them she's going to be a tough nut to crack and they'll be up against the best and most expensive lawyers in the country. Given the LA connection, they may even bring over a flash attorney from the States. It's my guess these two are just the vanguard. There's probably a whole team of them, dressed to the nines.'

'You realise she could walk?' Hinkson said.

'Let's hope forensics come up with the goods.' Jones dropped her head. She was desperate for sleep and knew her day had only just begun.

'And Lander's going to stand by her?'

'Looks like it.'

'But she may have had a hand in his father's murder.'

'When a man loves a woman…' Jones tried to smile. 'I had him down as ruthless, not stupid.'

'We'll see,' Hinkson said. She shrugged and asked after Lizzie.

'Discharged later today, all being well. Her doctors are waiting for results…scans, blood tests.'

'If she did shoot Simpkiss…'

'The IPCC's hovering, waiting for ballistics and forensics. Mitigating circumstances, got to be, hasn't it?'

'Not up to us, is it? And George?'

Jones shook her head.

'At Richard Lander's funeral you asked me more or less the same question. Then, he'd given up the fight to save his marriage. Now he's fighting to save his life. I looked in on him this morning. It's touch and go. We'll know later this afternoon. He's had to have another operation to remove pellets embedded in major organs.'

'I've contacted his wife.'

'I know what she'll be praying for.'

Hinkson's face was set grim. 'Go home and get some rest. You're going to need it.'

'Home's a crime scene. I could take Lizzie up to the flat in London.'

'I need you in spitting distance. You never know when you might be needed. I've got a cabin about an hour's drive from here. It's in a cove down the coast, near Lamorna. Yours if you need it. Whatever, you should take some time, give you and Lizzie a chance to get things into perspective.'

'So, what are you saying? I'm no longer in the driving seat?'

'You'll expect Kate Madison to be charged with both murders?'

'Yes. Probably.'

'If she is, we'll have to hand things over to Charlie Hobson and the Met.'

'After we've done the hard graft? No way.'

'The senior force always takes precedence. Besides, Magistrates may defer to the Central Criminal Court in London.'

'The Old Bailey? But that'll play into Madison's hands. Her lawyers will have a field day, milking the public gallery and the press. I've sweated blood over this. They can't do that.'

'They can, and you've just proved my point. You need to get away. Get some rest. Things will cut up rough over the next few days. You'll need a clear head.'

Hinkson put her arm round her shoulder and led her to the door. 'Lizzie's not the only one IPCC are interested in. It'll be you and me under the microscope - our handling of events leading up to the incident at the cottage.'

'If there's any flack, it'll be down to me.'

Hinkson turned Jones round. 'See that desk?'

'Ma'am?'

'That's where the buck stops.'

Jones picked up essentials from a convenience store, and drove to the cottage where she found SOCO sifting for clues. She was allowed to pack and put a couple of small suitcases in the Sebring, but only after DCI Bannerman, the crime scene's SIO, had vetted them. He wanted to make sure, he said, that nothing was removed that might inform the investigation. He'd appeared apologetic – she wasn't sure – and, for the second time that day she felt angry with him but this time her anger was accompanied, completely irrationally, by a desire to smack his face. Yeah, she needed to get away.

The afternoon seemed to drag and Jones fell asleep in a chair by her bed. When Lizzie woke, she squeezed her hand, and smiled.

'Hi,' Lizzie said, and Jones burst into to tears.

The doctor was called and, after he'd examined her and made them both promise they'd check with a local GP if either of them were concerned, he left them to get ready for the journey to Lamorna.

Of the coves along the south coast of Cornwall, few are more remote than St Loys. Hinkson had given Jones directions, but it was her description of the location that resonated as they inched their way towards the bolthole. It was off the beaten track, the Superintendent had told her, and the wooded valley ended in a rocky beach that was shaped like a child's drawing of an incomplete heart exposed to the ravages of nature.

The wooden cabin was hidden among hedgerows and trees two hundred metres from the shoreline. Inside it was cosy. The living area was one room with a kitchen, a dining area with table and four chairs, and a lounge with sofa and armchair huddled around an open fireplace. There were two bedrooms - one double, one with two single beds - and a small bathroom.

Outside, they stood on the veranda. It was just wide enough for two deck chairs and a side table. Out at sea, waves were topped with white horses that seemed to be teaming up with an easterly wind for an assault on the rocky beach.

Jones put her arm round Lizzie, wondering when she'd break the silence that had lasted from the moment Jones had started sobbing in the hospital.

'Pub in Lamorna?' she asked.

Lizzie looked up from the mirror she was using to check her face.

'No? OK. Quiet night in.' Jones held up a carrier bag. 'I'll put these in the fridge and we'll curl up by the fire. Have an early night.'

10

They went to bed early. Lizzie turned her back and the sedatives the doctor had prescribed knocked her out. Jones was restless throughout the night. She blamed herself for what happened. If only she'd handled it differently - called in a TAG team, or armed Tregunna. He'd done the training and although he hadn't been selected for the task force, she could have gone to Hinkson and made a case for issuing a handgun. Would it have made any difference, she wondered? Or would they both have been killed – Tregunna and Lizzie - and be lying next to one another in the morgue?

As the sun rose, she fell asleep.

During breakfast, she remembered a letter that she'd received from Albert. She fished it out of her handbag and showed it to Lizzie. Albert and Alice were about to embark on a cruise: a vacation to mark their retirement. They hoped they were well and would come and see them when they got back.

Lizzie folded the letter, put it back in its envelope and, as she placed it on the table, Jones covered her hand with hers and they looked at each other. Lizzie got up, walked round the table and sat on her lap, cradling her in her arms and burying her head into her chest. They sat like that until tears began to flow, raw emotion, both bodies convulsing.

It was some time before they got up and walked down to the beach.

At ten-thirty, they drove into Lamorna, determined to make the most of their downtime. They listened to a concerto on the car radio and looked at each other as if they knew they'd face music of a different kind when they got back to the real world.

They stopped for a coffee in the *Lamorna Wink*. The pub was quiet, almost deserted, which suited them.

'What are we going to do?' Lizzie said.

'About?'

'My face, for a start.' She smiled, her lip swollen, then dropped her head. 'I can't go back to the cottage, not after what's happened.'

Jones looked at her, hesitating. 'And I don't think I could give it up. It's all I have left of my parents.'

'I know. I'm sorry.'

'You could accept Charlie Hobson's offer.'

'And transfer to London? Work under Charlie.'

'Wouldn't be the first time.' Lizzie cracked a smile but couldn't hide her torment.

They sat in silence.

'I've had a call,' Lizzie said, eventually. 'They want me to audition for that tour of Asia.'

'Audition?'

'Can't blame them. They can't risk me freezing in front of a packed house.'

'You're sure you're ready?'

'I've turned it down, so they may not bother again.'

'Of course they will.'

'Not if I'm out of circulation for too long. Not with a fat lip. I need to be in London.'

'That may have to wait.'

'Until they know one way or the other?'

'If you did turn the gun on him...'

Lizzie dropped her head.

'Madison goes before local Magistrates tomorrow afternoon,' Jones said, looking at her over the rim of her coffee cup. 'I want to be there. She's not the only one on trial. If the judge dismisses the case against her, or she goes to trial and is acquitted, it'll be my professional competence on the line.'

'You brought her to justice. It'll be the system that lets you down.'

'You believe she's guilty, then?'

Lizzie reached across and squeezed her hand. 'Last night, I had nightmares. That young Constable sprawled on the sofa, blood pouring from him. I smelt Simpkiss's breath and saw the look in his eyes as he levelled the shotgun at me...He circles me several times like a predator toying with its prey. He orders me to strip. He's going to rape me. I try to reason with him, but he's having none of it. He tells me I'm to be traded for Kate's freedom. I can feel a shotgun in my hand and pump bullet after bullet into him.' Lizzie face began to crumble. 'Kate's his sister.'

'Stepsister. And you'll be a material witness.'

'And if I'm called, she'll be convicted.'

'That's not what I'm concerned about.'

'The cross examination?'

'The defence will do everything to discredit you. Tear you apart. I don't want to risk a relapse.'

'Not your call.'

'It could set you back months.'

'Not with you by my side.'

At the end of the lounge, the bartender switched on a large flat screen TV and they caught images of a crowd outside the Magistrates Court in Truro.

'If we don't face this together, we'll never be able to move on.'

'And you want us to move on, together?' Jones asked.

Lizzie sat back, drained her coffee, and then without making eye contact she said, 'Before we met, my life was one long round of airport lounges, hotel suites, concert halls, post production parties, and receptions. I lived in a gilded cage, a protected world of a privileged few blessed with talent and the good fortune to be able to share it with millions.' She looked up. 'Then I met you. And at first things were great. But in the last few days I've spent time with a serial killer, been shadowed by surveillance, watched a young man die, and I've been shot. I may even have killed someone. I've been beaten up, hospitalised, and I'm struggling to cope with the after-affects.' She looked at her lap and the large tissue she'd wrapped round her fingers. Tears trickled down her cheek. She looked up. 'What do you think I should do, Lydia? What would you do?'

Jones didn't have an answer. She got up and walked round the table, pulled Lizzie to her feet, wiped away her tears, and took her in her arms.

It seemed like an eternity, before Lizzie said, 'I can't promise it'll be easy but I might regret turning my back on something as special as our love.'

'I'd hate to lose you.'

'Yeah, me too.' Lizzie pushed away. She dabbed her nose and wiped her eyes, smudging mascara and making her look like a child's stuffed panda. 'Think I'll go powder my nose.'

Jones watched her disappear through the door leading to the pub's loo, then glanced at the TV and caught the BBC news at the top of the hour. The newsreader was staring straight into the camera...

It's two days since Kate Madison was arrested and, in one of the most high profile cases for many years, we go live to the Magistrates Court in Truro to hear from our correspondent, Mike Porter.

Yes. Thanks, Angali. Police enquiries have focussed on the deaths of Geoffrey D'Ancey and Chris Baldwin. Tomorrow, we hope to bring you the Court's ruling. Is there a prima facie case to answer? And, if so, will Kate Madison be remanded in custody or released on bail?

Isn't it unusual for someone accused of murder to be granted bail?

The guidelines are very specific. The Court will need to consider whether the accused is likely to abscond, re-offend or threaten material witnesses? Kate Madison's arrest has captured the public imagination precisely because her legal team has insisted that the police evidence is circumstantial and she has no case to answer.

Innocent until proven guilty?

Precisely.

And if she is committed for trial?

Proceedings are likely to be transferred to London where Geoffrey D'Ancey was killed and where Chris Baldwin lived and worked. Either way, if bail is granted, Miss Madison will be home tomorrow evening.

During his rare appearances, Stewart Lander's taken time to talk to the media and argue his fiancée's case.

He's stood by her, refused to believe she's capable of murder and has openly declared his love for her. But his business has suffered.

Initially there was a run on shares, but the market has settled in the past twenty-four hours.

And she's consistently refuted the charges?

Absolutely. She's admitted being with Geoffrey D'Ancey on the night he died. She'd accepted his invitation and went to his room to get information that she felt she needed to make her first show a success. She had a drink with him. He made a pass at her, but she didn't sleep with him. She maintains that when she left at about eight-thirty, he was very much alive. And, given her well-publicised fear of water, it is not clear how the prosecution intend to prove that she killed Chris Baldwin.

We don't know how the Magistrate will rule but, if this does go to trial, comparisons have already been made with several celebrity trials in the States. It's beginning to sound like something Hollywood might want to get its teeth into.

Before his death Richard Lander had invited the BBC to make a documentary about Rosemullion's restoration and I understand that his son intends to honour that commitment this weekend.

11

They made an early start - tidying the cabin and washing dishes left in the sink overnight - and then packed the two small cases with more dirty clothes than clean.

It had rained heavily overnight and the track leading to the main road was strewn with mud and leaves. They skirted Lamorna, picked up the A394 east of Penzance, and had just turned onto the A39 when Jones glanced at the Sebring's petrol gauge and pulled into the next service station. As the attendant filled the tank, Jones noticed him glance at Lizzie's injuries as she slept in the passenger seat. At least there was nothing permanent. The swelling had reduced significantly and the bruising had mellowed to a shade of bluish purple.

The attendant's offered to check the Sebring's engine oil. Jones declined and paid cash and was about to pull out into the traffic when she saw blue lights flashing in her rear view mirror.

She nudged Lizzie. 'We've got company.'

She took her feet off the dash and sat up. 'Speed trap?'

'On a forecourt?'

They looked at each other, and burst into a fit of giggles.

'Bit of decorum,' Jones said. 'We're in enough trouble as it is without upsetting the wooden tops.'

She pulled into a cleaning bay, took out her warrant card and waited for the two officers to catch up.

They took their time and seemed to be consulting notes before they got out, put on their peaked caps, and strolled towards the Sebring. One of them paused to check its number plate, then recognised Jones.

He saluted and then said, 'Sorry, Guv, but we've got orders to escort Miss James to Lemon Street.'

'You're not going to tell us why, are you Constable?'

'Would, if I knew.'

'We'll follow you.'

'Thing is, Guv...'

'It's OK.' Lizzie lent across, looked up at the officer and smiled a crooked smile. 'I'll come quietly.' She gathered her things and opened the passenger door.

'Thing is, Guv...' the officer said, again.

'What?' Jones said.

'They want to see you as well.'

Jones followed the patrol car to Lemon Street, concerned that she may not be able to see Lizzie until after the IPCC had determined her fate one way or another and, when Lizzie turned round and pulled a face, Jones only just managed to hold back the tears.

She checked in with the duty Sergeant who told her *they* were in Superintendent Hinkson's office and warned her that there was enough firepower to sink an Armada.

She took the lift to the fourth floor where she found the flotilla chatting over freshly brewed coffee and a technician connecting a laptop to a projector.

'Ah, Lydia,' DCI Bannerman put his coffee down. 'It's good of you to join us.'

She wanted to say, 'Not that I had much choice...' but bit her tongue, and said. 'Congratulations on your promotion.'

'Thank you, that's very kind.'

She let the condescension slide – not that she had much option – but she hoped he'd have the decency to return the compliment.

He didn't.

Not a good sign.

Bannerman walked over to the refreshment table and she watched him say something to a tall, angular woman in a sharp suit. The woman looked at Jones, nodded, took her coffee and sat down at the head of a conference table squeezed into Hinkson's office.

Hinkson poured a coffee, brought it over, handed it to her, and said, quietly. 'You've heard the news, I suppose?'

'What?'

'The Magistrate's hearing?'

'No.'

'Brought forward, this morning, Madison released on bail pending further enquiries.'

'Fuck.'

'My sentiments entirely.'

'I wanted to be there.'

'Referred to Central Criminal Court, in London, and assuming Magistrates at The Old Bailey don't bottle it, you'll be part of Commander Hobson's Major Incident Team.'

Jones snorted.

'A problem?'

'Lizzie suggested I'd enjoy working under Charlie again.'

'And?'

'She was teasing.'

'Wouldn't be a bad call.'

'In a couple of years, maybe.'

Hinkson nodded in the direction of the woman sitting at the head of the table.

'Lucinda Crane. IPCC. Don't mess with her and don't be fooled by Sir Giles, the old fart looking out of the window. He's Chair of the Police Authority. But the person with the real clout is talking to the DCI. He came down from London this morning.'

Jones had noticed him when she entered the room. He was tall, heavy set, his suit slightly crumpled, his hair slightly dishevelled - probably just stepped off the flight into Newquay, she guessed. She watched as he laughed and backslapped DCI Bannerman. She was, unaccountably, irritated by his self-confidence.

'Home Office.' Hinkson said.

'Home...What? Why?'

'I think we're about to find out.' Hinkson took her forearm. 'Now's the time to learn how to count to ten, Lydia.'

Jones was invited to sit at the other end of the table from Lucinda Crane. From there she had a clear view of a large clock on the wall above Crane's head and felt like someone condemned to watching a career slip away.

'How was your holiday?' Crane said, closing a folder and looking up.

'Sorry, Ma'am?'

'Your holiday, Inspector?'

'It'll be good to get back to work.'

'Not what I asked.'

'Did the trick, I suppose.'

'I'd appreciate it if you'd phrase your answers so that we don't have to second-guess what you mean.' Crane's face was deadpan, but Jones noticed a slight lift of an eyebrow, as if she needed to underscore her authority. 'I don't need to remind any of you that anything that's said in these four walls is not only confidential but may also be the subject of further enquiries.'

289

Crane dispensed with introductions, passed round reports prepared by DCI Bannerman, the IPCC and the CPS, and spent the next twenty minutes detailing the events leading to the arrest of Kate Madison.

Jones turned pages and highlighted specific parts of the reports. To be fair, she felt they'd done a good job.

'Questions?' Crane closed the reports and checked her wristwatch.

'Your first murder enquiry as SIO?' Sir Giles asked.

'Yes,' Jones said.

'Then you are to be congratulated.'

His bite's much worse…

'Sir?'

'Miss Madison is facing serious charges and it seems you've been able to provide CPS with some good, solid evidence.'

Good. Solid.

'Good enough to secure a conviction?'

'We're still waiting for forensic reports…'

'A bit hasty, perhaps, arresting her when you did?'

'If I'm right and her history's anything…'

'If, Inspector?'

Jones felt detached, as an intruder might - listening, but unable to influence proceedings - and, when Lucinda Crane turned and looked at her, she felt like a prisoner of war with a gun held to her temple.

'You wouldn't have been able to pull this off on your own, Inspector.'

The trap was well camouflaged and Jones fell right in. 'I had a good team working for me.'

'One of whom is dead.' Lucinda Crane lent back in her chair. 'And another's on life-support.'

'George is OK?'

'Hasn't been your priority, has he?' Sir Giles said. 'On holiday, Inspector, whilst a member of your team is fighting for his life?'

'It was my suggestion,' Hinkson said, and would have left it there, but Jones couldn't.

'I asked about DS Tregunna,' she said, 'and I'd appreciate an answer.'

The room fell silent and Jones swore she could hear her heart thumping and Lucinda Crane's teeth grinding.

'We've arranged for you to see him after we're done,' Hinkson said, hoping Jones would take the hint.

She didn't. 'And Lizzie?' she asked.

'Lizzie?'

'Elizabeth James.'

'Ah, yes.' Crane invited Bannerman to take the floor.

'The ballistics report...' He opened a folder. 'DC Andy Thompson was unarmed when he was shot and died from his wounds. DS Tregunna had traces of gunshot residue on his right hand.'

'George fired the shotgun?' Jones hesitated. 'I don't understand.'

'Neither do we yet, not until we hear from Miss James and interview the DS. We're assuming that, despite his injuries, George Tregunna managed to fire the shotgun, then staggered out into the garden to try to get help.'

'And Lizzie?'

'Is being interviewed by the IPCC.' Bannerman checked the report. 'Tests confirm that she used pepper spray on the gunman, but you'll be pleased to know there were no traces of gunshot residue.'

'So, she didn't...'

'No,' Bannerman said, 'Lizzie didn't shoot anyone.'

As much as she tried to fight them back, Jones couldn't stop the tears and everyone waited until she blew her nose and wiped her eyes.

'Inspector,' Lucinda Crane said, 'we will need to talk to you again.'

Before Jones could say anything there was a rap on the door. It was opened by a member of the civilian staff who was carrying several sheets of A4, an envelope, and a small holdall. 'DI Jones?' she said, looking at the faces turned towards her.

Jones hurried over, thanked her, read the notes, then reread the information she'd been waiting for since she'd interviewed Tim Rivers in his Social Services office near The Elephant and Castle.

'Inspector?' Lucinda Green said.

Jones drifted back to her place, stood behind her chair and allowed the sheets to spill onto the table. 'After her arrest, I interviewed Miss Madison and asked her if she'd seen or been in touch with her stepbrother recently. She told us she hadn't seen him for several years. We've had two sets of fingerprints analysed. They belong to two people...Peter Brooks, arrested outside a nightclub about ten years ago and Tony Simpkiss, the man killed at the cottage. Both men have the *same* fingerprints. The same, not similar.' She waited for a reaction. 'Brooks and Simpkiss are, therefore, one and the same.'

'Miss Madison may well have lied to you about her stepbrother,' Sir Giles said, 'but the fingerprints don't prove she killed anyone.'

'No, you're right, it's just another piece of circumstantial evidence.'

Jones opened the holdall.

'We found shoes at Frank Walker's boatyard. They belonged to Chris Baldwin. At first we thought Baldwin might have been involved in the murder of Richard Lander. He wasn't. But these...' she pulled out a pair of trainers, 'were taken off Tony Simpkiss during his post mortem.'

She turned one of them over. 'As you can see, they have a distinctive pattern on the sole. Impressions were taken at the boathouse where Frank Walker was stabbed and in the copse where Richard Lander was killed. Forensic evidence places Peter Brooks, aka Tony Simpkiss, at both crime scenes. He knocked Richard Lander off his horse, smashed his head on a rock, removed his riding hat and snapped his neck...and then he silenced Frank Walker.

The room was silent and Jones noticed the man from the Home Office look up, his pen poised. 'Inspector,' he said. 'I'd like to congratulate you. The reports I read on my way here, coupled with what I've heard during this meeting, make a compelling case against Kate Madison.'

Jones said nothing, cautious.

'But do we have enough to secure a conviction?'

'I'd like to think so.'

'So would I. And so would the Prime Minister. You see,' he said. He hesitated, and appeared to choose his words carefully. 'Washington's Department of Justice has issued an arrest warrant, in the name of Alison Fairweather. They intend to extradite her.'

'Can they do that?' Jones asked.

'Yes, they can, under the terms of the 2003 Act.'

'And all of our evidence is brushed aside?'

'If theirs is more likely to secure a conviction.'

'After all we've been through? Just like that? The cavalry comes charging over the hill and...' Jones shook her head.

Again, the room fell silent until Lucinda Green said, 'Inspector, we understand your frustration, but securing a conviction is paramount, you'd agree?'

'Of course.'

'Then, please, bear with us. We have something that might *clinch the deal*, as our American cousins would say.'

Crane nodded at the technician, who opened the laptop, switched on the projector and focused its beam on the wall beneath the clock. Crane waited until everyone had turned to face the screen and then smiled at the man from the Home Office.

'We have a movie, of sorts' he said, 'that will explain why the US Justice Department are so keen to talk to Alison Fairweather...your Miss Madison. The clips are edited from extensive footage taken by domestic spy-wear surveillance cameras in the home of a well-known media tycoon. The footage contains images of him, on several different occasions, in his bedroom, indulging in a variety of sexual activities. We're assuming that his 'guests' were unaware they were being recorded and that he replayed them for his own amusement. The footage is available for CPS use, should they be interested, but I don't intend to waste time with a re-run this morning.' He looked around the table. 'We know Alison Fairweather was his lover and there are several recordings of them, together. Again, I don't intend to bore you. However, I do want to show you one clip.' He nodded at the technician. 'The time and date are shown at the bottom right of the screen. The rest will be self-explanatory.'

They'd left the Magistrate's Court immediately after the hearing. Kate Madison clung to Stewart Lander as they pushed their way through a throng of reporters and, as the Rolls pulled out into traffic, she hid her face from a dozen photographers. She clung to him throughout the journey, sobbing, thanking him over and over, telling him how much she loved him and how she would make it up to him, make him proud, repay him for standing by her, for fighting her corner and *being there* for her.

When they got home she wanted to talk. She told him about the police interrogation and how unpleasant and intimidating it had been. She told him how isolated she'd felt and how frightening it had been to be locked up in a cell overnight.

She cried and it was nearly an hour before she was calm. But, eventually, she was able to smile, weakly at first. Then, she asked him to leave, to give her time, time alone, time to freshen up and put her face back on.

He gave her half-an-hour, then Stewart Lander stood in her bedroom, silhouetted against sunlight streaming through the window. He could hear her singing in the bathroom. He was carrying a tray and put it down on the linen-box at the foot of the bed and waited.

She came out of the bathroom, dressed in a silk robe, towelling her hair.

He picked up the tray.

'Lunch? Oh, Stewart, that's so sweet.'

She fluffed up pillows and sat on the bed.

'You must stop spoiling me like this. I'll never get into my dress. A few weeks, that's all I have. I'll make you the proudest man on earth.'

'I wouldn't worry about it,' he said.

'What do you mean?'

'You have nothing to prove.'

'After all you've done for me. All the trust and love you've shown. I want everything to be perfect.'

'It will be. Anyway, I couldn't have you languishing in jail, could I? I needed you here. How else could we have a fairy-tale ending?'

'You ok?'

'Yes. Fine.' He placed the tray on her lap.

'Do I look a mess?' she asked.

'You look tired. Stressed. Not surprising, all things considered.'

'But someone you'll want to wake up to each morning?'

'You're beautiful. You know you are.'

'And the luckiest girl in the world.'

'You don't have to worry about the future.'

'I know, all this, and you to look after me.'

She gathered the silk around her.

'Today's going to be chaotic,' she said. 'They're putting up the marquee and the place is crawling with television crew, technicians, and God knows how many others? I want strict orders. I'm not to be disturbed. I'm going to try on my dress. It's unlucky for you to see the dress before the wedding. OK?'

'I wouldn't want to spoil the party.'

'Not long now and we'll be married and when I'm acquitted we'll have that long, lazy honeymoon we've promised each other.'

Stewart turned and walked over to the window. He looked down at the lawn and the copse where his father had died. 'You think you'll be acquitted?' he said.

'Of course. I'm innocent.' She waited for him to say something. 'You do believe me, don't you?'

'It doesn't matter what I believe, does it?'

'Of course it does. It's important.'

He continued to stare out of the window.

'Stewart, what is it? Not getting cold feet, are you?'

'Like I said, I've got a lot on my mind. The film's behind schedule and the investor's are on my back. The helicopter keeps misfiring. It's due a service. I'm flying it to RAF Benson this afternoon. I want another crack at that simulator. John will leave me at Benson and fly the helicopter across the channel to a service centre north of Paris.'

'What about the documentary? They'll be shooting over the weekend.'

'They've already interviewed father and me. They'll edit that and add archive footage and commentary from the architect and landscaper. It'll be fine. I'll be away a week. I've left instructions with the staff.'

'Oh, you don't have to worry about the staff. I'm very happy to manage the estate, especially now that Albert has retired.' She smiled at him. 'I thought you were very generous, by the way, allowing them to keep the cottage on the estate.'

'It's no more than they deserve. Is it a problem?'

'No...'

'Glad to hear it.'

'Stewart? Are you sure you're OK? You seem edgy.'

'Busy,' he said. 'Loose ends.'

She popped a strawberry into her mouth, pushed the tray away and patted the bed next to her.

'Come here,' she said and threw herself back onto the pillows. She raised her arms above her head and exposed her breasts. 'Before you go?' He sat beside her and she kissed him, using her tongue to push a morsel of strawberry into his mouth. 'If you're going to be away for a week...'

He looked at his watch. 'Why not,' he said. 'Give John a chance to get things ready.' He picked up the tray, placed it on the writing desk in the bay window and, by the time he'd turned around, she'd thrown back the covers.

He sat on the edge of the bed and slipped his hand under the robe and found the softness of her skin and the fullness of her breasts.

*

297

CCTV picks up Alison Fairweather as she punches in a security code and waits for the electrically operated gates to swing open.

She's wearing her hair down - blond curls framing her face and settling below her shoulders. She's carrying a handbag and wearing sunglasses, high heels, a short skirt and a floral blouse that flutters in the light breeze. It's mid-afternoon and the Californian sun casts short shadows across the gravel forecourt and portico entrance of an LA mansion.

She removes her sunglasses and lets herself in, and the film cuts to the bedroom, where a young woman is straddling a middle-aged man. Both are naked and the sound is indistinct, monosyllabic. The viewing angle cuts from one camera to another. There are four cameras - one in the ceiling, one on each side of the bed, and one behind the headboard.

The door opens and Alison Fairweather stands there, seemingly unmoved by what's happening. She waits, watching, and then pulls a handgun from her handbag and levels it at the young woman.

She says something – again indistinct – and, as she steps forward, she fires five times, twice into the young woman, and three times into the man who's seen pleading with her.

She stows the handgun, turns and walks out of shot. The CCTV camera picks her up again as she slips on her sunglasses, walks through the security gates and hails a taxi.

The man from the Home Office waited, as if wanting to give everyone a chance to assimilate what they'd seen - its significance pretty obvious. 'I'm sure you'll agree, Inspector,' he said, 'that between us, we have enough to put Kate Madison away for a very long time.'

298

'She'll serve the majority of her sentence in the US?'

'Yes.'

'Justice of sorts, I suppose.'

Jones felt angry, dissatisfied. All she really wanted to do was to find Lizzie and go home, but then realised she didn't have a home to go to – not as long as SOCO were there. She puffed out her cheeks, exhaled forcefully, shook her head and sighed. 'Why weren't the cameras found when LAPD investigated the murders?'

'They were well hidden and only came to light after the house was sold and new owners embarked on a programme of renovation.' He asked the technician to eject the DVD and passed it to Jones. 'If she'd been content to stay behind the scenes, our assistant producer may have got away with it but, like a moth to a flame...' He smiled, got up and packed his brief case. 'Well done, Inspector, I'll make sure the PM gets to hear of your efforts.'

There was a knock on the door. It opened and Brenda McLeish stood there, grinning.

'Yes, Sergeant?' Superintendent Hinkson said.

'Sorry, Ma'am. It's George. He's come round from the op and, for some inexplicable reason, he's asking for the Guv.'

The Superintendent turned to Jones.

'George can wait. Bring Madison in. Show her the movie. See how long it takes before she realises she can't wriggle out of this one.'

'I could open a book, Ma'am,' McLeish said. 'A fiver a punt, closest scoops the pot.'

'Brenda.'

'Sorry, Guv.'

Jones turned to Hinkson. 'Lizzie, Ma'am?'

'Deal with Madison first. When you're done, you can take her back to Lamorna, relax, have a meal and a glass or three of Rioja. Just mind you take it easy driving back to the hut.'

'I could keep an eye on them, Ma'am,' McLeish said. 'Act as chauffeur.'

'Brenda.'

'Yes, Guv? Sorry Guv.'

Jones smiled.

Hinkson looked across the table.

'Well, Inspector, what are you waiting for?'

Kate Madison woke from a light sleep and found her bed empty. Stewart had been rough with her - taken her - and she'd enjoyed it, really enjoyed it, something she'd never thought she'd be able to do again.

She grinned.

Has it really been ten years? I'd left school late...a career's talk...young WPC from the Met.

Then Stewart sat beside me, gave me his card, said he wanted me to get in touch.

So, I did. Took ten years and it's been one hell of a journey.

But look at me now.

Set for life.

She heard the helicopter and guessed that Stewart and Hartley were running the standard pre-flight checks. She smiled, threw the duvet off, screamed, punched the air, and then collapsed back onto the pillows.

She giggled.

My own helicopter? Fuck me.

The engines shut down, calm returned, and the guard dogs stopped barking.

'Not long now,' she thought, 'and I'll be alone.'

She couldn't wait.

She showered, pampering herself with oils, her hands caressing her body, softening it, smoothing it, conscious of Stewart's enjoyment of her and her desire to satisfy her own sexuality. She dried herself and then spent time looking in one of several mirrors, posing, pouting, and preening.

Finally, she removed the wedding gown from a walk-in wardrobe and slipped it on. She was naked beneath, and enjoyed the sensation of the silk on her skin.

She smiled at her reflection. White - such a purifying colour - the colour of innocence, of virtue, of piety, of renewal. What was past was past. The dress symbolised the transformation in her fortune. She was to be married, wealthy beyond her wildest dreams, courted by the rich and famous. The guest list read like a Who's Who from the world of entertainment, television cameras would be outside the church and a glossy magazine would publish photographs taken at the reception.

She had no idea where he would take her for their honeymoon. It would have to be somewhere isolated... an island in The Caribbean, maybe..?

She didn't hear him come in, and his reflection in one of the full-length mirrors startled her. She turned to see John Hartley, dressed in overalls and wearing gloves. She watched him place a rucksack on the floor.

'Is everything all right? You're meant to be flying to Oxford with Mr Lander.'

He didn't remove his sunglasses and stood, barring her way out.

He didn't smile.

Multiple images in mirrors around the room confused and disorientated her momentarily.

301

She felt cold suddenly, threatened, and anxious.

He kicked the door closed.

'What are you doing?' she asked.

'I've come to say goodbye,' he said, and stayed where he was.

'I don't understand.'

'You don't recognise me do you?'

'Should I?'

'Oh, I think so, don't you, Jenny?' He removed his sunglasses, pulled open the overall and undid his shirt. 'Perhaps this will jog your memory?' The operation had patched the knife wound, but left an ugly scar, like half an orange compressed into his chest.

'Jon? Jonathan Harrison?'

Her eyes darted around the room.

'There's no escape,' Hartley said. 'It's soundproof. A panic room. Remember? The lock's only accessible from the inside. It would take an hour, at least, to cut through the door.' He replaced his sunglasses and placed a hand on a large button by the door. 'You could try pressing this to summon help.' He took a gun from the rucksack. 'This is a Glock semi-automatic.' He pulled a slim metal object from a pocket. 'And this is a silencer. When they are combined like this...' He made sure it was attached securely. 'The sound of the gun is barely audible. Even if you stood on the other side of this door, you wouldn't know a shot's been fired.' He smiled. 'You'll hear it, of course.'

'What are you going to do?'

'All I wanted was a kiss. A kiss. That's all.' His voice was calm, and quiet. 'I spent several months in hospital, but the scars were just the beginning. You accused me of trying to rape you and that hounded me everywhere I went.'

'For God's sake, Jonathan...'

'John. Call me John. Jonathan was reported missing in Afghanistan. I was badly burnt.' He peeled back one of his gloves. 'But I saw an opportunity to escape the sentence that you'd handed down. I disappeared and reinvented myself. Called myself John, just in case anyone recognised me and called out my name.'

'You'd do that to your parents? They must have been devastated.'

'They lost their son the day you cried rape. I'll go back to Afghanistan, give it a couple of months, recover from the *amnesia* that's robbed me of my identity, and make a tearful, hero's return.'

'You're sick. You won't get away with this.'

'Oh, but I will. All that military training, you see. I know how to cover my tracks. The CCTV I've installed here hasn't been commissioned. It not even switched on, so there'll be no record of the helicopter taking off, just the vague recollections of people too busy to check the time.'

'Stewart? He'll be waiting, wondering where you are. Come looking for you.'

'You think?'

His question hung in the air and she used the lull to work out a way of getting to the button on the wall. There were no windows, no other doors, and no obvious escape route. But the button...

'I was a child,' she said, quietly.

'You lied and inflicted more misery than any knife could. Just think about it, Jenny, if I'd tried to lead a normal life – had a wife and kids – and you went on trial for murder. How long would it have been before someone dug up the past? Can you imagine the distress caused by disclosures during your trial? The dirt dragged into millions of homes, my family's life ruined, my parents hounded by the press?'

303

She moved a step to one side. He seemed not to have noticed. She was closer to him now, no more than a few meters.

'You should've stayed in LA, Jenny. But you had to return, didn't you? What? Did you blow them both away - sugar daddy and the young thing who'd taken your place? Don't look so surprised. I've done my homework, read newspaper accounts, put two and two together.'

'You have no idea what my life's been like.' She used words as cover. She took several steps forward and was standing within striking distance.

'The whole world knows your sordid little tale,' he said. 'Your lawyers and your PR team have made sure of that, but few of us know what an accomplished liar you are.' And then, as though signalling the game was over, he crossed his arms in front of his chest, holding the gun so that the silencer ran alongside his cheek. 'I'd spent years searching for you, then, one evening, I happened across a crowd in Leicester Square who'd gathered to catch a glimpse of the stars in your fiancé's latest film. And there you were, his beautiful love-interest, walking down the red carpet. There were features in magazines and speculation about the beauty who'd stolen his heart. My search was over and everything fell into place. I've been this close to you. Just biding my time.'

'You're insane.'

'Probably. But who'd blame me for my insanity?' He paused. 'I can't risk a trial. I wouldn't have been able to bear it if you'd been sent down for life. Out of reach. I've waited too long.'

'You won't get away with this.'

'Oh, I will. I'll have the perfect alibi.'He smiled. 'The police will investigate your death, of course and may decide John Hartley was responsible. But they'll never be sure, not without a body.'

'A body?'

'John Hartley's.'

'I don't understand.'

'I wouldn't let it worry your pretty little head.'

She looked at the button next to the door.

'How thoughtful of you,' he said, 'to dress for your execution.' He levelled the gun at her. 'The button on the wall?' He smiled. 'Go for it. Be my guest.'

'Bastard!' She rushed at him, fists flaying.

He hit her once, square on the bridge of the nose, and sent her reeling backwards. She stumbled over her dress, smashed into the dressing table, and collapsed on the floor. She sat up and wiped blood from her face and smeared it on her dress. She struggled to her feet, arms outstretched towards him. 'Please, Jon. Please. I beg you.'

He emptied two rounds into her. The impact sent her sprawling across the room and into racks of clothing. She snatched at designer outfits, dragging them from their hangers, and then slumped to the floor, pulling clothing on top of her, blood pumping from her chest and mouth. She sat like a grotesque doll, her wedding gown soaked in crimson, her blue eyes wide with shock.

'Please,' she managed, but his next shot took out her left eye. The bullet exited at the back of her skull, spraying brain matter over mirrored doors.

He didn't bother with a fourth bullet.

He removed his protective clothing and gloves and slipped them into the rucksack along with the Glock and its silencer.

He opened the door, set the alarm, walked across the bedroom, checked the corridor, closed the door behind him, and made his way down the staircase and moved unhurriedly through the throng of contractors.

*

305

Stewart Lander was sitting in the pilot's seat as the roar of the helicopter's engine reached take-off speed.

Harrison clambered beside him, placed the rucksack on the back seat and pulled on the co-pilot's headset.

They glanced at one another, and then Lander pulled the paddle back and the helicopter lifted off the ground.

'Take it easy,' Harrison shouted above the crescendo. 'We'll need to nurse her all the way.'

They circled above the house, swept over lawns and past stables, and then banked north.

'Heading our way, d'you think?' Harrison nodded at a convoy led by a patrol car with flashing blue lights.

'Probably the intrepid Inspector Jones with more of her inane questions.' Lander looked at Harrison. 'Don't worry. I'll sort her out when I get back. Besides, it's too late now, isn't it?'

'You sure you don't want me to take over?'

'No. I haven't felt this good for a very long time.'

Harrison adjusted his headset. 'We have clearance for RAF Benson and from there I'll head for Paris.'

'And ditch off the French coast?'

'Yes.'

Lander handed him an envelope.

'Twenty-thousand and a passport,' he said.

'And the balance?' Harrison said.

'When you make it back from Afghanistan.'

'Half a million's a lot to pay out.'

'Not if we start a bidding war for the exclusive rights to your story.'